HOSTAGE

SAMANTHA GIBSON

PUBLISHED BY

SIGMA'S
BOOKSHELF

MINNETONKA, MN 55305
WWW.SIGMASBOOKSHELF.COM

Acknowledgements

Writing my first book was difficult, but thanks to writer Dennis Vogen, my English teacher, Deena Zauft, and a couple of my peers at school, this has been achievable. Thank you for taking your time to help me out with this. I would have never gotten this far without you.

Chapter 1

Last day of School

My name is Serina Ange. I am the daughter of the one and only Marcus Ange. He is the boss at Limie.co, also known as Limie. The business is a huge marketplace for apps, mostly for communication. Limie.co operates out of one of the most prized buildings in New York. It towers over the building next door, which happens to be its direct competitor.

Every single year at the same time, the two companies compete to see which of them can bring in more money in a thirty-day span of time. This tends to be the one month of the year when I'm home alone and have no way of getting money for food. So, once I get wind of the fact that the month is coming up, I do a whole bunch of shopping, filling the house with food so I can survive for the month while my father is gone. He is so into the competition he doesn't even bother coming home. He sleeps in his office night after night until his group wins.

Speaking of my father, it's thanks to him that I'm popular at school. But not the healthy kind of popular. Students pretend to be my friend just because they think I have money. The joke is on them. It's actually my father with the money, not me. He only gives me money for groceries, and every once in a while I get a little bit extra when I ask for cash to go shopping or to the cinema. My father spends his money on himself and his interests. It's disgusting.

Being popular seems like this awesome thing because you have a whole group of friends. Your life seems perfect; you're one of those girls who get anything they want, the perfect outfits, the perfect family, the perfect star football or hockey boyfriend that everyone seems to faun over. Dean Parry would definitely be one of those people.

Anyway, how about we change the subject? My mother passed when I was only eight years old. I'm an only child, which makes it kind of lonely since my father is always at the office. When my mother was still alive, she and I would play all the time. She would always have breakfast waiting in the morning, making eggs and bacon into a smiley expression for me. Every day when I came home from school, I would yell, "I'm home!" as I came through the door and she would come down the stairs, welcoming me with a warm smile. I miss those times.

Ever since she died, my father has spent more time in his office then he did before. It's like he doesn't care about me. Sometimes I would write in my journals while I was alone at home, "He only loves me because I look like her." But all that gets covered up with, "She did it again," or, "This happened at school once again."

Speaking of school, I have buddies here and there, but since everyone comes to me for money, who knows if they're fake like everyone else. I decided long ago not to trust the kids at school. I back away from everyone, keep to myself, and try to keep my last name a secret as much as possible, which isn't easy. It's usually all over the news, and so is my father's face. I wish I could live a normal life, like other kids. Not possible. *I want to run away*. I often write that in my journals in fact. There are pages and pages filled with these words. For a long time, I've dreamed about leaving town with the boyfriend I don't have, and heading off into the sunset. Sadly, it's a fantasy I'll never achieve.

My morning routine is to get up, take a shower, dry my hair, put on clothes, make breakfast then depart for school. On the nights he actually sleeps at home, my father is usually already gone before I leave the house. So much for any kind of father-daughter relationship.

I rarely wear nice clothes anymore. I only dress nicely on designated days when I know my father will be on my back about looking nice for this random event that I don't even need to go to. Today, I decided to wear a loose-fitting dark green sweatshirt with black leggings and sneakers. I put my hair up in a messy bun, but don't feel like bothering with makeup. It isn't a good thing to put on your face every day because it increases the chance of acne. I usually wear it anyway though to cover up the pimples on my forehead.

One thing about me is that I am very self-conscious about my face and how I look. Even if I don't wear cute clothes, at least I usually have some makeup on my face to cover my acne. Anyway, even though I looked like crap at school today, a peer of mine came up to my side and conversed with me.

"Serina, I love your outfit!" says one of the annoying ones. Not trying to be rude, but people who come up to me and pretend to be nice because they know my father has money annoy the hell out of me.

I still laugh and reply, "Oh, thanks, Joyce."

Why do people like my style so much when everyone else's is so much better than mine?

Joyce runs ahead to catch up with her other friends. I look on with envy as I trail behind them, my hand on my backpack strap as it hangs from my right arm. I wish I could have friends like hers. Seeing people around me like that, having fun, laughing with their friends makes me jealous. I try to ignore it. I stare down at my phone and scroll through the Instagram feed. I see posts every day about everyone's life. *Annoying.*

I put my phone in my sweatshirt pocket and I look ahead. I see the school. *If only I'd disappear.*

There are times where I do wish that—I wish that I would disappear and be gone from this sickening world that I live in. Especially social media. People are there just to brag about their experiences and their fun times, or there are the ones who only post about depressing shit just to get people's attention because let's be real. Who posts something about anything so personal out to the world about yourself being depressed? Yet again, all in my opinion. When I scroll through and look at these posts—starting with cafes, it's only another wish that comes to mind. It would be great to have a group of people to go to cafes with, drink some coffee, eat some ice cream, talk about all the drama occurring in school. Maybe some people are just not meant to be like that.

I keep scrolling.

"Best day of my life! Thank you all for coming! Love you!" Birthday posts. Everyone is smiling. All those presents, the treats, the activities. I have never experienced anything like that I can cherish. Just birthdays with my family.

Maybe one day I'll get a good career and make some friends at work. After work, they'll maybe want to come to my place for a party and some booze. And maybe one day I'll have a boyfriend with whom I can spend time by a campfire, holding some warm sweet creamed coffee and enjoying some music.

Who am I kidding? My significant other will most likely

be my dog. I mean, who would like me? There has to be somebody out there for me though doesn't there? If there's any chance, I'll take it because I'm sure nobody has a crush on me that goes to my school. I'm sure of it. Well, maybe this guy named Elijah might; but who knows. All I know is that he asked me to a school dance a while back.

"Hey, Serina?"

"Oh hey, Elijah, right?"

He nodded at me, overall looked nervous though. "Are you going with anybody to the dance this Friday?"

I gave out a laugh. "What? Me? No, why?"

"Would you come there with me?" He paused and his words all jumbled up. "I mean, as friends because if you're not going with anyone it must get lonely if your friends leave you. I mean, uh, there has to be somebody by your side the whole dance and—yeah."

"Sorry, I would love to, but I have a family thing going on."

I lied. And I shouldn't have. I wonder how things would have gone if I had accepted his offer. After he asked, we both headed to our classes. It was already near the end of the day so I just faked being sick and headed home early.

Maybe I would have a better life right now if I had a cute boyfriend, a boyfriend who was kind and would help me with my situation at home. A boyfriend who would make me feel safe and happy. There we go again with the maybe.

My train of thought finally shifts back to reality as I climb the stairs and enter the school building. My first order of business is to buy some drinks (non-alcoholic) for my so-called friends, then I head off to my classes. I am smart.

Not trying to brag or anything, but I have always been the top student in my class. There were a couple of AP classes that I took here and there. Some people would make fun of me for taking those, seeing how they always think that people with money have a better future ahead of them guaranteed. Lies! Money doesn't control where you go in life. You decide that on your own.

It's probably because I'm smart that students in my classes keep on pestering me to help them with their studies. I've found a good way to get them to go away though. When someone says, "Morning, Serina. Can you write my essay for me?" I respond. "If you pay me. Longer the length, the more money."

"What!? No way! You have enough money as it is," the kid will say and mainly storm off and be angry. Not for long though. They always come crawling back saying that they're sorry. *Pests*.

By the end of the day, I'm drained. I want to go home, see my dog, and lay in bed. But I know that's not going to happen. After school today, I'm supposed to go somewhere where something happens and I get some kind of "reward." Something like that. Honestly, I don't feel like going. I exit the school doors and say goodbye to the people I was talking with down the hall from our locker bay. Walking with my hand on my backpack strap again, still dangling from my right shoulder.

Right before I left the school proximity on that fateful day, one of the girls who was a part of the award ceremony I was supposed to attend tapped my shoulder and said, "Hey! Serina!"

Somehow my backpack fell to the ground. "Oh my god. I am so sorry, Serina!" She bent down onto her knees and picked up the folders that fell out of the bag.

"It's fine. My fault." I don't really know her that well.

I do know that she is one of the few people who hadn't said anything about my father's money just yet. "Thank you."

She handed me my bag and I threw it back on my shoulder. "Did you need something?"

"Uh, yeah actually." She was the nervous type, clumsy, smart, cute, but not hot. "Do you want to head to the event together? I know it starts in like an hour but I thought it would be nice."

"Sorry, I can't go."

"But you're getting the most important award there! It's going to be so awesome. So many students will think of you and think of that award. Ah, it's like a dream." She seemed too excited about the moment.

"I'll be there but I have to head home first. How about—" I paused and thought for a moment—"you save a spot for me until I arrive? It would be appreciated." I smiled. *Please accept my offer.*

"Of course! Yeah, I'll save a seat for you, Serina."

"By the way, what's your name? I don't think I ever got it." Hopefully, I didn't sound too rude.

"Oh, it's Mariah." She was filled with happiness, adding an extra tint of sugar after I told her to save a seat for me. "So, I'll see you there?"

"Yeah, I'll see you." I started to walk home with Mariah waving to me behind my back. I stuck up my hand and waved without looking at her.

It started to sprinkle when I was about halfway home. I looked up. A pretentious storm was coming, or at least what my eyes told me. *Just great.* I pulled my hood over my head and I stared at my feet as I proceeded to walk on the path. There were no cars, no students walking on the same street. It was peaceful for a while. I lifted my head and stared up at the sky. Some raindrops had fallen into my eye and it stung. I rubbed them with my hand then looked ahead of me to continue walking.

Just then, out of nowhere, a person appeared and started to walk towards me, on the same side of the sidewalk that I was walking on. I tried to overlook it and move to the side to get out of their way, but they just slid over so they would be in front of me. What was this person's problem? Whatever! I couldn't handle this anymore. I wasn't in school, so I didn't care anymore.

If they bump into me, they bump into me, their fault. I just need to go home and sleep, pet my dog, eat some eggs or something, anything to get me away from people.

A few moments later, we were in front of one another. I looked up at the person who appeared to be about six feet tall at most. I couldn't see their face. This person also had a hood over their head, but I didn't think too much of it because I also had my hood up. I tried to get past them, but they wouldn't move.

I made an austere expression. "What the fuck is your problem, man?" I didn't swear much in public, but I was just too accentuated. It was weird at first when we were both stopped in the middle of the sidewalk. We just stared at each other. Beneath his hood, I didn't see the color of skin. It was just black. I got a closer look and there was something over his face. I couldn't figure out what it was, but instantly a red flag appeared.

Before I had the chance to clear the red flags, it was too late. I saw that he lifted his hand and put it behind me. My automatic reaction was to back away but I couldn't move. He kept me in place as his other hand went to my face. He was holding a cloth. It smelled horrible. "I didn't want to have to do this." His voice seemed sincere.

Everything went black.

Chapter 2

A Black Face

"Serina Ange? Is Serina here?"

"She should be, soon," Mariah said with little hope she would come. "Or—Hopefully." She ended up bringing Serina's award home with her, hoping to give it to her the next day at school.

* * *

My wish, unfortunately, came true.

"I'm very sorry to inform you that one of our students, Serina Ange, has recently been reported missing. If you have any information on her whereabouts, or where you saw her last, or if anything bothers you about this incident, please go to the counselors. They will be in the library for the next two weeks for anyone to talk."

No one came. No one bothered. All everyone thought was, *She's a rich girl. She'll buy her way out of trouble. Well, now there's no one to give me the money,*

Or at least that's what I think was going through their heads. I could see that girl, Mariah, saving a seat for me at the awards ceremony, expecting me.

She must be crushed, being lied to like that.

I felt bad—sort of. But it wasn't my fault, entirely. No, I didn't want to go to the event, but being there would have been better than where I was at that moment.

I woke up in an obscure room. Thinking was the only thing I could do. The last thing I remembered was facing this tall person and then I got attacked by them. They made it so I couldn't struggle and whispered into my ear, "Please, I don't want to do this."

Fuck that! I don't believe what they say. Does this mean I got kidnapped? Now, I'm here, in a room that smells and looks sickening. What I see right now that is—my eyes start to adjust to the darkness a bit— the walls around me. I conclude that I'm in a basement of some sort. The walls are stone. So is the floor. If you touch it, your body might as well be an icicle.

Normally in movies or videos that I've seen on YouTube, the kidnapper would put the girl in the basement, so people on the outside wouldn't notice that the kidnapper had a girl inside of their house.

Don't ask why I know that. I have always been interested in crime and kidnapping, and I still am, just not as much as I had been years ago.

I jumped as I heard footsteps behind me. Heavy footsteps creaking down the stairs. Either they were the footsteps of some kind of witch who knew I was awake even if they were in another room, or there were cameras, right? When I looked behind me, the door opened and the light turned on.

I was in a small room with no windows. It looked like

a tiny square room connected to a basement. The ceiling was wooden. There was a thick pole in the middle near where I was lying. I got up hastily and went to the nearest wall and put my back up to it, my eyes wide. There was a person in the doorway. Their shadow was large.

My kidnapper is now down in the basement with me.

But of course, I couldn't see their face. They had a black mask on. The mask had holes for the eyes and a hole for their mouth. It went down the kidnapper's neck half-way.

I guess they don't want me to know their identity. They might plan to let me go. If they planned to kill me, I wouldn't think they'd care if I have seen what they looked like.

"Who are you?" I clenched my fist in anger. I wasn't going to be scared right now. I expected an answer like, "I am your worst enemy," or something cliche like that. But to my surprise, they didn't respond to me. "I asked you a question, damn it." My voice got more stern.

"That," there was a little pause, "don't matter." They just stood there, stepping a tad closer, halting by the pole in the middle of the room. They leaned against it, continuing to look at me. "Please, calm down. I told you that I don't want to do this."

They must see me trembling, I'm trying not to look startled, but I don't think that's working out too well. Liar!

"Get me the hell out of here!" Even though my head was still a bit fuzzy, I ran past whoever they were out the door into another room with a carpet; a finished basement. I ran up the stairs that were located on the right. I ran all the way through the other door at the top and I saw the front door of the house in front of me, a bit to the right. I heard their footsteps crawling behind me.

Faster, Serina.

At that moment, I was frozen. I looked around. There was a closet on the left with two sliding doors. A living room was on the right. There was a large window in the living room, but it was covered with brown-tinted curtains. Without realizing how much time had passed, I felt a hand grasp onto my wrist. I jumped. The door was right in front of me, and I could've gone for it, but it's not like it was open anyway. What abductor would be that stupid? I turned around and looked at them. One of their legs was down on the first step, their head looking up at me, eyes looking fierce. *Crap.*

Why was this happening to me? Why did they seem so eerie? Kidnappers are not supposed to act like that, right? I'm assuming, maybe this is some kind of prank. Foolish, I have no friends and I don't talk to any of my family.

I blinked. I was still frozen. It was just like that time on the sidewalk. We just stared at each other. I tried to pull away, but their grip got even tighter.

Based on my kidnapper's figure and strength, I'll say it's a guy.

His grip would not leave my wrist, so I sort of gave up. Instead of bringing me back downstairs, he stepped up that one stair that his leg was still back on, he closed the basement door behind him and locked it with a key, all while still holding onto me, looking at me. My kidnapper brought me upstairs. It was silent. He didn't talk, and I didn't try to say anything.

He brought me into a room.

There is a bed—it looks pretty comfortable. Hey wait! What am I thinking? This is absolute bullshit!

He let go of my wrist, pushed me a bit into the room, closed the door and walked out. A click was heard. He probably locked the door, but I just had to make sure. I put my hand on the doorknob and twisted it. It was locked.

There was only one thing I could do. I sat down on the edge of the bed, knowing that there was nothing else I could do. There were no windows in this room, no light switch that I could see, no ceiling fan. I wasn't tied up or anything.

Why not? I feel like a kidnapper is supposed to tie up their victims to stop them from trying anything. Maybe he's testing me?

There were a couple of lights around the room, including fairy lights hanging up against the wall. There was an air purifier that looked like a rock on the desk. I turned on the fairy lights first. They let off a yellowish tint of light. After that, I turned the switch on the rock. That gave off an orange and yellow light. It was already filled up with water, and I could smell lavender coming through the vent.

There was also a lamp next to the bed on a bookshelf filled with books. I turned that on as well. The desk lamp was a shade of pastel pink. The light pointed down at a fake cactus. The room was cute.

This can't be his room unless the person who took me is a girl. I'm pretty sure a guy wouldn't have this in their room. It doesn't even have any video games—no offense to any females.

The walls were a light gray and the ceiling white. My bare feet swept across the delicate carpet as I looked around the room some more. I looked at the walls, the desk, and the frames that were hanging on the wall. Frames of what looked like to be a happy family: a mother, a father, two sons, and a daughter.

I don't get why I was put in this room. I groaned. I had no choice but to sit back down on the bed.

It would be nice if I could see the outdoors again, maybe some sunshine. I wonder what there is to do in this room anyway.

There were books, which I thought could double as weapons. I slid a bit down the bed, keeping at the edge of the bed facing a bookshelf, and I looked through the books. I grabbed a few books off the shelf and thumbed through them. A lot of them seemed to be realistic fiction, or at least that's the conclusion I made based on the pages I browsed through.

I came across a book called *Kindness for Weakness*, which is a book about a teen going to jail. *Seems interesting.* I set it on top of the bookshelf just in case I didn't find something more interesting. I pulled out another book called *Self-Destruction*, which is about a teen going to jail for—love?

I think I'll read this one. I want to know how this all goes down. Maybe she falls in love with a troublemaker?

I didn't even bother putting the other book back in place.

If my kidnapper wants me to be in this room, then this is my room and I can mess it up however I want because—screw it!

I plopped on the bed and sighed, then opened the book

and started reading. A while passed. The book was pretty interesting. I finished it in a couple of hours and set it down beside me on the bed and stared up at the ceiling.

After a while, I realized I was starving, so I got out of bed and went to the door again. I knocked on it and called out, "Hey! I'm hungry." I waited for an answer. "Can you at least get me some food, Kidnapper?" My stomach growled, the door unlocked.

What else could I call this guy?

At first, I was surprised. Maybe it was a coincidence? I twisted the doorknob to open the door, only to see my kidnapper with his black mask on in front of me. I looked deeply into his eyes. I could see their color now. They were blue. If you looked deeply into his eyes and concentrated, I bet it would look like an ocean. "What are you hungry for?" He spoke with such a deep and smooth voice. It seemed as if it had no emotion in it though.

He wasn't enjoying himself at all—I mean, who would under the circumstances?

"Pizza." A quick response. Pizza didn't sound very appetizing at the moment, but the word still popped out of my mouth.

"Well, I made chicken and rice tonight so you better eat up. Let's go." He took my wrist again and dragged me all the way downstairs, through the living room and into the kitchen. He didn't say anything. The only noise was a ticking clock. It was so awkward.

I have to say something.

"So what, you poisoned my food? Maybe drugged my drink? What's all this for?"

Me being skeptical as always I guess you could say. Of course he didn't fucking answer me. I swear! I am going to punch him in the goddamn face.

He let go of my hand and sat down at the table. I could have just gotten up and ran out the front door, but I didn't. I sat down across the table from him where the plates were already set. There was a glass of milk, chicken and rice in the middle of the table and he decided to dig in, placing some food on his plate. He looked at me. "Aren't you going to eat?"

I nodded, not saying anything in return.

See how he likes it.

I grabbed my utensils and started to move some food onto my plate. I was hesitant to start eating. What if this stuff was poisoned or drugged?

Maybe I'm just overthinking things.

I put some of the rice on my spoon and held it up in front of my face. I looked up at my kidnapper. He still had that stupid mask on while enjoying his meal.

What the hell? How does he even eat with the mask on? He can't even open his mouth that wide. How does he do that? Maybe he's done it before. Maybe there were other girls before me.

I put the spoon in my mouth and started to eat.

It's going pretty good. I'm not throwing up. I'm not passing out.

"Is it good?" he asked, breaking the silence. I nodded and he nodded back. "Good—" He then stood up with an empty plate and glass and walked towards the sink. He was finished eating already. He didn't eat that much. There wasn't much food on the table and there was plenty for me.

I continued to eat as my kidnapper was washing a couple of dishes at the sink. I glanced over at the door but something was holding me back. Once I was done eating, I stood up and set my dishes on the counter next to the sink. He turned his head to look at me, staring at me for a good ten seconds before turning back to the sink. It felt off. I felt the tension. I should have made a run for it. But I didn't.

I closed my eyes and took a deep breath. Suddenly, his finger came onto my lips. I couldn't talk. I couldn't move.

Damn it!

"Go to your room." He seemed calmer now.

Why can't I just stay here?

With me being who I was, I didn't say anything. I was completely frozen once again. My kidnapper had taken my wrist another time, letting his finger slowly leave my mouth. Turning towards the stairs, he brought me down to the same room as before. He then closed the door. I heard a click, and was locked in again. There was nothing I could do.

When I was upstairs, I had many chances to run. I could've probably gotten away too, but if you think about it, this life I'm living right now is more pleasant than what I'm used to. No school, no fake ass people, no father—not like he was there for me anyway. The only thing I miss is my dog. I hope you are okay, Ritz.

I thought about the movies I've seen and the books I've read. No kidnapper I had known about had never been this nice. I thought I would be tortured, maybe raped. But my kidnapper was taking care of me. Sure, he had his flaws, but just maybe they weren't so bad.

This is my new story, and I like it.

Chapter 3

Secrets

I t was in the midst of the night. I grabbed another book from the shelf and held it open to page two-hundred forty-six. To be honest, I just opened up to this page and stared at the words.

Soon enough the words disappeared and I was just staring at blank pages. I blinked, then placed the book back in its original place after closing the cover. That's when I realized that half of the books that were on the bookshelf earlier were missing. I kneeled on the carpet and picked through the books, trying to remember which ones were still in the room, and which ones were missing.

That didn't work out too well. I didn't remember anything except the two books that I had pulled aside when I first arrived. I picked up the book that I had just put down moments ago and opened it up. The words were still not on the pages. They were still blank.

I set the book open on the floor and rubbed my eyes, hoping when I opened them the words would be back onto the pages of the book. Good thing when my lids opened, the words were back on the page. I sighed with relief, closed the book and put it back on the bookshelf.

I said to myself, "I thought I was going crazy for a second

there, Jesus." I sat on the bed, wondering what the hell to do in this room.

I looked around and I noticed that some of the frames on the wall were missing, just as the books were. It was the family photos, the parents, the children. Maybe my kidnapper took them down because it was him. One of the sons was him. I should have paid more attention. Maybe I could have figured out what he looks like under that stupid mask he always has on, or what he used to look like. At least I got the information that he has two siblings, a mother, and a father. They looked like a happy family—or at least what I remember looking at. All of them were smiling and standing in front of an ocean, barefoot on the sand.

Honestly, now I'm feeling a bit jealous. I should just go to bed now, take a nap or something...

When I woke up, I opened my eyes. I don't know what time it was, but it was bright. It must have been morning. I was wrong. When I woke up a bit more, I heard waves and some birds. I felt a breeze, my hair flowing a bit, cold air on my face. I sat up in bed and looked around.

I was on a beach, and in front of me was an ocean with waves crashing. The water getting so close to the bed on the sand but not quite touching me, or getting anything wet that I was on. I looked around some more, seeing stars and moons on the sand, in the sand, surrounding me. It looked like it was some kind of orange sandstone. I look at the bright blue sky, a seagull flying above me squawks then flies away.

I smiled. It was peaceful. Even if I didn't know what is happening or where I am. I must've been in a dream. A sweet dream.

It didn't last long. I blinked and I was in the same room

I fell asleep in. I was sitting up in bed, smiling. I clenched the bed sheets slightly. My smile faded. I lay back down on my bed. "That dream should've lasted longer," I said out loud.

I closed my eyes, but unable to fall back asleep I opened them and stared up at the ceiling, and that's when I heard a knock on my door. My kidnapper walked into the room. I tilted my head back and looked at him. He was smiling.

Why?

"That was a nice dream wasn't it?"
"Huh?" I was perplexed.

How did he know?

"How did you know?"
"Just a guess. You're smiling." I wasn't really unless he had cameras in the room where he was watching me. *Gross!* "It just made me happy," he paused, "to see you smile."
"Uh—Yeah, thanks." I looked away from him, not wanting to talk.

He didn't say anything and shut the door, probably locking it after it shut.

That was weird. Maybe he does have some kind of camera around in the room where he's secretly watching me through those creepy lenses. I better not get naked. I chuckle to myself.
My next thought is to look over at the closet. I hadn't checked it out yet. If this is a girl's room, the clothes would most likely give me the answer. I stand up. The bed looking like a mess, but that's okay. I get to the closet doors and open them.

There were—surprisingly—clothes, girl clothes. There

were dresses, blouses, cute clothes, aesthetic outfits. I looked at what I was wearing.

I guess I wouldn't mind a change. To be honest, I don't think he'll watch me but if he does, I hope he jerks off because I have an amazing body. I'm joking.

I saw a knitted sweater. It was pink, not to mention, very soft. I didn't know what material it was made of, but I didn't care. I took off the sweatshirt I had on, leaving me in a black bra. I put on the sweater. It fit.

There was a dresser in this closet below the shirts that were hanging on a railing. I looked through the drawers. Thankfully, there were clothes in there as well. I picked out pants that would look good with the shirt. They were black ripped jeans. I pulled down the pants I had on, putting on the jeans. They were a bit tight, however.

Sooner or later I will get used to them. Might even make some of the fat go away on my thighs.

I chuckled to myself again.

I didn't have any socks on my feet either. They were freezing. I looked through the drawers more and found some socks, fuzzy ones. They had black with white stripes. I put them on. They were comfortable—warm, perfect. I couldn't see what I looked like because there was no mirror in the room. I decided that once my kidnapper unlocked the door again, I would head straight to the restroom.

That's another thing people ask me about. Why I call bathrooms restrooms. Ever since I was little, somebody told me to not call bathrooms, bathrooms, but restrooms because there's some kind of difference. I mean, I can still call bathrooms, bathrooms, but only at my house. The person said once you are in a public place, or somebody else's living space, you must call it a restroom, not a bathroom, because for some reason they said it seemed to be inappropriate, not polite. Ever since then, I have called them restrooms, even in my own house—not supposed to but I still do. It just kind of stuck with me all these years. It's weird. Sometimes I do call them bathrooms though. It wasn't my entire life that I called them restrooms, so it's only natural to subconsciously do that once in a while.

Speaking of my childhood, it was pretty interesting. I'm not going to try and tell you my problems at home, but I can tell you about this one friend I had. He was home-schooled. His name was Jameson Smith. He was a pretty sweet kid, a little older than me but that didn't stop us from hanging out. We lived in the same neighborhood, which was nice so we could hang out after I was done with school and on the weekends. Jameson and I did almost everything together—until I had to move. I moved to a different town, the one over, a different school. I haven't seen or spoken to him since.

When I was packing up to move, I went over to his place. I assumed he would open the door right away, but no one did. To think that my last days in that town, I never got to say goodbye to my best friend.

To be completely honest, I don't remember what Jameson looked like. I never even met his family. I only remember some little bits and pieces, like us hanging in his tree house while nobody was home, us laughing and having fun. Gosh, I miss the old days. I wonder if somehow I'll meet him again. If my mother were still alive she would know all the information, like where he lives, and if we could meet up again, but she's not here anymore.

A tear came to my eye. I finished getting dressed in new clothing. I left my original clothes in the corner of the closet, then walked over to the bed and sat down. I knew I was unable to sleep again, so I couldn't do that. There was nothing to do.

A while passed, then my kidnapper came up to my room and unlocked the door, not coming in, not saying anything but I still heard the door click. I went to the door and opened it. He wasn't there either.

Does this mean I have free time to roam? I walk out into the hallway, looking around. There's a door in front of me. I open it. It's the restroom. To the left, there's another door down the hall a bit. I open that door and what's in it is a room. I look around. This must be his room.

The bedsheets were gray. So were his pillows. The walls were white. The carpet was a light brown. There was nothing special. Nothing on the walls. No special lights. It was empty. There was a nightstand with nothing on top of it. I looked through the two drawers. Nothing. There was a dresser in front of the bed against the wall, but nothing on top of it. I looked through the four drawers that were there and found what I assume were his clothes. I decided to close that up and stop looking before I found anything that my kidnapper might not want me to see, like his Spider-Man undergarments.

Kidding. I have no idea what undergarments he has. Frankly, I don't want to find out.

The last thing to check in this room was the walk-in closet, of course. I noticed it had windows in it, but they were really tiny, just big enough to let in a little bit of light so I didn't both to try to look out of them into the yard.

I did venture into the closet though. I was a little room filled with hanging clothes. There wasn't much color. Not much for dress clothing either. I shrugged and that's when I saw a hatch in the floor in the right corner of the closet. It looked like it wasn't supposed to be there. The carpet around the square was all torn up. It just didn't look like it was supposed to be a part of the house.

I walked over to it and noticed it didn't have a lock on it. I didn't try to open it, although, I wonder what's in there, a box filled with weapons? Drugs? Maybe it's a secret passage to go somewhere.

Hah, what am I saying? Maybe it's just those photos and books he decided to hide away from me. Of course, he wouldn't have a secret passage or anything like that because that shit only happens in books and movies.

I left his room. Nothing special but that hatch. To the right of my room were the stairs that go downstairs. I went down them, not seeing my kidnapper anywhere.

I noticed the front door, the living room, the kitchen, like usual. I hadn't had a good look at the kitchen yet so I looked there.

It's pretty decent, not the best but better than my own. There's not much food in the fridge, or cupboards.

It was boring so I went to the right of the kitchen. There was a little opening for the back glass sliding doors that led into the backyard. There was also a door. I tried opening the door, thinking it must be another bedroom of some sort, but it was locked. I turned back around into the kitchen, out to the living room, now standing in front of the basement door, the place I woke up in. I put my hand on the knob and twisted. As soon as I opened it, cold air hit my face. I instantly got goosebumps.

I don't remember it being so cold down here. You could freeze to death—and I'm not joking around this time.

I went down the stairs.

If my kidnapper is down here, he's one hell of a devil for doing so.

Once I reached the bottom, I found a large area of a finished basement. It had the same light brown carpet as the other rooms, white walls, a white ceiling, and one thing you wouldn't expect to find in a basement—a minibar in the corner of this big space. I checked the minibar out. It was like an actual bar place, the counter where you tell the person on the other side, "Slide me another" or something like that. There were drinks. Alcoholic and normal ones, along with a mini fridge which didn't seem to be working. It was clean.

Weird! It looks like none of the bottles have been drunk yet except one, Tennessee whiskey. Does he like that stuff? I think I remember trying it once but I thought it was gross.

I didn't touch or go through the bar. I just walked away to a room that was connected with the first area. It was the part where it was unfinished, the room that I woke up in. I walked in there. Even though I was wearing fuzzy warm socks, the coldness of the stone floor went right through me, sending shivers up my legs, and resulting in goosebumps.

I rubbed my arms in an attempt to warm myself up.

If you think about it, this corner of the house is below my kidnapper's room, weird. There isn't much in this room. It is

*just an unfinished room with a little dark space in the left
corner. No way I am going to look what's over there. It is dark
for one, and for two, maybe there are spiders and insects. Yuck!*

"Hey."

The sound of that voice startled me after it being so quiet
for a while. I turned around, not scared anymore since
I knew it was my kidnapper, just by his voice. "What the
hell? You scared the shit out of me! What?"

"Get out of here and go upstairs." He sounded serious,
like I wasn't supposed to be down here for a reason.

"Why, you hiding something from me, kidnapper?"
I stepped closer to him and acted a bit childish. Honestly,
I don't know why I did that. I could have just gone upstairs
as instructed.

"Just," he paused, "go upstairs, please."

He even used the word, please.

"Fine!" I walked past him, out of the room, my feet slowly
getting warmer and my whole body warming up as I got
up to the living room. My body was soon back to a normal
temperature, only my hands still needed to be warmed up.

My kidnapper was right behind me. "What do you want
to have for dinner?"

I knew this question already. "What do you have in mind?"

I heard him chuckle beneath his breath. I sat on the
couch. He sat as well, but on the opposite side. "Just some
steak and potatoes."

It was silent for a couple of minutes until I decided to
speak up. We weren't even staring at each other. It was just
us looking around the room, not looking at each other at
all. "So, can I ask you something?"

"What is it?"

"Why are you so nice to me?"

He stood up. "I have to start making the food now before it gets too late. I don't want you wandering around in the basement, so stay up here or go to your room."

"Yeah," I said. It was obvious I wasn't going to get an answer out of him. "Sure."

I went up to my room.

It's mine because he just said it is—I guess. I lay in bed, wishing I had my laptop or phone to go on, but now I can only imagine playing Pac-Man on the ceiling.

I accidentally fell asleep. When I woke up, nothing was unusual until I saw there was a sticky note on my door. It read, "Food is downstairs. Heat it if you're hungry. I'll be gone for a couple of hours, I need to do something. DO NOT GO IN BASEMENT." The ending surprised me a bit, all caps and everything.

He means business!

I took the note off my door, walked over to the little bookshelf of mine and took off a sticky note from a stack of sticky notes that were in the room and started to write something on it. After writing, I put my kidnapper's sticky note behind my own, went out into the hall and put sticky notes on his door for him to read my message once he's back. I was standing in front of his bedroom door, reading my note to myself just to make sure I did everything correctly. I nodded, my stomach growled, and that's when I went downstairs to get some food. There was more than enough steak and potatoes for me to eat.

Sometimes I wonder, does he leave this much for me just so

I have enough food to eat? Another way of him, my kidnapper, being just a "friend" of mine? Maybe, who knows.

I took some, not all. There was no way I was going to finish all of that anyway. I heated the plate of food up in the microwave and sat down on the couch. I turned on the television to give me something to do while I was waiting for the beeping to go off. I found a great show that my mother and I used to watch when I was little: *Jane the Virgin*.

"Do you want to watch it with me?"
My mother always gave off the greatest smile, like there was nothing wrong in her life.
"Sure!"
I was young, so in the show. I didn't get many of the adult jokes, but my mom did. She'd always laugh. "Why are you laughing?"
"Nothing you would understand." She paused and looked at me. "You'll know when you're a bit older, Serina. We can re-watch it and laugh together."

The beeping went off. I noticed my eyes were a bit teary from remembering that memory, but it was fine. I shook it off and went to get my food. I came back with a fork in my hand, a plate in the other and I sat. A new season of *Jane the Virgin* came out recently. I was intrigued by what it would be because of the cliffhanger

Then I remembered that I didn't want to start watching it until I watched the season before it, so I could remember most of it. When it was on, while I was eating, however, I decided to watch out of nostalgia.

I imagined my mother sitting next to me on the couch, right beside me, watching *Jane the Virgin*. We were laughing together, like when I was younger. I looked off to the side and smiled. Slowly, my smile went away. My eyes turned red as tears fell.

"I'm so stupid!" I said out loud, as I set my plate down and rubbed my eyes.

I wish you were still here, mom—I wish you were still with me. I wish it was father, not you.

I don't even know who I was talking to, but a little part of me wanted to get this feeling out of me. I feel responsible for my mother's death, or at least my father did say I was responsible. A stab wound I'll never get rid of.

I heard a click. Looking up with tears still falling down my cheeks, my kidnapper walked in through the front door, holding a bag.

"Here you go." He handed me a cup of coffee and I sat on the couch with a blanket over my shoulders, my eyes still puffy from crying.

"Thanks." I took a sip and sat there. We sat there in awkward silence. I'm sure he has no idea what to say at this point.

"Do you want to sleep out here tonight, or what do you want to do?"

What?

"Why would I want to sleep out in the living room?"

He hesitated. Maybe he just said that because it was the first thing that came to his mind he thought may console me. "I don't know. More spacious, and there is a television."

"I want to go home. I want to see my dog. I want to be in my own house, my bed." I looked at him with the mug still in hand, the heat going to my hands, spreading out through my body.

"I can't allow that. I'm sorry."

"Why not?" My right leg started to bounce uncontrollably. "Why am I here? Why was I brought here? Why am I here? Why did you kidnap me?"

"I didn't kidnap you. I'm not a kidnapper." His voice cracked a bit, even if it was just a little one, I still noticed it.

"Hell, it sure looks like you are. It sure looks like you fucking did. Just let me out." I stood up and set the mug on the coffee table, the blanket falling off my shoulders. I needed to think more about myself.

He stood up and came after me. "You're not leaving."

"Whatever! I walked to the front door and grabbed the knob. I didn't see him lock it.

"I said, you're not leaving!" He grabbed my arm harshly, pulling me back.

"Yes I am, let me go!" I pushed him back.

"Serina!" His eyebrows furrowed. Then, he pinned me against the wall and looked directly into my eyes, keeping a good grip in place so I couldn't move much. I spit in his face. He smirked.

"What the hell is your problem? You fucked up in the head or something?"

Only a psychopath would smirk.

He slapped me. He began backing away, wiping his face, then looked at me. My face said it all. I was surprised by what happened.

He actually slapped me.

"Go to your room."

"We're not related! I'm not your girlfriend. I'm not your friend. We're strangers. We don't know each other! That is not my damn room. This shit isn't mine at all!"

"I know you, Serina. You just forgot me! You LEFT me!" His eyes were glossy. "You left me!"

"I don't know who the fuck you are! You're just a creep who kidnapped a girl with money!" I paused. "Is that what you want? Money?"

I hadn't thought about it much before. But yeah, why would he bring me here in the first place unless he was looking for money?

"No, I don't—" He stopped his sentence and shook his head. "I do—I want your money. Give me $10,000. Then you'll be set free, and everything will be fine with our lives." My kidnapper's tone changed.

What he said just now, is it true?

"What? We can't just hand out a large amount of money to you like that! Maybe $5,000 but not $10,000! Are you crazy?"

"I guess I am."

"I'm leaving." I went to the front door and opened it. It was nighttime, but who cares? I walked outside and felt the breeze against my skin. The breeze I hadn't felt in such a long time.

"Oh no you don't!"

My kidnapper put a hand over my mouth and the other arm around my waist, bringing me back inside.

He's quite strong. He always wins.

My muffled scream through his fingers was not that loud. No one in the neighborhood could have possibly heard me.

That was dumb. That was stupid.

He slammed the door shut with his foot, which made him stumble over and I fell on top of him. The air was pushed out of my lungs. He pushed me off of him and sat up coughing. He must've had the air knocked out of his lungs as well.

This was my chance. I headed to the door one more time, but he got up hastily behind me and grabbed me again. That's when I saw what looked to be black house spiders on the walls and the door. Everything around me became dark, and the first thing I thought about was screaming. I was scared. I screamed. That's when the kidnapper let go of me. I dropped to the floor down to my knees, my face buried within them, and I started to cry.

Crying twice in one night, he must think I'm weak.

My lids popped open, I looked around. I heard a train go off in the distance. I heard somebody whisper beside my ear, "Beyond and under the floors, through the wall, the stone is cold."

"Who are you!" My head went down to my knees again and I felt a hand grasp my shoulder. I jumped in fear but it was just my kidnapper.

"It's me. It's me! What the hell is going on!?"

I bet he was confused, but not as confused as me! I think I'm going crazy.

I repeated what I was thinking out loud, "I think I'm going crazy."

Chapter 4

Trust is Brewing

It was only Mariah who was in the room. The teachers did say to meet if you have any information that may help authorities find Serina. She was the only one who showed up, wearing ripped blue jeans and a striped long sleeve shirt, tucked in with a black belt around her waist.

"Where is everyone else? Serina's friends?" Mariah was confused about why she was the only one there. She imagined Serina had everything—good friends, money, a big house, good grades—but she was mistaken.

"I don't know." That's all the teacher could respond with. "What did you say when you got here?" Ms. Ling sat down in a chair, across from Mariah. "You were going to the ceremony with her?"

"Oh yes—" Mariah described how Serina was going to go home and then meet her at the ceremony. She explained that she never showed up and the seat saving idea went into the dumpster. Right then and there, Mariah started to cry. "I really thought she was going to come. She seemed so nice to me and—" her words got caught, bubbles getting stuck in her throat.

"It's okay, take your time."

* * *

I woke up the next morning feeling a bit dopey—or at least it felt like morning. I sat up in bed and rubbed my eyes. I thought I was home, so I stood up and walked out the door. I walked down the stairs, not realizing I was not in my house but somebody else's. When I got downstairs I said, "Good morning mom," as I used to when I was little. "What's for breakfast?" I looked up and rubbed my eyes one more time to see a man with a mask standing in an unfamiliar kitchen.

"Eggs," he said with a bland voice.

I quickly remembered everything. How I was kidnapped, how I wasn't home, how it wasn't the good old times when I was a kid. Feeling too embarrassed to speak, I sat down at a stool with the plate of food being set in front of me. I began to eat, knowing that it wouldn't be poisoned. The breakfast was good, although it could have used a bit more salt or some other flavor, and fewer egg yokes.

Once I was finished eating, I left my plate there and stood up. By the time I had finished, my kidnapper was sitting and watching television in the living room.

One of my hobbies is writing. I'm most likely the first one in my family to have an interest in writing. I usually write poems or short stories. There's no way in hell I could write a whole goddamn novel or book. I'm not that talented. But I do, at some points, just write randomly—what happened throughout the day, what I hope will happen in the future.

That gave me an idea. Since I haven't written in so long, I miss it. Since my kidnapper is being so nice to me I'm sure he won't mind giving me a notebook and pen.

"Hey, kidnapper!" I walked over behind the couch he was sitting on. "Do you have a notebook and pen I could use?"

"Why do you need it?" he asked.

"I get bored in the room, in this house. At least I can do a bit of doodling and shit, right? You gave me a comfortable bed. You're taking care of me, kidnapper of mine."

"Stop calling me a kidnapper!" He exclaimed, then walked to a nearby closet and opened it. "Here, you can have a notebook and a pen. Happy now?"

He walked back with a small bound pastel pink notebook and a black pen. I took it out of his hands and stood up, inches away from him.

"Thank you." I held the notebook and pen up to my chest and stared at him. After a bit of awkward staring, he got out of my way. "I'll be in my room, kidnapper." He shot me a look. It was a look I have never seen before. It was scary. I gulped.

"Okay, okay, fine!" Not wanting to be with him any longer, I headed back into my room.

I don't know how many days I have been in here. Probably a week I guess. My name is Serina Marie Ange, and I have been kidnapped by some weird guy in a black mask. All I know so far is that he has sharp blue eyes, a good body to go along with it. At least he's not chunky. If he were, I don't think I would be able to stand to be near him. LMAO.

I guess that I will be here until he lets me go. I don't even know what he wants. Maybe he wants my father's money. Maybe he heard of me because of my school and how much money I supposedly have. It's kind of stupid in my opinion. He did tell me one night though that he did want money, but there was a lot of sarcasm in his voice, I think.

I miss my dog Ritz. I bet she's laying in my bed

*right now waiting for me to get home from school.
I wonder if my father has been home. Hopefully, he
fed her. Because I swear, if I come back home after
this and find my dog dead in my bed because of
starvation, I am moving out of there and stealing
the money I need because screw him.*

*Where would I go? I have no idea. Why am
I writing this exactly? No idea. I guess it's a place
to write down my thoughts. I mean, if my kidnapper sees this, I don't think he'd care. What if
he's transgender? Gosh, whatever. It doesn't matter.
Till another day, diary. Oh gross, that's so stupid.
Whatever. I don't even know what to write. Maybe
if he gave me a room and this notebook and pen,
what if I can use him to get whatever I want too?
I should get to know him. He doesn't seem too bad.*

After writing a bit inside of the notebook, I wasn't sleepy
at all and the sun was about to set. So, I decided to get
myself out of bed. I put the notebook under the mattress,
just in case. I didn't want this kidnapper of mine to find
it and decide to read it. Now that would be embarrassing.

I went to look for him and noticed that his bedroom
door was open. I knocked quietly on the side of the wall,
peeking my head through the doorway. "Hey!

He looked over his shoulder and turned off his phone.
"What do you want?"

"I'm just bored and it seems like we could be friends.
I mean, you don't seem like a killer or a rapist kidnapper
that everyone tends to think kidnappers are."

"I'm not a kidnapper!" He turned his head back around
away from me. I decided to walk into the room and sit down
on the corner of the bed, and looked at him.

"Well, I was on my way home, and woke up here, and I can't really leave so—yeah basically you're a kidnapper. But a nice one." I smiled.

"Sure, whatever. I guess I am a 'nice kidnapper', but what if I were a mean one? I could be mean to you, Serina." He locked his eyes with mine and he gave me a little smirk.

"Oh yeah sure. Whatever you say, Kidnapper."

"Jimmy." He paused and sat up in bed. "My name is Jimmy Coral."

"Jimmy," I repeated. "Well, it's nice to meet you." He nodded, not saying a word after that. He yawned. "Oh sorry, are you tired? I can leave."

"No, no. It's fine. I like the company."

"Hmm okay. Whatever you say, Jimmy Coral."

"Do you remember me, Serina?" he asked suddenly.

"As I said before, I don't know you. How would I remember someone who I haven't even met before, huh?" He blinked.

"You'll find out sooner or later, and it will be too late." He scoffed.

There was very little talking after that. I guess there wasn't much to talk about and it got kind of awkward. I liked how we were getting closer though. I learned his name, but every time I got closer to knowing him, he seemed to think that I already do.

Still, this can give me the greater advantage. I can get to know him, get on his good side and sooner or later he can let me go. Maybe we can go shopping together, or I can get him locked up in jail.

Sure, he seemed like a nice kidnapper but at the same time he did kidnap me, and so far, wouldn't let me leave. There wasn't much I could do about that.

There is still this little voice in the back of my head saying to not leave because this can be a better life than what I was living before. I know his name, but how much more can I figure out? One thing that bothers me is his mask because I didn't know what he looks like. I mean, if I ever do report him, I bet there are millions of Jimmy's walking on this planet right now.

Jimmy got out of bed. I stood up and looked at him. "Where are you going?"

"Do you want to watch a movie?" he asked as he motioned for me to come sit next to him.

"How? There's no television in this room."

"Just sit down, you'll see." I did what he said. I sat down. I was still at the edge of the bed when I heard a click, and that's when a projector screen showed up on the wall in front of me. I tilted my head, confused. "The TV in this room isn't as fancy as the one downstairs, but I do have this projector that can play movies."

"Oh," I scooted back up to the back wall of his bed, facing the wall still. "That's nice."

"I guess." Jimmy sat next to me, his back against the back of his bed as well. He had a mini-remote in his hand. "What do you want to watch?"

"I don't really care, anything you choose will be fine." I looked at him. He didn't look back.

"Okay." With a single click of a button, I looked to the wall and the movie *Frozen* appeared on the wall.

"Do you like this movie?" I asked.

"I guess you can say it's one of my favorites." He turned to me as I turned towards him. He beamed.

I couldn't help but smile back, although it might have been weak since I've never seen him smile. "That's good," I paused, still thinking of him smiling. "I've never seen it."

"What? Really? Well, you better pay attention to the movie, it's a good one."

"No, I meant this is the first time I've seen you smile." His eyes widened a bit. He must have realized he was showing too much of his true self. The smile went away and he turned his head.

"Well, let's just get this started."

"Yeah, okay."

Halfway through the movie, I looked over at Jimmy to see if he was still awake because he didn't answer a question I asked him a while ago. I just figured he didn't respond like he sometimes does, which is low key kind of annoying.

He was not awake. There he was, lying in his bed with me next to him. He was asleep.

This is my chance. This is my chance to see what he looks like. He's asleep.

I got up slowly out of the bed. I needed to see what he looked like. I needed to take off that mask. I tip-toed over to the other side of the bed and looked down at him sleeping.

Trust me—I'm not a creep.

My hands went up to his mask—the *Frozen* movie playing in the background—I was inches away from his face and I touched the mask, my hands shaking. His eyes opened. His pupils got used to the little light that was lighting up the room from the projector. My hands quickly receded from his mask and down to my sides.

"Hi." My voice was wobbly.

"Hi, do you—" He hesitated. "Do you need something?"

"No, no. Nothing at all. I just wanted to tell you I'm heading back to my room." I faked a smile at him and backed up a couple of inches near the door.

"Oh, okay." He sat up and rubbed his eyes and pulled down his mask a bit. "What do you want in the morning?"

"Pancakes would be nice." My body was still shaking. Not as much as a couple of minutes ago, but I kept telling myself to stop.

What if he notices?

"I'm getting really tired, I'm going to go to bed now." I bit the inside of my cheek, hoping that would help stop the shaking. I walked through the doorway.

"Wait, Serina?"

Crap! "Yes?" I peeked my head back into the room.

"Never mind, goodnight."

"Yeah, night."

* * *

It was the next morning, and the smell of pancakes filled the entire house, forcing me to wake up with sparkles in my eyes. Jimmy had made pancakes that morning, unless he was just tricking me with some pancake spray or something just to get me out of bed.

Is that even a thing?

I went downstairs where the stench of the pancakes just became more intense. I looked at Jimmy and there he was in a white apron with black letters across his ass saying, "Eat

It" for some odd reason. He was standing there, flipping mini pancakes, still with his mask on.

Does he ever take it off or is he keeping that stupid thing on just for my sake, for me not to find out what he looks like?

He turned around with a plate of mini pancakes in his hand. Seeing me must have startled him. So much, in fact, it caused the plate to fall onto the floor, making a loud crash. Glass ended up all over. My eyes squinted and my whole body tensed up from the crash. A couple of seconds later my eyes opened again.

"I'm sorry, I didn't mean to startle you." I walked into the kitchen making sure not to step on any of the shards. "I just smelled the pancakes and—"

I got cut off. "Get out of the kitchen, it's dangerous." His hand shooed me away like I was a puppy sent to the corner after pissing on the carpet and in need of a time out.

"I—"

"Go into the living room, Serina." Our eyes locked and I slowly walked backward, my feet on the carpet, now in the living room. Jimmy grabbed a broom from the kitchen closet and started to sweep up the glass, or as much as he could sweep up. He also picked up the mini pancakes that fell to the floor and threw them in the garbage.

Right after that he put more pancakes onto a plate and brought the plate out to the living room. I stood there, staring at him the whole time like the creep I am. "Here." He handed me the plate and I took it.

"All for me?"

"The ones that fell to the floor were for you but now you can have mine. I don't eat breakfast that much anyway."

I nodded. "Right, okay. Are you sure? I mean we can split?"

"I'm sure. Please just go sit down and eat. I have to go

run some errands and I trust you not to make a mess of this place."

"You trust me?" I set the plate down on the coffee table in front of the couch and went to stand inches away from Jimmy. "Is that so?" I tilted my head just a bit.

"Don't think much of it," he said as he stepped back a couple of inches. "I need to go shopping once in a while and I don't want to be the 'mean kidnapper' you always talk about."

"Okay okay. Damn, so you don't like me? You just want to be a good kidnapper. I see." I kept on looking at him, his eyes were wandering and he was acting strange. I could just tell there was a slight shade of pink across his cheeks.

Is he embarrassed?

"Whatever, I'm leaving." He took the apron off and set it down at the kitchen counter and turned back to me. "I'll be back in a couple of hours."

"Can I come with you?"

"No," he said sternly. He walked past me and opened the front door. "I trust you, remember that." Then he shut the door behind him and left the house.

He left me alone in this house. He trusts me.

My mind was fazed. *I trust you.* Those words kept on playing through my head. The door was right in front of me. I could have opened it and escaped, but something prevented me from doing it. I walked a bit closer to the door and put my hand flat against it.

I heard the laughter of children and a dog bark. I went over to the right a bit and looked out the living room window. I saw two kids, maybe elementary school-aged.

They were walking their dog. It looked young. I remembered back to when Ritz was a puppy.

So cute!

I sighed and turned my head to the rest of the house, wondering what to do. Suddenly, something came into mind.

I can make Jimmy get even more on my side. I could clean the whole house. A deep clean just to make him happy. I should have a couple of hours before he comes back home.

I used to do that a lot back at home when father was at work and I was stuck at home on the weekends. I would clean the house for no apparent reason. I'd start with music. As it flowed throughout the house I would start at one corner of the house, always the kitchen. Sometimes when I would be cleaning, my father would come home early and yell at me for messing around with the house. "You put it in the wrong place!" he'd shout. Or, "Don't ever do this again, you hear that?" His voice was always so stern when he spoke to me. Sometimes I wonder, when people say your parents love you—I'm pretty sure father only loves me because of mother, but now she's gone. So, what's the point in loving me anyway? Am I right?

Enough of this depressing, sappy stuff. I shook my head.

Get the hell out of my head, memories.

The first step, music. I grabbed the television remote for the living room and turned on the TV. Since it was a remote for a Roku. It had YouTube and other apps. I searched for some random Christmas music. No idea why, but I did, and it played with a fireplace in the background for the video.

With the songs I knew, I sang along while cleaning up the house, thankfully not getting a noise complaint from the neighbors. Well, the music isn't that loud, but loud enough for me to hear it upstairs so, maybe it is?

A couple of hours later, I finished the kitchen, living room, most of the upstairs, my room. I was just finishing mine to be exact.

Wonder what's taking him so long to get back from wherever he went! I think he told me but how in the heck am I supposed to remember?

Once everything was done, I went to sit down on the couch, figuring I'd stay there until he returned.

Maybe I'll just lay down and rest my eyes for just a bit.

I ended up falling asleep. When I woke up from about an hour-long nap he still was not back. I sat up and rubbed my eyes.

What errands take this long to make?

I jinxed myself and he walked through the door. "Great timing," I said.

"What did you do?" He was looking around. I guess he noticed I cleaned up the place.

"I just cleaned." I paused, then stood up and walked over to him. Smiling I said, "Do you like it?"

"What the hell, Serina?" He looked straight at me. "What the hell? You went through my stuff and rearranged it? What if I had something special laying around and you just ruined it!"

"Sorry, I thought you would appreciate it and—"

"No, just no! Just, shut up!" That stupid mask was still on. "Sit down. I'll get some dinner ready. After you eat, you're going straight to bed."

I laughed a little. "You're not my dad, Jimmy."

He gave me a look that I've probably seen before. He was not liking the joke. I went to sit back down on the couch and stared up at the ceiling sighing. There was nothing I could do. He was in a bad mood, so I couldn't even try and ask to help him cook whatever he was cooking. There weren't any pan boiling up. There wasn't anything on the stove. The food was instead in a microwave.

Since when does he start making food in the microwave? I thought he was going to make a good meal, or at least ask me what I want for dinner like he has done most of the time so far.

I stood up and decided to use the restroom. When I was in there, I heard the microwave go off. Maybe he was heating something. As I was washing my hands and looking in the mirror, he knocked on my door.

"Have you finished in there yet?" He still sounded annoyed. I opened the door and walked through. "Finally." He paused. "You're eating in your room."

"What, why?" This was nothing like him unless I don't know him at all.

"Oh, and also, give me the notebook that I gave you. And don't even ask me why I need it, but I need it back."

"No! If anything, he'll take that notebook and read what I wrote in there. God, I was so stupid to write that.

"Give it back!" Jimmy grabbed onto my wrist with a lot of force. For a second, I was scared.

I pushed him back, running away from him and into my room, closing the door behind me. I guess he gave up on the notebook because he locked the door when I got in.

Chapter 5

The Past Can't Change

I was only a young child when I first experienced one of my father's and mother's fights. I don't know why it is stuck inside the back of my brain, but every time I think of my childhood, it comes up and I'm like, *How in the hell do I remember these things but I don't remember what happened—let's say—ten minutes ago.*

It was after school or on the weekend, I can't quite remember that part. My mother had a guy friend come over. His name was Julian. Of course, I wouldn't have understood what Julian and my mother had without somebody physically telling me what was going on between them at that age, but the one thing that I did know when this argument happened, was that father did not like Julian at all.

"Who the fuck is this?" I heard my father yell from my parents' bedroom. Mother told me about an hour or two earlier that they were going to watch a movie and not to bother them, so I didn't.

I sat in my room, minding my own business like the good daughter I am. "So what, you just decide to cheat on me now?" My father was still yelling. I was confused, so I left my room and went out into the hallway. I looked around the corner and there they were, all three of them, walking out of the bedroom.

I remember Julian didn't have on a shirt and had unbuttoned pants. Mother, however, was wearing a tank top and no pants, only her undergarment. My father was standing in front of the both of them, furious. He was fully clothed—I sure hoped he wouldn't get unclothed as I watched.

"So, you're just going to do this while our little girl is here, home, in her bedroom?" My father cast up his hands and walked towards Julian. He looked frightened to face my father.

The next thing that happened was my father clutched Julian by the side of his arms and launched him into a wall. My mother had gotten out of the way just in time. I jumped. Julian was not the only one who was scared. Right where Julian had been thrown, a hole was made in the wall and he was now on the floor.

My mother was crying hysterically. She got her phone out and tapped on a screen. "Yes, please, get over here as fast as you can! My husband—" Mother was talking to somebody on the phone. At the time, I didn't know who it was. She told them where we lived and stayed on the phone even after their conversation was over. That's when my father looked over his shoulder, and we made eye contact.

"See I fucking told you, woman! How much did you see, girl?" He stomped over to me. My heart started pounding furiously, the anxiety coursing through my veins. That feeling felt disgusting. I ran into my room and jumped onto my bed.

My room had purple painted walls, colorful bedsheets, a huge wardrobe and a large window by the bed with white see-through curtains. There were sirens in the distance. I knew it was the bad guys; as I called them when I was little.

My father looked out my bedroom window. He was the one scared now. He turned back out of my room, pushing my mother out of the way. What would have happened if the cops did not show up at that time? I have often wondered.

"I'm so sorry, I'm so sorry. Serina, my baby." My mother had tears streaming down her face, making me want to do the same thing, and I did. She and I cried.

When the cops came inside the house, they found us sitting on my bed in my bedroom. They asked my mother a bunch of questions. I didn't understand what they meant at the time. They also asked me a couple of questions. I didn't know how to respond. Thankfully, my mother responded for me.

That same night, me, my mother, and Julian all got into the same car with things that were special to us packed into a couple of bags. We drove away. I hadn't seen that purple painted wall since.

Julian and I had a great relationship after that though. After the incident, my father had made up some lie and explanation to the cops and got let go. After a couple of months of living in some random house, we moved into a different house. That was the last time I saw Julian. My father and mother moved back in together. There were no longer any fights. They were kissing, behaving like a normal married couple as they had before. My father loved my mother. I know that for sure. Maybe that's why he couldn't just move on. Because he loved her, and somewhere deep in my mother's heart, she loved him too. Or else, why would they still be together, making an image of a "happy family". It didn't last long— the new house, the lovely happy family—because then she died. After things got back to normal, I was no longer scared of my father.

When I do think of this time, before my mother died, it was a roller coaster. Am I afraid of him now? No, not really.

I haven't been around him much since my mother died so I don't even know what kind of person he is now, well except that he's an asshole who doesn't care about his daughter.

I wonder if he'll change if he knows his daughter got kidnapped. I wonder what he's thinking right this moment with me being gone for almost a week. I don't even know if that's how long it has been. More than a week? Honestly, I don't trust the clocks. I trust the sunshine and the night light. I haven't really kept track of how much time has passed because I don't care.

I did say this was a better life, but would it stay that way?

Chapter 6

Rocks and Bags

"It has been a while since I've seen Serina. I wonder where she is." There was a group of girls talking about Serina in school. The one that brought up Serina in the first place was a girl in black leggings, Adidas shoes, and a wild sweatshirt. Her long, blonde hair was caught up in her hood, but she didn't care.

"She's probably on some kind of rich vacation with her family." One of her best friends was wearing almost the same thing. These two wore matching clothing almost every day. Some people believe they're twins.

"I heard she has gone missing. What if she took most of her family's money and ran away with it?" said the last girl of the three. She had on a cute jean skirt—a little too short for dress code—with a white tank top tucked in. She had her brunette hair in a low ponytail.

Mariah heard all of this as she was walking by. The conversation took place only a couple of days after Serina had stopped showing up at school and disappeared from social media. "Hey, shut up okay! She's just missing. No one knows anything, so stop talking smack about her!"

"There goes the lesbian," one of the girls from the group called out to Mariah as she walked off. "I bet you're just protecting your girlfriend, lesbo!" They all giggled as Mariah clearly heard them and kept on walking. It bothered her, yes, but she tried to ignore it as best she could.

Mariah is still the only actually wondering what happened to Serina and worried for her. She still holds on to her reward from the ceremony and is hopeful she will get to give it to Serina one day. Mariah is probably the only person alive who cares for Serina's well-being and is willing to be her friend—or more.

As the group of girls who were gossiping about Serina was saying, Mariah is a lesbian, and she is in love with Serina. She and Serina have been going to school with each other for not even a year, yet she feels like she has known Serina for so much longer.

She used to live over ten hours away from where she lives now, in the town that Serina lives in. On her first day of school, most everyone shunned her because of her looks, but not Serina. She was nice to Mariah, and in her eyes Serina had everything. Mariah changed her clothing style, her hair, and then she started to wear contacts once in a while, all to be more like Serina, to be more like everyone else, so people would like her. Even though she was perfect the way she was before changing. The only thing that changed were those factors, but she did not get what she wanted. She didn't get to be popular like Serina. She didn't get talked to as much. Mariah was still a nobody who people made fun of. She tried so hard to change so people would like her, but nothing would work. This took a toll on her mental health.

Imagine a backpack. You carry it on your back everywhere you go, but every time you feel bad or someone puts you down, a heavy rock is added to the backpack, adding more weight on your shoulders to carry. That was Mariah's backpack.

Some people took rocks out of their bags on their back and put them inside of Mariah's bag, making it even harder to carry. Mariah herself couldn't get the rocks out of her bag because she couldn't take the bag off. She couldn't reach that far behind to help get the weight down.

But Serina could. Serina was Mariah's vision of a high school goddess. She was the one who took the rocks out of Mariah's bag. She was nice to her, didn't talk behind her back. She helped her. Mariah felt like she was someone to somebody—a friend. At the end of the day, instead of having nine rocks—heavyweight on your shoulders—she was now down to two light rocks.

Of course, no matter how many people want their bag to be empty, it never will because everyone has that guilt and sadness that they carry along with them. There's always something. There's always at least a small rock at the bottom of a person's bag.

Chapter 7

Go Home

Fuck!

Okay, after dinner I decided to go to bed. I thought everything was going alright until the next morning. Despite the thing that happened last night, I woke up to this terrible stench, like an old dumpster in the middle of an alley in New York. I tried to stretch out my body as I yawned, only to realize I have been tied up. My eyes widened. A cold sensation went through my body. I was back in the basement. The floor was cold, a stone-cold, goddamn floor I was on. What the hell happened to my little room with the bed and all the nice things in it? Did I do something to piss him off to put me down here?

If I do something else wrong, will he do something even more horrible to me? I mean I did refuse to give him the notebook, but I had a valid reason! It's not like I want him to know what I was thinking or planning. Good thing I hid the notebook. Just hope he doesn't find it.

If you think about it, maybe everything before this was just a dream, and I just woke up. Shit! If he comes down here, I swear I will spit in his face if that damn mask isn't in the way.

I heard footsteps. It was like he knew I was awake. Jimmy was on his way into my room to say good morning. I lifted my body so I could stand up, and that was when he walked in.

I tried to spit in his face, but missed. He was too far away from me. Good job, Serina.

"You asshole!" I shouted. All he did was tilt his head and smirk. "What the hell is wrong with you?"

The grin faded and he came up close to my ear. "Do you want your breakfast or not?" I nodded yes, feeling whipped. My hands clenched into fists and my nails dug into my hand, specifically, my right hand. All of the nails on my fingers had dug into my thumb, slowly beginning to dig into my skin. It hurt, but I couldn't stop it. My mind was empty.

"Well, good for you. I didn't make any. You're not getting breakfast." He stepped back. "You have to wait till dinner time comes around."

"What?" My back slid down and I was back on the floor. I looked around the basement that I was in. I felt something liquid on my thumb.

Shit! I made my thumb bleed. I couldn't look at it. I wonder how much I'm bleeding.

"What happened to your hand?" I didn't respond. My mind was still blank as my nails were still digging into my thumb. "Stop!" His voice accelerated. "What do you think you're doing?"

He took my hands and untied the rope. My hands were finally free and I sat there in silence. I was dead mentally, no matter how much I wanted to get up and go.

"Look at me! How many fingers am I holding up?"

How many fingers? How much blood did I lose? It couldn't have been that much. Maybe he's not medically talented, stupid.

He was in front of me now and I smiled at him. He looked worried. His hands held my hand as he looked at me. I stopped smiling. "I'm sorry."

Why did I apologize?

He got me up on my feet with my arm around his shoulders, bringing me out of the room, setting me on the carpet. I looked down at my hand, and there was the blood. I almost vomited. I looked up and I saw him. He had a red bag in his hand. My kidnapper took my hand again with a light touch. He set the bag beside me, took out some bandages, and started to clean up my thumb. It stung. My face scrunched up.

"Sorry!"

Why did he apologize? I feel like something is going on here, like he doesn't want to do this. What if Jimmy is being forced to do this? What if his family or loved ones are in trouble and he needs to do this to be able to save them? Or just maybe I'm going to get raped and then thrown out on the street.

I shivered. "It's going to be alright—"
"Why are you doing this?" I flat out asked him.

There was no point in asking questions inside my head that I can't answer. That's childish.

He didn't answer. He just continued working on my hand.
I could see right through him. He was trying his best to be the mean kidnapper that I always seemed to talk about,

but he just couldn't do it. I could tell that this was not who he was.

"There, promise me you won't do that again."

"Sure, yeah." That didn't mean, however, that I was just going to be nice to him anymore—unless necessary.

"You're staying down here until further notice. You got that?" He looked at me. "You cannot come upstairs, at all. Don't make any noise either."

Fine, I will obey your orders. It's not like it was any more fun up there. There is a bar downstairs and I can get wasted.

I nodded. "Good." He walked away. I walked behind him until he got to the stairs. My feet were slowly warming up on the carpet. I looked around.

"What am I supposed to do down here?" The plan of getting wasted was not a plan at all. The bar was empty. There wasn't anything there. There were also now two couches and a television down here.

Hey wait a minute, what?

Then it came to me. Jimmy was having people over. Why else would there be no alcohol, extra seating space, him being anxious, putting me down here where nobody up there can see me.

Oh, I see how it is. This is my chance to leave this house, tell them I need help but—he is going through all this trouble to impress whoever is coming over. Is it a girl? Does little kidnapper Jimmy here have a date? I chuckled to myself.

Oh hell yeah I'm going to mess it up!

* * *

It had been a couple of hours, but a little bit ago, I swore I smelled some good ass food. I was starving. I was chilling on one of the couches downstairs, relaxing until the audience had come on over.

Eventually, I decided to go up the stairs. The smell of the food was now much more clear. It smelled like turkey. I sniffed. There was also ham, maybe some potatoes and—carrots?

Man, how much more does he have up here?

I opened and closed the basement door, leaving the basement. Then I headed into the kitchen. I looked at the counter. It was filled with food. The place was even neater than I had left it after cleaning yesterday. I went to the counter and looked down at the ham, not turkey, but ham. I took a little piece of it and ate it.

Delicious!

"Hey, what are you doing up here?" He turned me around so my back was facing the food. I swallowed the ham and smiled slightly. "Oh, and you ate my food! Come on, Serina, I told you to stay downstairs!"

"When there's a smell that I cannot resist up here? Hell no," I paused. "You're having company over, aren't you? The extra couches, plenty of food, cleaning up even more than what I did, am I right?" I backed up my claim. He looked really nervous, even more so when a knock at the door was heard. I guessed they had arrived and I was right.

"Go downstairs, close the door behind you, and do not come upstairs, or else."

Well, I guess the couch would be nice to take a nap in while

*a bunch of people are here eating the food. I'm jealous. I'll be
down there in the not so hot basement of Jimmy's and freeze.
Gosh, what kind of world do we live in where girls are this
much unappreciated? I'm kidding.*

Before heading downstairs, I snatched the sweatshirt that
was lying on the floor and started to put it on. I heard
Jimmy sigh and I snickered as I reached the bottom of the
steps. A short time later, I heard voices—one, two, three,
no. There are at least five voices up there. I imagined a
married couple with a child, maybe Jimmy's sibling, and
the grandma, of course. The fifth person would have to be
another family member?

*They must think that Jimmy is just one wonderful guy who
has a good job and keeps his house cleaned, not a confused guy
with a girl trapped in his basement wanting to go home and
see her dog but unable to. Hey, that's me.*

I sat down on the couch and sighed, pulling my knees
up to my chest and laying my chin on top. "Downstairs!"
I heard a little kid's voice say.

*I don't know how young, but they said the word downstairs,
and I'm downstairs. Should I stay here, or should I go hide and
follow his majesty's orders?*

"Kyle! Don't go down there! It's unfinished and dangerous.
I don't want you to get hurt, buddy." That was Jimmy's
voice. I had never heard him say something so calm and
sweet. It sounded like he wasn't even the guy named Jimmy
up there that I knew.

The kid never did come downstairs, but as time passed,
I found myself wondering what would have happened if he had.

He came downstairs and looked at me. "Is that Jimmy's girlfriend?" That's everybody's instant thought when they see a girl at a guy's house. I look back at the kid and here come the other family members.

One of the guys in the back speaks. "Yes, she is." It was Jimmy. I wouldn't blame him though. He does have a reason for faking me to be his girlfriend. Since his family was down here, I'm sure he wouldn't wear that mask. What does he look like?

Dang, I wouldn't be able to imagine that. Although imagining the kid coming down here might have been interesting. So would being somebody's fake girlfriend. I sighed and lay my head back, staring at the ceiling.

What if that kid did come down here, for real? Would I see what my kidnapper looks like? Maybe I just need to stop thinking about it and sleep through all this. I'm not even sure if I should even be in this room. If the family won't come down here, why is it all cleaned up? It doesn't add up to me.

So, there's a kid named Kyle up there. I can hear their forks slide against their plates, the sound of laughter, Christmas music playing from the television. It makes me think of when I had a family moment like that. It makes me think—will I ever have something like that? What will become of me in the future?

The more time that went by, the more my mind got all clogged up with fog. I could barely see. I felt like hiding down in the basement was making me go crazy.

I'm pretty sure I'm hearing things too. There's this banging sound behind me, over by the unfinished room. Hey wait! Instead of my eyes being half-closed, they were all the way open. Looking behind me while still sitting on the couch, looking at the doorway, looking at the darkness of that room. It wasn't

my imagination because now I'm paying attention and some-
one or something is banging in that room. It could be from
upstairs, but when I hear it, it's up close, like it's calling out
to me. What do I do?

I followed the noise. If it was calling out to me, I would
go to it. I got up from the couch, walking into the room.
The noise got a whole lot louder. It was in the darkest corner
of the room that I hadn't checked out yet. It was so dark in
the corner where the noise was coming from, there was no
way in hell I was going over there without a flashlight or a
hammer just for safety.

I backed away slowly. That's when I heard a voice come
from the corner. The banging stopped. "Come here pretty!
Let me out! I'm begging you!"

"What?" My voice cracked. My throat was dry. It was
like I couldn't speak. I didn't run out of the room. I froze
up. I stayed because I think some part of me wanted to
know who this person was and why they were in Jimmy's
basement. Was he a victim just like me?

"Get me out of these damn chains!" There it was again,
that voice, that creepy laugh that went along with it.

"Who are you?" My voice was still weak.

He laughed again. "Let me at her! Let me at her!" I could
tell by the sound of his voice that he was smiling. Then the
banging started up again. A loud thud followed, then silence.
There was a person in that corner unless it was some kind
of recording, but I doubt that it was.

My kidnapper, Jimmy, is hiding two people inside of his house,
in his basement. One is crazy, one is just here. Either I have
to talk to Jimmy about it myself, and he'll tell me. Or I'll ask,
he won't tell me and I will find a flashlight and a hammer or
something to protect myself with, and I will go down here into

that corner and free that poor man. I wonder how long he's been here. Based on his mental state, I think he's been down here for a while—with no special abilities that I have.

Once the family leaves, or his visitors, whoever they are, I will storm up there and the first thing that will come out of my mouth will be, Why is there somebody else in your basement?

I made my way up the stairs as a couple of cars drove out of view of the living room window. Jimmy looked at me, of course, with his mask on. "Why is there somebody else in your basement?" I asked. "I waited down there like a good victim I am. Stayed out of your way, and your dinner."

He didn't answer my question. "Speaking of dinner, it is out in the kitchen if you want some. There's still food left. Oh, and you probably just imagined it. I gave you a drug to make sure you'd stay in the basement rather than ruining my little dinner."

Never mind.

"A drug, oh wow, smooth. Hey, Jimmy, I got a question for you." I walked into the kitchen. "Would you kindly not drug me? I followed your orders like I was asked. I cleaned the house for you. I'm not fighting back, and I'm being good. So why are you being so bad to me? You don't trust me?"

Of course if the tables were turned and I was the kidnapper, I wouldn't be so trusting either. The only good thing out in that world is my dog.

"Stop asking so many questions and maybe I will get to learn to trust you."

Oh yeah, sure, whatever you say.

I dished up some food. There weren't too many left-overs, but at least it was food. I was starving. He didn't get me breakfast. He had me down in the basement for the whole day.

Out of spite, I think I'm going to stay in the basement.

"Oh and you can come out of the basement now. I don't want you down there anymore so take your food upstairs into your room and eat there then go to sleep. I'll see you in the morning."

Oh, well, never mind—again. "Breakfast?"

"No."

Damn, I was hoping for him to say yes.

Jimmy got up close to me while I was holding my plate in the kitchen, not going to my room yet. He got a drink out of the fridge. Since he was so close, I smelled his cologne. It smelled nice. I wanted to compliment him myself instead of complimenting him in my mind but I couldn't bring myself to it. I shouldn't compliment my kidnapper.

I could imagine his hair being all done with gel. His blue eyes sparkling, his white teeth smiling and maybe even dimples on the side of his cheeks. The nice button-up he had on right now, the tan pants with the belt around his waist, the white socks, showing no skin. I could just imagine what he looks like without the mask on—without him hiding his face from me.

Is that weird to think about? I think he looks cute, although I don't know what his face looks like. When I think of it, I should've looked further into those photos because it was family photos. I might have found out what he looked like, but I didn't.

I felt my heart pumping. I can hear my heart beating. My eyes are so heavy. My throat is so dry. I can barely feel my feet. There's an anvil inside of my stomach. I weigh so much right now, I feel heavy all around.

I set the plate down, not finishing my food. Why did I suddenly feel like I was going to pass out? My kidnapper looked at me, his lips moved. I couldn't make out what he was saying until it rendered through my head.

"Are you alright?"

"Yeah, just tired I guess. I'm going to bed now." Was I tired? I'm not sure, but suddenly I didn't feel like eating anymore because it felt like if I did I'd burst out my guts and shit my pants.

Now that's gross. More than gross, that's sickening.

I ended up walking out of the kitchen slowly, up the stairs, dragging my feet, my eyes half-closed. I guess sleep was the best thing for me right now. When I went to bed, it felt like I had slept for days.

My eyes felt so light, everything around me was warm. I opened my eyes. I was laying on my left side, my arm resting below my head and the other up close to my chest. The first thing I noticed was the pillow. It felt weird. It felt softer than usual but it also felt like a pine tree. Then the next thing I noticed was a little boy in front of me. He was laying on his right side, his left hand was on my cheek. I couldn't move. I should be afraid of this but I feel warm, warm on the inside. The boy had white hair. There was an angel ring on top of his head. The energy of red and the happiness of yellow. It was the only thing that lit up the place I was in, yet I could see around me. Did it light up the whole room?

My back felt weird. I turned my head around my shoulder and saw hospital IV bags, the cords wiring up into my back. It didn't bother me that much, but the fact that did bother me was that the machine that had my heart rate on it. It was connected and powered up to my back as well. I was confused. I sat up and looked at the medical stuff beside the bed I was in. I turned back around, expecting the boy to still be there staring at me, and I was right. He looked so happy when I opened my eyes, although now, he looks like he was pretty tired with huge bags under his eyes, yet he still looks happy. My hand moved to his cheek. It was soft. Then the room instantly went cold.

I blinked. When my lids opened up again, I was laying on my left side on the same bed, staring at a blank wall. I sat up, my back hurt even more than before and I looked to see if anything was connected to it this time. There was. I had a cord plugged into my back like a charger cord but way larger. It reached one shoulder blade to the other. I followed the wire and it was connected to a power strip on the floor. When I sat on the edge of the bed, my feet didn't touch the ground. I looked at myself, and I looked just like the little kid that I saw earlier. The only difference was that I didn't feel any of the happiness he had, and I didn't smile. I also did not have the angel ring above my head, but the room was still lit.

There was a black phone charger cord also connected to the power strip. I followed that cord and found out there was a phone to the right side of me lying on the bed. Once I touched it, there was a ding. The phone received a text message and I read it, "Go home." The room around me started to get brighter and brighter and brighter. Until I was forced to shut my eyes only to hear Jimmy's voice a few seconds later.

"Serina? Serina!" His face was up close to mine. I was back in his house. I blinked a couple of times, confused. "What did you see? What happened?" He forcefully sat me up in the bed and grabbed onto my shoulders.

What did I see? This makes no sense.

"Charger cords—a lot of cords—"
"Is that all?" I nodded, even though it wasn't the truth. I remembered the boy, the message on the phone, but it didn't give me an answer, did it?

It said to go home, but I can't. There has to be some kind of reason for that message.

I pushed Jimmy lightly out of the way and walked out of the room. My throat was so dry. I had to get some water or something. It felt like I had never had a sip of water in my life. So, I went downstairs, my kidnapper following me.

Jimmy knows I was seeing something, and I feel like he knows that cords were not the only thing that I saw.

As I reached the kitchen and grabbed myself some water, I drank it. My eyes closed, feeling the water travel down my throat made me feel free.

This is the best water I've ever tasted.

While I finished the cup, my mind became more clear.

Jimmy is still by my side. He knows that I'm not telling him something. He knows things that I don't know either, and until he tells me, I won't tell him.

"I'm fine, can you give me some space, please?" I said.

"Yeah," he replied, stepping back away from me.

Thoughts had been rushing through my head. I leaned against the kitchen counter and thought to myself.

There's a person in the basement. I'm sure of it. But there's no way I'm going down there without a light. I've said that many times. Somewhere around this house there has to be a flashlight or something. Isn't it like a "need-to-have"? There's also the story with Jimmy. What if he has something to do with this? Well, of course, he has to with the person living in his basement.

The dreams, or nightmares, whatever you call them. They're neither. I had them about twice, I think, and each of those times when I woke up to reality, he was there saying something related to what I had just experienced. Like he was inside my mind almost.

If you think about it, Jimmy is hiding a bunch of secrets. The room that's always locked is one of them. Going out for "errands," which I don't believe for a minute, is another one.

There are so many things that I don't know yet. Like if I will stay here and be the victim who isn't a victim anymore? I just don't get it.

My mind was racing for about eight minutes. I was surprised my kidnapper left me alone. I wondered, if I were to get closer, would he start to trust me with these secrets he has?

Gosh, a thought just came into my mind.

What if there are two people other than myself who are in this house? I shake my head and get off the counter. Jimmy is in the living room and his leg is shaking violently. I walk upstairs without saying a word. I don't think he noticed.

I went back into my room and looked under my mattress. I grabbed the notebook that thankfully was still there along with the pen and I started to write.

I don't know what date it is, but I'm still here. Recently I believe Jimmy's family had visited and I was stuck down in the basement. But because of this, I learned something—there is somebody down in his basement. I'm going to figure out who, get a flashlight or something. And there are plenty more secrets, the room, his life, this house, and why? I thought Jimmy was a pretty nice guy, but the more I know about him, the more I question myself and him and everything.

Pros: He seems pretty fit, nice—especially around his family. Takes care of me (to the best of his kidnapper abilities) I guess.

Cons: He's a kidnapper, and might be a murderer. There's a person in his basement. There's a secret locked room. I don't know where we are right now. He goes out secretly and mysteriously.

Gosh, there are a lot more cons than pros. This might be bad. But it's like pros cancel out the cons, yeah? When you think about it, whenever there's a large amount of bad in a person, it always gets covered up by what's good, and we're blinded by the fact that this person is bad for us. In some cases, I mean. Sometimes, it doesn't work out that way but hey, I'm just writing down random words on a piece of paper, right?

One day I will read this notebook—all these pages and never forget this moment. If I ever do, let's be honest, who will forget a tragedy like this? But there is, however, one thing I do not want to forget about. These dreams I keep having. They feel so real. I've never had them before and it's just crazy to think that it's always the same thing where I wake up in my bed and there's a new surrounding around me. It's peaceful—or at least the first time was—and it's scary and confusing like the last one I had with all the wires and the boy. The boy was warm, I don't know how to explain it, but I hope to see that boy again someday. He might be the reason I want to keep having these dreams of mine. That's crazy, isn't it? To think that only a simple boy could control what I think and do.

Chapter 8

The Kiss

Is it a day? Night? Afternoon? There is no calendar or clock to tell the time. Well, maybe I lied. There is a clock out in the kitchen on the stove and microwave, but how should I know if they're not switched up? The only way I'll find out what time it is, or if it's day or night, is when I go downstairs and see the light shining through the living room curtains. My everyday routine, I guess, is to wake up after I sleep, no idea how long I've slept. I go see if it's day or night. Right now, today when I woke up, it was night. The next day? Maybe I just slept an hour? It's confusing to me, to be honest.

Time. It's a concept. "Time flies, time drags. We think of time as a one-way motion, from the past, through the present, and into the future. Life moves from the past to the future in such a way that what happens now and what will happen is always the result of what has happened in the past."

Jimmy wasn't in the room. He wasn't anywhere to be found to tell you the truth, and I was hungry. I didn't care if he yelled at me for making food. I was going to do it because I was hungry.

I'm just surprised he didn't lock me up in my room.

I opened the refrigerator and looked inside. Instantly, I knew what I was going to eat: eggs.

I took out the egg carton and set it on the counter, then I got a pan out, turned on the stove and set it down. He had one of the nice stoves—an electric one. These stoves have been trending lately because of their modern abilities. I grabbed the butter out of its container that was already on the counter and put just a slice onto the pan. I let it melt. That's when I opened the carton, took an egg out, and cracked it at the edge of the counter lightly. It made a small crack on the side. I held it over the pan and put my thumbs into the crack, splitting the shell into two, and let the yoke fall onto the surface. It made a pleasing sizzling noise.

I had to quickly throw the shell away and get another egg before the first egg had started to cook. I did the same steps with the second egg, then the third, and the fourth. Once all of the eggs were on there, they started to cook, and with a rubber scraper I moved around the eggs and mixed them, the yoke of the egg spread around and was mixed too.

After just five minutes, my eggs started to look like scrambled eggs and I took them off the heat. Next came my favorite part of the cooking process—thankfully Jimmy had slices of square cheese and spices. I grabbed a small cup filled with just a little bit of water and a lid that fit over the top of the pan. I had to do this step quickly. I put three slices of cheese on top of the eggs in the pan and poured the water into the pan carefully. I put the lid on. This makes the cheese melt faster.

Some people judge me for how I make my eggs, but they're

just jealous. They say that the heat coming off the eggs would melt the cheese but I don't want to wait for the eggs to melt the cheese then have my food cold while I eat it.

After waiting a couple of seconds, I took the lid off and put it in the sink. I grabbed the rubber scraper once again and mixed in melted cheese with the eggs. Lastly, spices.

Usually I just put a tiny little bit of salt onto the eggs and pepper—the more the pepper, the better! I believe it tastes better.

I got a plate and filled it up with the eggs and put the pan in the sink. This was going to be a great breakfast dinner.

After walking into the living room, I turned on the television and found something to watch. It had been a while since Jimmy left. I was sort of wondering what he was doing out so late but hey, this was my time. I could try and figure out the dude from downstairs, maybe I could even kill two birds with one stone and figure out what was in that locked room as well.

After finishing my food, I put the dishes into the sink and wandered off to find a flashlight or a match. For some reason, I stopped and thought to myself.

I'm too tired, and I have all the time in the world to look into that, right? No actually, I'm just too lazy.

Was that the real reason? I guess being lazy was what saved me. Right as I was thinking about my next move, Jimmy walked through his front door and I went up to him to greet him. "Welcome back from your journey." I put my hands behind my back. He looked a bit sweaty. "Where did you go anyway?"

"Just some errands and I ran a bit. Why do you care?"

"I was hungry and I made eggs." I turned around and shrugged.

I guess it is better if I do something about these mysteries if he's gone.

"When will you be out on errands again?" I asked.

"Probably in about a week. I don't know. Whenever I leave. Why?" Maybe he was getting a bit suspicious so I should stop talking about it.

"Just wondering. I gotta know when I'm going to get my food, right?" I laughed it off and plopped myself onto the couch. "So, what're we going to do now?"

"You mean, what are you going to do now?" He paused and stretched a bit. "I'm going to my room."

What great company, I thought.

"Have fun, whatever." But before he went up, I saw that he took a glass of water up with him. Most likely not important but if there was some kind of sleep medicine I could sneak in there when he was not looking—

Wait what am I thinking? He'll for sure get pissed at me for that. He'll know I was the one who did it.

Looking up at the ceiling, there was nothing to do but think.

How could I get closer to him? Make him love me? I guess that'll work, he's a kidnapper. I bet he'll fall for love easily.

Yes, that's it. Well, no I don't want to fall in love with some-body who I don't actually love. That's just fake, stupid. Maybe with fake loving him I would learn to love him, but that's not right. Plus, he probably doesn't even like me like that anyway, right? Gosh, what am I thinking?

Since there was nothing else to do, I went to go see what he was doing up in his bedroom. I peeked my head through the doorway and saw him sitting there at the edge of his bed, which was a little weird. Not to mention when I walked in a bit further the glass of water was on the floor in front of him. It was half empty.

"Jimmy?" There was no response. I tried again. "Hey, you alright?" Maybe he died. I went closer to him and tapped him on the shoulder.

Yeah, he's not dead.

He turned his face towards mine with his eyes wide.

I scared him.

"Sorry," I said.

Why is he on edge?

"Serina." He stood up. There was something wrong. The atmosphere around us felt off when he stood up. His hand grabbed onto my left arm lightly, and he just looked at me. Towering above me, our eye contact was fierce. Neither of us blinked.

That's when things got even weirder. His face leaned in closer to mine. Before I realized it, our lips were touching. With my eyes wide, I had no idea what to do. I was frozen. I had to move away.

This is so—I don't know how to explain it. One moment

I'm thinking of fake falling in love with him, and the next he's pressing his lips against mine. He kissed me.

"Wait. Wait. Wait. What the hell?" I put my hand on his chest, pushing him back. "You're my kidnapper. Why the fuck did you just kiss me?"

To my concern, nobody just kisses anybody like that, but the question that keeps on lingering now is—

"I—" He stepped away and turned around. "Go to your room. I just wanted to see how you'd react. Now I know."

"Well, don't do it ever again." My hand was hovering over my lips. My pointer finger rested on my bottom lip, and I was standing there while my mind raced.

Why? What? Is he telling the truth? This isn't real, this has to be a dream.

He turned back around and smirked. He went up to me and put his arm around my waist, his hand on my lower back. "How was it?"

I pushed him away again as I felt myself get flustered.

Get it together, Serina.

"It was gross. You're a bad kisser. Don't touch me." I turned around and left the room.

I guess I kind of lied when I said he was a bad kisser because, to be honest, or at least from the other kisses I've had in the past, he was not bad. The question that keeps lingering—why did I enjoy it? Enjoy the feeling? Great, now all that was on my mind was that kiss. The thoughts flowing through my head, coming in and out. I was confused.

I went into my room and closed the door behind me, hoping he wasn't following. He wasn't. I paced around, both my hands resting on my hips as I rendered what just happened over and over again on repeat like a popular song on the radio station.

* * *

The next morning seemed to be a bit normal—at least it was morning and I didn't sleep the whole day. What happened yesterday was still stuck in my head. Right away when I saw his face, that moment, what happened in his room, it was replaying again. I felt a bit of tension between us. I knew in his mind he was seeing the same thing. He was thinking about the kiss as well.

We didn't have any breakfast or anything to eat. We didn't speak to one another. It was like we were strangers passing on the street. Only this time he didn't drug me and bring me to his house. I was already there.

Things were silent. We worried about ourselves, and honestly, it was boring. I liked how we were, kind of fighting and a little talking here and there.

It's better than being silent with each other and acting like everything is wrong. I mean, don't get me wrong, things are wrong because he kidnapped me, and I'm here; but it's also my fault for staying. I get why things were silent, but it's so different.

One thing about this "fake" or weird romance moment where we looked like we were a thing, now it seems like we're strangers. It seems like neither of us wants to talk to the other because we're both embarrassed by what happened. Maybe Jimmy is more scared than I am to talk to him since he was the one who made the move. Unless, he was telling the truth about just seeing my reaction, but still.

It's crazy how things happen like that. One moment you can be strangers, the next friends, followed by best friends, and later suited lovers. Sooner or later those beloveds will become strangers.

It's crazy how you can have something with someone, and a couple of months later it's all in the past and everyone acts like nothing happened. The love between two people gone just like that. It's heartbreaking.

"Shit." There was a knock at the door. Both of our minds were cleared from the kiss. From love, now the focus shifted to the police car parked on the side of the road. "You need to hide. I don't care where but hide."

Why should I hide? This could be my chance to escape. Like I just said, it's my fault for staying, and right now, the police are at Jimmy's doorstep. It's my fault for not reaching out to them.

I ran upstairs, being as quiet as possible as he opened the door. There was this feeling inside of me that I should stay and for some reason when I saw the cops and when there was a safe way to get out and get Jimmy in trouble, when it was right in front of me, the feeling inside of me was stronger to stay.

"Hello sir, have you seen this girl? Her name is Serina Ange. She has been missing for a while now."

"I haven't, sorry to tell you that. I hope she gets found."

Jimmy is pretty good at this, speaking normally, not freaking out about the police at his door while I'm at the top of the steps listening in to their conversation. Jut then I had a thought. Has he ever done this kind of thing before? Lying to the cops, straight to their faces.

"Then you wouldn't mind if we search the house. Don't

worry, it won't take long." Something must have gone wrong. Usually, they'd leave. Did they see something suspicious about Jimmy? That's when I decided to find a place to hide.

I don't blame Jimmy for letting them in. I would too if they came to my house. It'll just make you look more suspicious if you say no to them and refuse. They'll probably have the right to go in by force anyway.

I heard the front door close. I was looking in my room for somewhere to hide. There was nowhere but the closet, but if the police looked in there, I'd be found. One thing came to mind. The hatch that I saw in Jimmy's room that one time, I could go there. I quietly tip-toed to his room. When I opened the door to the closet it made a little squeak. I winced, hopefully, nothing was heard. Getting in, closing the doors behind me while I found the hatch in the darkness, I heard no voices or footsteps headed my way.

Thankfully, I did find it and I remembered where the hatch was. I couldn't remember if there was a lock or not— or if there was one in the first place—the lock didn't work because the hatch opened.

A flash of cold air blew in my face. It must have been the basement. Maybe it led somewhere, but I couldn't think of that now. I needed to hide before the police got upstairs. I jumped down, closing the hatch as I went. There was a slight bang, not that much surprise though, it was quite the fall. Once I was down there, I looked up at the hatch, barely seeing it because of the darkness surrounding me. I couldn't reach back up to the top of the room, so if that was the way out, I might just be stuck down here.

I heard chains moving in the same room I was in not even a minute after I dropped. "Pretty, let me out of these chains.

LET ME OUT!" This strange voice wasn't my kidnapper's voice. I was in a dark room. The voice was yelling.

I hope this place is soundproof.

"You're very pretty, pretty, pretty, pretty." I felt like I had heard this voice before.

"What?" My voice cracked. It was like I couldn't speak. I was confused for one, but mostly scared. Scared of what was down here with me, and scared about the police, scared about Jimmy.

"My brother made the right choice. A very pretty girl, very pretty!" There it was again, that voice, that creepy laugh. I focused on his words and I was looking around me, trying to see which direction the voice was coming from.

Brother—he said brother, that his brother made the right choice. Jimmy?

I stepped back as a man showed up right in front of me. I backed up not even two inches and I hit a wall. "There's no way out of here pretty, no way out. If there was, I would be out of here by now."

Who is this? Why does he keep on calling me pretty? Repeating the word like it is the word of the day?

I looked at the chains wrapped around his neck and his feet. His arms were behind his back, most likely chained as well. I looked at his face. It was too dark to notice the features of it, but I did know that he was injured. There was blood on the ground, blood on his face. It looked like one of his eyes was about to pop out of his skull. His body looked small, skinny, and frail.

"Who are you?" My voice was still raw. I tried to whisper.

He laughed again. "Let me at her, let me at her!" He smiled. His teeth were barely there. He had maybe three teeth at most.

What the hell am I supposed to do? I can't get back up. I can't get any further away from this person. I can't scream. I can't yell for help because nobody will hear me and the cops are inside of his house. They can't hear me, right? They would be here. This room must be soundproofed, otherwise they would be here by now, right? I don't know what to do. I'm freaking out. I don't know who this is. What if he has something infectious that I will get? I mean, look at him! This will have to be a page in the journal. I have to remember this moment. I have to ask Jimmy about this guy. But there's nothing I can do now.

Silence.

The room I was in became quiet. I looked around. The beat-up guy who was chained was not as close as he was before. Relief went through my body as my tensed up muscles relaxed just a bit. There was nothing I could do but wait. Wait in this room, this dangerous yet silent room, for Jimmy to come get me the hell out.

If he even finds me that is.

Chapter 9

Ritz

Mariah was finding it hard to focus on the task ahead, taking notes in science class. She definitely heard the ripping paper as her fellow students pulled paper out of their notebooks to write down notes. But she barely noticed the students around her who were messing around instead of doing their work; and talking to the person next to them.

There were twenty-four students in the class and seventeen of them were boys, so the majority of the class was made up of males. Mariah turned her head when she heard one of the students whisper Serina's name. The rumors had been spreading throughout the school for days, but that's all they were—rumors. Nobody knew what had happened to Serina.

Mariah's head turned again when she heard a buzzing noise in the background. It was coming from the projector even though nothing was yet showing up on the SMART board in front of the class.

Mariah tried to tune into the whispering students' conversation again, but was distracted by the teacher, Mrs. Swanson, as she handed out neon green sheets. Two students stared ahead, but not at their screens. The teacher wasn't paying attention though because she was answering the question of a shy girl in the class. The teacher seemed cool about the answer, whatever it was. She closed the door to block out the noises in the hall, the whispers, the laughing.

The assignment was to put bullet points on the side of the paper and write down what was on the screen with their bullet points. About seven minutes had passed when the teacher said, "Does anybody need more time?" As she walked around, her heels clicked against the hard floor.

After finishing their assignment, the students started to do a little quiz on the computers. The name of the quiz was "Pretest: Earth in the Solar System". After they finished, the teacher brought the answers up on the screen, and then polled the students to find out how they had done. Mariah got a few right and a few wrong, but she didn't really care much. She just put an "x" over the questions she missed and moved on.

One of the questions was about moons, and if any of the planets has more than one moon. It was true. Turns out that most of the planets have more than one moon. Who knew?

The class was silent, looking at the teacher while she went over more of the questions, reminding them about the review they had done the day before. There were two "student pets" in the classroom who always raised their hands and answered correctly (almost every time). The teacher backed their answer ups, sharing more information to make it more believable—talking about the shifting of tectonic plates and the underwater rocks. The majority of the answers for this mini quiz were C. Like somebody once said, Mariah thought, "When in doubt, choose answer C."

Just like the two who always raised their hands, there were always the two people who were best friends in the back row of the class who messed around and didn't listen while the teacher was trying to teach. One of the people gossiped and whispered about one of the students who answered a lot of questions. They snickered behind their backs.

"Is the sun going to keep going and going forever?"

"No," the students replied in unison to the teacher. Mariah thought at that moment that everybody in her class could be robots. She laughed to herself just a bit, quiet enough that nobody else in the class heard.

"In four and a half billion years the sun might go out," shared the teacher. Even though it could be a serious thing in the future, not many students were bothered by this. Was it because they don't have to worry about it?

"Are things in space moving?" she asked next. The class was silent. Since she didn't get a verbal response, she continued, "They are. The stars, galaxies, and nebulas. Everything is expanding. That's the theory of our expanding universe. Stars appear to be moving, but why?"

One of the students raised a hand, and shouted out, "The earth is moving."

"Correct."

Half of the class got most of the questions on the quiz correct. Once everyone was done going over the quiz, a lot of the guys crumpled up their paper into balls and threw them in the garbage. One athletic kid threw his paper ball towards the garbage can from his seat, as if it was a basketball hoop. Of course he failed. Rather than doing the right thing and picking it up though, he just left it there on the ground next to the garbage.

Mrs. Swanson got off track and started to tell stories. "I dreamed once that the moon is made out of rubber and it came down, so I kicked it back into the sky," she said. Some students laughed it off, but not in a mean way. The teacher was laughing with them.

Another story came after that. A student in the front row of the classroom shared that he had once stuck tweezers into an outlet because he was bored. His exact words were, "I did it so I could become a flamethrower. He also shared that he got shocked, but no fire resulted.

The class got off topic and now all the other students started to talk about incidents that happened when they were younger, and their experiences with shocking themselves. While those conversations happened, they were told to grab their evidence notebooks. A couple of people went to get their notebook if they didn't have them already. Now it was time to take notes in science class. Of course, being the high school students that they were, most of them messed around while they did it.

More conversation echoed off each wall as the teacher spoke with Steven, the student who told the story of the flamethrower, more in-depth of what happened in his situation.

Ms. Swanson has a "board of shame" where she sticks up gum and candy wrappers that she finds on the ground. When there are too many wrappers on the board, she will ban whatever treat the wrapper came from for all of her classes. This annoyed Mariah. She didn't understand why students can't just put their trash in the trash can.

After everybody took their seats, the teacher put the slide from her computer up on the screen. The title on the smart board was "CER Model." There were markers that came along with the smart board where you could write notes on the board. That's what the teacher did. She put notes on the board, the same ones she had written the other day. The teacher explained the notes and waited for a little bit between sections so the students could write them down.

CER Model

1. **Claim - Answer to a question (one sentence).
   "I think that....**

2. **Evidence - Provide at least two pieces of evidence
   from the text that support your claim (2 sentences)
   Factual info.**

3. **Reasoning - Explains how the evidence supports
   your claim. "My evidence is... which supports
   my claim that..."**

She held up the neon green sheet in front of the class
and devoted a whole speech to it. Showing the claim, evidence, and reasoning that were on there, she then rambled
on about the homework assignment students were being
given that related to the violent history of the solar system.
There were questions the student had to answer on one
side of the paper, and she said something about cutting
something out of a magazine. Mariah missed what she had
said originally, but tuned back in when she heard, "This
will be a requirement. Something that has to do with the
moon and the Earth. Then, you will find a pair of scissors.
You will take them and open back up the paper. You cut
through one layer, cutting through the dotted lines shown
on the paper on half of the paper, not across the whole thing.
It's going to look something like this. Tomorrow I will be
sure to have our tape dispensers out so we can tape them
in our evidence notebook."

One of the students interrupted Mrs. Swanson, reminding her that it would be Saturday tomorrow. Not only do
students forget that it's a Friday, teachers do the same thing.
"Oh shoot. We don't have school tomorrow," she said, then
continued explaining the assignment students would have
to work on over the weekend.

Then with the remaining time in the class, Mrs. Swanson snuck in a little more instruction. "What does geo mean?" she asked the class, putting her hands together by her waist.

"Earth," a student called out.

"Isn't it clever how Latin works? Latin is a very difficult language to learn." A student laughed under his breath, but loud enough for basically anyone who was paying attention to their surroundings to hear him.

Even though there were only a few minutes left in the class period, the teacher continued showing pictures explaining heliocentric and geocentric models, and asking questions. "Why do you think the geocentric model was popular for so long? What do you think caused people to begin to favor the heliocentric model?"

Realizing class would be over with momentarily, nobody answered. The students instead started packing up their things, and when the bell rang they quickly got up and rushed out the door to head home.

It was the weekend now, and Mariah was on her bus ride home. She sat closest to the window and looked out and through the glass, seeing all the houses fly by. Sometimes seeing what was happening inside of a house.

The bus passed a light blue house with a large window in the front. There were curtains. However, they were not closed. Because of this, what Mariah's eyes saw was something you don't see every day. A middle-aged guy was dancing with what seemed to look like a younger kid. She smiled slightly at the sight, which reminded her of when she used to be care-free and dance in the living room like that. A couple of minutes later, the bus reached her stop. She stood up and got off the bus, suddenly encountering a blast of cold air. She hadn't brought a jacket to school that day and rushed towards the house.

Usually, when Mariah gets home her mother, Nellie, is home in her office working. Mariah's mother always cooks dinner right before school ends so when her daughter gets home, she has something to eat.

"Philly cheesesteak, my favorite!" Instantly Mariah smelled the food coming from the kitchen. She dropped her school stuff on the living room floor as she went to say hello to her mother face-to-face in her office. "Thanks, mom." She smiled, happily.

Her mother looked at her tiredly and nodded, smiling as well. "Ah, don't say thanks. Just eat up."

"What about you?" Mariah asked. "Should I leave some food for you and dad?"

"We'll be fine. You go eat, alright?" Nellie went back to work.

Mariah's family is quite poor, or at least less rich than Serina's. Her father works all the time, but always comes home every day with a smile on his face and enough energy in his system until everybody goes to bed in the house. It warmed Mariah's heart that he did this because of her and Nellie, but it also pained her at the same time because of how much her father had to deal with.

Philly cheesesteak is a treat they have once every two months, even though it costs more than their typical meal. Sure, making it at home is less expensive than going out, but the meal still costs between twenty and thirty bucks. Mariah's family lives paycheck to paycheck. They barely have enough money every month for expenses like rent and generating heat in the house.

Mariah ate quite fast, especially when her taste buds favored the food that was about to be digested. She had about three hours of free time before she had to begin anything school-related. Homework, shower, get ready for the next day. That was her usual week schedule. But luckily for Mariah, it was a Friday, and frankly, she forgot that fact, thinking there was school tomorrow.

"Mom, I'm going out for a bit. I'll be back!" She yelled, opening the front door and walking out. The blue sky looked amazing as she looked up and admired it. She then smiled at the green trees and nature that surrounded her.

Some days Mariah would take walks. Nellie would sometimes join in, but this time Mariah wanted to be alone. Being alone means a lot more thoughts could come to mind, like overthinking for example.

Serina was on her mind, particularly what the other students said about the "rich girl" who went missing at school. She was disgusted by how people reacted to this type of situation, something that shouldn't be joked about because it was a real thing that happened in the real world. Mariah believed in that fact a lot, and she was willing to do anything—well almost anything—to make things "right" in her opinion.

As she was walking, she shook her head, not wanting Serina to be on her mind because lately she had been on her mind a lot. A lot as in the amount of time that Serina had been missing? No, Mariah had been thinking about Serina for a lot longer than that. Ever since they had met, in fact. Ever since Mariah had set eyes on Serina, it was like a virus went inside her motherboard, her brain.

After probably an hour passed, Mariah was ready to head on back home when she spotted a dog, a Cairn Terrier with a warm ivory color coat mixed in with beige. The little guy looked lost, so Mariah rushed to its rescue.

First, she checked the dog's collar. Luckily there was one because if there wasn't it would have been harder looking for its owner. She said the name on the tag out loud to herself, "Ritz." After looking around and seeing no possible owner around, she picked up the dog, careful like it was a human baby, and started walking home.

"Cute name, Ritz," she said, smiling at the little dog.

By the time they showed up back home, Nellie was very nice about it. They came up with the idea of keeping the dog until they found its owner. Ritz now had a little foster home. Mariah liked this idea because after a half-hour of being with Ritz, she loved him to the bottom of her heart and couldn't let him go. Mariah promised herself and her parents that she would take care of the dog, feed it, give it water, take it on walks, everything. That was the main reason her parents agreed to let her keep the dog for now, despite not having much money to take care of the animal.

A night of hanging out between Mariah and Ritz was pretty interesting. They were both lying upside down in her bed, looking at each other. Mariah made conversation with the dog who most likely had no idea what she was saying, but they still looked at each other intently, and it made Mariah's night. When it was time for her to get some shut eye, she laid down under the covers with the dog in her room, the door closed. Ritz went under the covers as well and snuggled up by Mariah's legs. He got some shut-eye as well. Although, when it was morning, Mariah got up only to see that Ritz was gone.

"Ritz?" She said tiredly, getting the blankets off of her, looking around her room. She started to freak out a bit. "Was it a dream? No, it couldn't have been." She continued to look and once she was in doubt, a little bark came from the other side of the house. Mariah instantly headed in the direction the noise had come from, seeing the dog wagging his tail with her dad, Joe. "Dad."

"I took this little guy out for a morning walk. Hope you don't mind." That was a relief for Mariah. She thought it must've been a dream or that Ritz ran away.

"Thank God! I almost had a heart attack when I woke up and saw him missing." Mariah picked the dog up and kissed it, laughing a bit.

"A heart attack?" Joe laughed. "This dog must be important to you."

"He sure is, but I know we have to find his owner." She
gave off a sad smile.

Later in the day, her parents made missing dog fliers.
They got some companies and other places around town
to help look for the owner. They put the papers all around,
hoping for the owner to show up and claim Ritz. Nobody
came the first day the papers were handed out. Mariah and
her new best friend talked again all night, laying in bed,
having fun. They were both having a blast.

* * *

"Mariah!" Ritz was wagging his tail. He seemed to know
what was about to come. He ran out of the room with his
little legs and barked happily when he saw a guy standing
in Mariah's living room. "This man, Marcus Ange, claims
to be Ritz's owner."

Marcus held his hand out. "It's a pleasure to meet you.
I've heard that you've been taking good care of Ritz for us,"
he paused and smiled. "Thank you." Mariah shook his
hand then she couldn't help but ask if he was Serina's father.

"Mariah, please." Nellie thought it was inconsiderate
because of the loss the father might be feeling.

"Oh no, it's quite fine. Yes, I am her father. It sure is
something that she's—" He hesitated on saying the next
word, "missing." Clearing his throat afterward. "Anyway,
I should really bring Ritz back home and give him his
favorite dinner. Thank you guys again. I appreciate this,
and Serina will too."

After Mr. Ange and Ritz left, a strange feeling came over
Mariah. She had this lingering thought that she would never
see him again. Not to mention she couldn't believe she had

just met the one and only Serina's father. Mariah pondered about this for a while.

She.

Met.

Serina's.

Father.

This was crazy for her. She never thought she would meet him. Mariah felt kind of empty. She felt lonely. She could've learned more about Serina from Marcus. She could have given him the award she has been keeping for Serina. She could have done a lot of things, but she didn't.

Ritz was gone. Serina was gone. Mariah was back to only having a select few friends, and of course her parents at home.

"It was Serina's dog." Mariah said out loud, trying to take it in. "Her dog. I can't believe that I touched her dog." She loved Ritz even more knowing that he was Serina's. Even if he might not be with her now, he would always be in her heart. But that didn't compare to the happiness she felt knowing she had touched something that Serina cherishes with all her heart.

"Mariah, sweetie, I'm sorry it was so soon that the little guy found its caretaker, but now he's back home, back to his owners. It will be alright." Nellie set a hand on her daughter's shoulder, consoling her as she noticed Mariah's expression and sad smile.

"It's alright. I'm alright," she paused and smiled at her mother with that same smile. "I'll be in my room if you need me."

Mariah's family hadn't really watched much television in their life, so whatever was on the news or anything special like that, the only way they'd hear from it is from friends, family, and peers. If something big happened, they'd be some of the last people in the town to know because they weren't really interested in that type of stuff. Or they weren't interested in that type of stuff before. Mariah only really got into the news and information of what's happening around the world—around her town—because of Serina's disappearance. Will there be any more news? Has she been saved? Found dead? She wasn't a detective. She couldn't do anything for Serina, but if there was just the slightest chance she knew where she was, Mariah would definitely not have hesitated to go save her, to save a person she really cares about.

Chapter 10

The Death of a Family Member

I couldn't get any sleep, not while I was down here with him. My eyes were so heavy, it was hard to keep them open, to stay awake. Good thing this beat-up guy didn't stay quiet for long, otherwise I may have closed my eyes and fallen asleep already. Just the right time for something bad to happen.

"What are you doing over there, pretty?" The chains rattled. I looked up from my hands as his body crawled like an animal over to me. Seeing his face clearly, I almost threw up.

"Same old, same old." I figured out by the time I was down here that he didn't freak out as much when we were having some decent conversation.

It's not the best though.

"I'm hungry. Brother will bring me food soon." He licked his lips, and scooted closer towards me. A sadistic laugh filled the room. "I could always just eat you."

I stood up, wiping off some dirt and placing my back flat against the wall behind me. "What the hell man, that's creepy!" Those words spat out of my mouth.

Oh no.

"I'm not creepy!" He screamed, jumping just a bit, freaking out. I knew this was going to happen. He shouted at the top of his lungs, hitting his own legs and pulling on the chains that were attached to him. "Not creepy!" If anything, this guy was self-conscious about himself even though he may not seem like it.

"Okay, okay! Calm down. Can I ask you a question?"

"Pretty, pretty. I'm not creepy!" Of course, he wasn't going to answer my question right now. Maybe later, once he calmed down.

This was the third freak out so far that he'd had right in front of me. I wondered how many times he freaked out when I was in the room above him while cleaning the house. I heard nothing. To think that he was down here the whole time is weird to think about. How something is so close, but so far from your reach?

"I love this time of day—" The person who was stuck with me down here pointed over at the wall. "I used to be able to reach that wall and look out the hole, and see all the kids playing."

Okay, creepy.

I wasn't connected to anything. I wasn't tied down by chains, so I could go over there and look out the hole.

Maybe it can be some kind of entertainment while I'm down here, right? Or am I becoming just like him? Speaking of him. I think I'll just give him a name. He looks like a Barthamieal, Bart for short.

Bart stopped talking and sat down on the heels of his

feet, slowly letting his ass hit the ground as his knees came closer to his chest. He rocked like a child. I shook my head. Sometimes people need to be alone. I felt a little safer now that I had gotten used to his movements.

Gosh, I sound like such a bitch saying "movements" and all these other things about Barthamieal.

I walked over to the wall that he had pointed at and looked around for the hole. Since we were underground I thought the hole would be somewhere near the top. I started at the top left corner and went from there. The middle of the wall was where the hole was.

Well, more to the right, which wasn't symmetrical; but you know what, I don't care. The only thing that really bothers me about unsymmetrical stuff is if it's unsymmetrical in a video game that I play.

I went up on my tippy toes.

I'm too short for this.

I looked through the hole, and surprisingly I could see a lot more than what I had imagined. Bushes were surrounding the hole, but there was just enough room between the two bushes that I could see the sidewalk, the road, the front lawn, part of the sky.

It seems peaceful after looking around a dark room and seeing all the cobwebs. Gross!

There was a little boy, and he seemed to have a sibling with him, a girl? I couldn't really tell from where I was.

The little one was holding a red ball and throwing it up into the air. He also started to kick it. I smiled a bit. It seemed like fun.

I wish I never grew up.

As I was watching them, it seemed like the older sister was not having much fun. Her little brother threw the ball up into the air, smiling up at it and waiting for it to come back down so he could catch it. That didn't happen. The girl knocked the ball in the air, making the ball end up in Jimmy's yard. It ended up right in front of the peephole.

All I see is red now.

The boy laughed loud enough for me to hear him, but it seemed so quiet from where I was. He must have thought his sister was just playing with him. That was rude of her.

I got a bit closer to the wall. My chest basically against it, and I tried to get a better view, trying to keep my balance. The red that I saw started to move. The next thing I knew, I saw the boy looking straight into my eyes with no expression. Then his eyes opened, wider than usual. His mouth moved like he was saying something, but I couldn't hear exactly what. I tried to read it his lips. No luck at that.

I continued to stare through the hole. Did he see me? He must have because his little finger went across the hole from the outside and tried to wave to me. I realized that he could see me. He was trying to make contact. I blinked twice, trying to tell him, "Hey I'm here. I see you."

I don't think he got the idea though. Before losing a staring contest with this random boy, he turned around quickly with the ball in his palms and stood up. He ran back to his sister and I watched them walk down the sidewalk.

The boy looked behind his shoulder before turning back and looking up at his older sister.

Shit!

The more I think about it, the higher the chance I could have been saved because the boy could have gone to the door, and given Jimmy some kind of idea that I'm down here, but I guess not. Too late.

My feet went flat on the floor and I sighed, turning back to see what Bart was doing. He was laying on the ground, so I assumed he was asleep.

My eyes still felt heavy, and I decided it was a good time to take a little break. Plus, Barthemial was sleeping. What could he do, right? I let myself drift off to sleep.

* * *

"Ryan!"

Looks like my nap time is over, unless I'm just beginning a new dream.

To be honest, the nap was amazing. I had lots of dreams, and I felt refreshed when my eyes had opened. However, those feelings didn't last too long.

Uh oh.

"Serina!?" I saw Jimmy standing in the room, hovering over Bart's sleeping body.

"You finally found me? I didn't think it would take this long." I stood up, continuing to talk. "Your friend here though was pretty interesting."

"Yeah, so interesting he's dead." I heard the sarcasm in the first part, but he was serious when he told me that Barthemial had died.

"What do you mean. He was just sleeping." I paused, thinking it over. "Wait, no way." I didn't check if he was actually asleep. I just assumed.

"Yes, way. What did you do to him down here? Did you feed him something? Touch him? Anything?" He walked towards me and put his hands on my shoulders. It was not a light touch. "Tell me now, Serina!"

Fuck, I messed up. I screwed up. I cannot believe myself. I can't tell if Jimmy is pissed at me, or silently breaking down on the inside which is why he is acting out. All I can tell right now is that I feel absolutely terrible.

I was supposed to do something, I guess. I was down here with him and it seemed like Jimmy really cared for Barthemial, despite having him stuck down here looking like he wasn't taken care of at all. Maybe he had a reason. Maybe he was born like that?

It couldn't be. I'm overthinking. This can't be real. This has to be a dream. I screwed up. Serina, you can't just tell yourself that everything will be okay because it's not. You know deep down that.

I could see it in his eyes. He was sad. He was serious. He was sorry. I couldn't put an emotion to it. Maybe he saw the same thing in my eyes. I heard the eyes are the gateway to the soul. You can see what a person is feeling based upon what their eyes say.

"I'm sorry." I looked at Bart laying on the floor then back at Jimmy. "I didn't know anything was wrong. I didn't do anything to him. I thought he was just sleeping!"

"I thought you ran away, Serina!" He let go of me and stormed off in the other direction, the opposite side of the room that I was in. "God! You had me so scared. I thought you left, and I thought something could have happened to you."

He was scared? I fell silent.

"It has been days. I thought you left the house, and you weren't coming back. I've tried everything. Maybe I wasn't trying hard enough to make you stay." He paused, his voice calming down. "It has been years."

"Hey, Jimmy, why would I leave? Tell me that." I walked over to him.

"Because I took you hostage. Can't you see? I'm a maniac. I'm stupid. You probably want to go home, but I'm keeping you here."

"Did I ever say once, to your face, that I did not like this? That I wanted to go home? Did I try to run away when you left the house? When you were asleep? No, Jimmy, I didn't." I grabbed his hand, and forced him to look at me. "This right now, me living with you, it's been the best thing that has happened to me in months. I don't want to go home."

Now he was the speechless one. "You really mean that?" Finally, I let go of his hand and it rested by his side. "You don't want to leave?"

"Well, maybe a little, but I don't know how to explain it. It's a lot to explain, and I'm sure you don't want to listen."

"No, no," Jimmy answered fairly quickly, "I do want to know. I'm here, I'm listening."

I'm here.

My chest felt like it was being lifted somehow. Something felt different. My chest felt weird. My heart, maybe?

Somebody who wants to listen to me. Somebody to under-stand me. Could I trust him?

"Okay—let's just get out of here first."

"I'll boost you up, and I'll tell you where to get a ladder." He bent down on his knees. "Then, I'll make you some food. You must be hungry."

I nodded and followed his instructions. He boosted me up through the hatch door like he said he was going to. Once I was up there I looked down at the dark room below, heat warming up my body slowly yet surely as I remembered how soft the carpet is. Jimmy told me that the ladder was in the room by the kitchen, the locked door. I reminded him that the door was locked and he told me where the key was. It was behind his television in a little box—a weird place for it, but an easy place to remember.

I felt bad leaving him there all alone, but he was down there with someone who he clearly cared about.

That leaves me wondering if he really cares about Bart. If he does, why did Jimmy have me up here, but him down in a freezing room? I'll be sure to ask him that after we have this serious talk about why I want to stay and why this is better than the last couple of months that I've lived on this earth.

Inside the box was a small key, just one, on a thin red string. I went downstairs, through the kitchen, the sunlight meeting my face through the windows. I reached the door and there it was. After wondering what was in this room, I would finally get to see.

My hand reached for the knob and it unlocked. He wasn't lying. I mean, I wasn't doubting him in the first place, right? To my surprise, it was just a bunch of boxes. This was a storage room. There were boxes that said "kitchen", and boxes that said "Maya", whoever that was. Without taking much of a look at the rest of the boxes that were in the room, I found the ladder leaning against the wall in the far back corner. It was red and silver. I went over there and picked it up.

I'm not going to lie. It was kind of heavy, but that's okay. My goal isn't to become more muscular.

"Should I just drop it down?" Jimmy was waiting down there, next to Bart. He looked up at me, and held his hands up.
"Just drop it down slowly. I'll grab it and set it down, then I'll climb up."

It's like he's done this before with someone. He knows what he's doing.

I did what he said, putting the ladder down. He took it and climbed up, giving me a gentle smile as he closed the hatch door and left the ladder there.

Good thing it wasn't an inch taller or maybe we couldn't have closed the hatch, and I don't think that would be a good thing if the cops come here again. They'd call me and Jimmy murderers.

"So," I stared at him as he began to speak. "What do you want to eat?" Totally putting on a fake mask over his face about Barthemial, I knew deep inside he was hurting, and that he cared for him; but he wasn't showing it because he wanted to listen to me, to my feelings, my life, me.
I replied as I started to walk out of his bedroom and downstairs. "Surprise me."

I honestly have no idea what I want to eat, really anything I guess because I'm so hungry that like a cow I could eat grass if I really wanted to.

I sat down on the couch, closing my eyes. My mind focused on my breathing. I could feel my chest rise and fall. My mind felt like there was wind flowing from one ear to the other, cooling down my head. There was so much emotion within the air, getting denser as me and Jimmy got closer to one another.

Right now—I don't know why—but I feel like saying everything that's on my chest, asking all these questions, yelling about my father, everything. I just want to feel good, uplifted. I want to feel something other than regret, sorrow, anxiety. I guess you could say everyone has a face mask.

"I just heated some leftovers I had from last night. It's some stuffing and mashed potatoes." He brought over the hot plate of food. I smelled it and it smelled amazing. I just wanted to dig in. "Hopefully it's enough."

I took the plate and nodded. "It's enough. Thank you, Jimmy."

I knew it was coming soon—the talk, him listening, me talking.

"I guess you want me to explain? Start from the beginning?"

"If you're willing, I'm here." He sat next to me, looking at me with caring eyes. His eyes said he was telling the truth.

You can trust him.

Sometimes I'm just not okay with sharing my life story,

what happens at home, because I always get so emotional and the last time I tried to share it with somebody, the last time I told anybody anything that has to deal with me and my family, they lied. They were not telling the truth when they had said they could keep a secret, that I could trust them. But I know I can trust Jimmy because I know he's not like the others. He is different. Is that weird to say?

"It's probably stupid. You might think that it's something small that I shouldn't worry about but it really does affect me—" I started slow.

How do I put this into words?

"I won't judge you one bit. It can be our little secret if you want. I won't tell anyone." He put a hand on my shoulder consoling me. "I promise."

"My family wants me to be perfect, to be sane, my father especially. He wants the perfect daughter who has good grades, who is not ugly, but is sweet and funny. I'm everything he wants me to be." I started to speak a little faster, a little louder, getting more comfortable and angry.

"He doesn't even come home most of the time. I have to cook meals myself. I have to miss mother by myself because it seems like he doesn't give a fuck about anything she left behind. It's like he wasn't even in love," I paused, "but I know that's not true because they were in love but—that doesn't change the fact that he wasn't here for me, how he isn't here for me. He's probably working right now in his goddamn office, thinking I'm just at a friend's house."

"The people at school don't care. Everyone just wants to associate with me because my family is rich. It's stupid how people think they can just use me and I'm even more stupid for letting them. I'm not even that rich!" I threw my hands in the air and rubbed my face, groaning.

"I only get money from my father sometimes. He doesn't just give it to me. I don't have a job because he won't let me get one. He just wants me to stay home and clean the house and when I want money to go to the movies or anything like that with friends, he will give it to me. That's not a way to live because if he dies, just like my mother did, then I have nothing and I won't be able to take care of myself, you know? It's like he somehow just mentally messes with me, and it makes me so scared that I think something bad will happen to my dog because I know my father doesn't take care of a single thing in the house. It's stupid."

"Serina, it's not stupid. I'm sure Ritz is just fine."

"It is though!" A thought came to mind.

Wait! How did he know my dog's name when I never even told him?

But I ignored it and kept on rambling about the main subject, on my mind. "The reason why I don't want to leave and go home is I ask myself, what's the difference?"

What was the difference?

"If I stay here and don't go to school, I don't have to worry about much anymore. I don't have to talk to fake people. I don't even have any friends to talk to, to vent to, to go to the mall with, and everyone else in my school is doing everything every other high school kid should be able to do. If I return home, I clean. I am the goddamn housewife my father wants me to be."

"Here, you're not a housewife. Here, you will never have to be a housewife—"

I cut him off. "Yes, here I don't have to follow any rules based on my gender. Here I can be who I want to be. Here

I can actually talk to somebody who will listen and who will have my back."

"Like a lover would—" He mumbled something after he said that. I looked at him confused?

"What?"

What did he say after that?

He shrugged as if to say never mind. "I mean, you're not wrong. A lover would do that, yes, but we're not lovers." I heard what he said the first time but in the second part, I didn't quite get.

"Yeah!" It seemed like Jimmy was hesitant. "We're not lovers."

"Do you want to hear more?" I changed the subject when I noticed things were getting a little tense. "I can tell you a whole lot more and just say random things to make this conversation keep going unless you have stuff to do or anything."

"I ain't got nothing to do but care for you, and run errands for the house. "

Is that all he really does though?

"What about a job? What do you have a career in? What did you go to college for?" He burst out laughing. I was confused. "What?"

"How old do you think I am?" He looked at me, catching his breath.

I stood there looking at him, waiting for him to tell me how old he is, but he was just waiting for me to answer. "Oh! Uh, I don't know."

"I'm the same age as you, almost, just a bit older."

No way, well, I guess this makes sense. I haven't even seen his face because he always has a mask on. After a while, to be honest, my mind totally blanked out on the mask and I saw him like him. I don't really see him as that weird guy who has a black mask over his face. I can imagine what he looks like under the mask. Maybe that's why my mind is blanking it out.

"Damn, same age but a little older." I repeated what he said. "I have a question, not trying to change the subject because I do want to know more about you and how I have never met you but," he was smiling at me, listening, "why do you wear that mask all the time?" At that moment, the smile turned into a sad smile, a wide grin, kind of like a Duchenne smile.

"I know I said that I'm here for you, Serina. I really am, but I cannot show you my face," he sighed, "not yet at least. Just give me time."

"Why?"

"If you saw my face right now, I'd be scared that you would leave. And I really don't want you to leave."

I get it. I know what you're saying and you didn't lie to me, or you better not have. I can trust you. I wanted to say that to his face, that I get what he's saying, but I won't say anything. I'm not sure what it has to deal with exactly, but I know the fear that he is feeling.

"I think we should make dinner together tonight. What do you say?" I changed the subject, something where we wouldn't just have to talk, but we'd actually have something to do.

"Together?" He chuckled. "But you can't cook, can you?"

"I can cook. I'm totally a chef. Did you not hear that I cook for myself at home?" He made me laugh by laughing. I couldn't help myself. Laughter is after all contagious.

"We'll see about that. Just don't burn down my house, alright?" He stood up and started to walk towards the kitchen. I got up and followed.

"Yeah, yeah, whatever."

Chapter 11

Fire hot as Hell

We didn't end up burning the house down—thankfully! We did make some wonderful baklava though. I thought the end product would have looked like the pictures, but let's be honest, no food looks precisely like the images. The food was supposed to be a rich, sweet dessert, filled with nuts. Honey and syrup would be used to hold it all together and in our case, we used just syrup.

Evidently, we did learn some things while following the recipe—don't skip any directions. We didn't know what step we missed, but it must've been something important because it turned out not at all as it was supposed to—more like a lava cake.

During the whole procedure, Jimmy and I had bumped into each other a lot, and because of that, there was a ton of laughter. I guess it was nice. One of the things I was happy about was that I didn't feel overwhelmed. He did not get mad at me for any reason, and I did not mess up. Well, if I did, then whoops.

Part of me is glad that I still have this notebook to write in even though it's basically a summary of some sort. I'm happy that I have something to just write all my thoughts down in instead of bottling them up in my mind.

To be honest, if I were stuck in a room all day with just a notebook and pencil, I would write everything on my mind, no matter how weird or how strange it might be. It would be something to do and who knows, some things that I may write down might be something I had not even known before or acknowledged myself.

Imagine reading this ten years later.

"Hey, Serina?" I closed the notebook and turned to the male who spoke to me, my kidnapper. After we ate our food, we decided to go and do our own things. Jimmy started to wash the dishes and clean a bit while I just went up to my room and did random things, like write in a notebook.

"Yes?"

"Just checking in, I guess." He wiped his hands on his pants. "I'm going to take a shower then head off the bed. You should probably go to bed as well. Get that beauty rest."

"Oh yeah, sure, because I need it." I used sarcasm, and he caught on.

"Yep, totally. Because right now you look like a total toad."

"Hey!" I got off the bed, leaving the notebook on the mattress. I went up to him while he stood in the doorway. I ended up punching him lightly in the chest. "Not funny."

He laughed. "But you're laughing, and hey! That hurt." He took both my hands into his and smiled at me. The warmth of his hands as he held mine, I found that comforting. Some part of me felt safe.

"What?"

"Nothing." He let go of me and walked out into the hall. "I'm off to take a shower. Don't bother me." When he walked off, I heard a laugh escape his mouth.

"Nerd," I muttered under my breath.

It's crazy how things happen, how our relationship changed, how my life changed, how his life changed—a lot of change. It all started with me being mad at him and confused because I was taken hostage, then I slowly realized how he took care of me and how this trust had grown into a lively rose.

And now, I wonder what will happen. I know at some point somebody will come looking for me. Maybe my father will be a father for once and find me. But at the same time, I hope he does not notice that I'm gone and, I hope that I can just stay here with Jimmy.

I sighed.

I guess I better get my beauty rest.

Mimicking his words, I lay down and gazed up. It always took a bit for me to fall asleep, but after a while with silence and the darkness of the room, my lids closed, and my breathing relaxed. I fell asleep.

The next thing that happened was not a good dream or me waking up to the smell of wonderful food Jimmy made. No, I woke up and I almost had a heart attack.

At first, I thought it was real, as always. It was another one of these dreams. I think the last time I had one of these was with the boy, and that's when Jimmy kind of went haywire. This time it was not warm, it was cold. I couldn't feel my body or move either. I was tied up to the same bed though. However, there were other beds hanging upside down beside me, just like how I was hanging upside down. I moved my head. Every single bed looked the same. The only difference was that I was the only one on a bed. I was the only one in this place.

There were black strings that were holding my body to the mattress, keeping me there. Silently still freaking out, I looked around to take in more of my surroundings. Even though I knew nothing could hurt me, I was scared.

Slowly, my fingertips started to get heated. They were now the only body part that felt a warm temperature. Then, I felt the warmth coming through the rest of my body. It's like the fingertips were the source. At first, it felt nice, just hanging there, my body warm and relaxed; but once it started to get too hot, that is when things changed. Starting from my fingers, my skin felt like it was burning, like it was in flames, slowly going up my body, spreading.

I tried to scream, yet nothing came out. Everything was silent. So much more was felt than what was seen on the outside. This was no longer relaxing, that's for sure. I just want to feel the warmth of that boy again.

I was still feeling the pain as my body burned, now up to my abdomen. I still couldn't move, which made it worse. It's like when you have a cramp when you're on your period and you rock back and forth to try to just get rid of the discomfort faster. Screaming in agony, the pain was getting more acute. I couldn't concentrate on what was in front of me anymore. Trying so hard to get out of this bed, but nothing was working. Feeling the pain throughout my body forced tears to my eyes, and the only thing that was physically a part of me—my head—showed that I was hurting.

"Freak, give me your lunch money!" I remembered a time from my childhood when kids used to beat me up and steal from me. It mainly happened when I was in middle school, sixth grade. Everyone had figured out that I was some rich kid—an ugly, rich kid.

"Why do you even style your hair like that, huh? You look just like a boy!" Words from my peers kept on spouting, burning into my heart.

"I need this money for food!" I cried at them. I really did need the food. My dad hadn't been home in a while and there was nothing I could really eat. Plus the free lunch was trash.

Not only did the kids at my school try and get my lunch money away from me and make fun of my hair, they would also do something that I'm sure everyone thought was just in that one high school drama. I went to the restroom without knowing the same group of kids had followed me in, males, females, who cares at this point which restroom we went in. Gender wasn't a thing right now.

They carried a large bag filled with garbage and liquid shit, and threw it over the stall I was in. Before I could react, I was sitting there pissing, covered with waste.

It's crazy how mean kids can be. It's worse when nobody notices or realizes it. You'll just be there in a dark corner, cowering like a baby chick who just hatched while larger, more grown-up chicks surround and bully you, make fun of you. It is not fun to deal with, trust me.

Have you ever had some breakfast for lunch at your school? Me too. The Wednesday after the throwing of the trash happened, a kid named Jacob had thrown a little plastic container filled with syrup from lunch at me, unaware. Not only did I have waste all over me that one day, now I was all sticky like a messy baby. What he said to me is something I'll never forget.

"Now your daddy can clean all that off for you." Snickering, he walked away.

At first, it made no sense to me. But then I started to think about it. It could mean two different things, and honestly, the second thing I thought of was not appropriate at all.

That's the problem with being this one rich kid in your school. People use you, people bully you, people mess with you. It's not really what people think on the outside.

"Being rich is so cool. You can do whatever you want." Oh yeah, sure, because that's all we're about. Screwing the jocks, and messing around throughout our whole lives because we do not need to worry about college. Sure.

Burning, blazing, ignited with flames—on the inside. Still, nothing is showing on the outside, no actual flames, nothing. All on the inside, all of the pain is coming from inside of me, but it feels as if it is on the outside too. As if it's all over. There is nothing that I can think about, not because I can't think of anything to get my mind off this pain, but because my mind is not allowing me to think about anything other than pain.

That's when I woke up. But the shock didn't stop. At least I could move now, although it didn't help. I fell off the bed and shrieked. I heard my voice. I don't think Jimmy heard. Usually, if I screamed or did something unusual, he would come right away. Yet he hadn't come.

One of my greatest fears is ending up alone with no one there to help me. And thinking about it, it hurts more when you used to have someone and they're not here anymore.

My body felt weird. It didn't hurt to move. It didn't hurt at all anymore. It was like the heat just vanished. As I was laying on the floor, staring up at the ceiling with my arms wrapped around my stomach, my thoughts came back to me, and I felt light. Not light-headed, well—maybe just a little bit, but I felt light as if I was a beautiful, yellow butterfly. It felt unreal to be completely honest. How one second I was recoiling in pain, the next I was on vacation.

I need to stop with these mood swings, for real! I miss Ritz, and it kind of hurts to say this too. However, I think I'm starting to miss my father a little bit too. Despite all of the things he's done and everything, he's still family, right? Isn't that what people say? I'm just scared of all things right now, scared of sleeping because I might have that same dream or a worse dream. It's crazy.

First, it started with me being on a beach, then meeting a wonderful warm boy, but why had it turned to this?

Is it because I feel like my life is finally getting somewhere, getting better? Even if I don't go to school anymore or I'm being spoiled by the person who took me.

I don't know. It's— whatever. I stood up, a little dizzy at first, but I got used to it quickly. I opened my door and looked around. The whole house was dark.

It must be the middle of the night, or is my mind playing tricks on me?

I took a left outside my door and opened up Jimmy's bedroom door. To my surprise, just a little one, he was gone. This explains why he did not come out and help me when I was screaming in literally the room next to him. I mean, I can't really complain because it stopped now. But, that pain I will never forget.

I backed away, not wanting to be in there too long, and closed the door as nothing happened. My eyes felt like they were brand new. My whole body felt like it was brand new.

I felt like a new person, but to make it even better I needed to wash my hair. "Jesus."

I went into the restroom and saw myself in the mirror. All this picking out clothes in the closet did not do well for me.

Sure, the outfit may be a little cute, I guess, but my hair is so oily you won't even imagine. Oopsies. I guess it's time to take a shower, finally.

The shower felt great, but it didn't wash away the fact that I'd had that weird dream. It was messing with my mind. I decided that maybe the best thing to do would be to focus on myself.

Isn't that what people say these days? I'm sounding like an old grandma, no offense. Focusing on your own mind is the best way to the soul. Really, some days it doesn't make sense, but right now, it makes perfect sense. I need to work on myself, and maybe everything will lighten up more for me.

Chapter 12

Happy Birthday

"But I swear I saw somebody!" A little kid's voice bellowed.

Of course his attitude annoyed his sister. "Liam, you did not see a person! It was probably some kind of sticker or some shit." She paused. "Fuck, don't tell mom I said that word."

Realizing the word she had said in her second phrase was even worse than the first one she said, "Whatever, just don't tell mom a word I said. Got that?"

It seemed like her little brother wasn't listening because he kept on blathering about that eyeball he saw in the wall. "But when I picked up my ball, I swear it was real! It even blinked at me, sis!"

"Just shut up already!" They went home.

On Monday, things got interesting. Mariah went to school as always and went to her classes as always. There was only one thing different though: the whispers. Most of the talk about Serina had died down. Everybody slowly started to forget that she was missing, and everybody started to forget she even existed. Some of the girls and boys who had messed with Serina in the past because of her father's money found somebody else to pick on.

Yet again, Mariah seemed like she was the only one who cared. "I heard from her father over the weekend."

She still talked to the counselors and people around the school about Serina. It seemed as if she was the only person who was not giving up.

"It seemed like he didn't care about his daughter at all, but more so about getting the dog back from us! Don't you think that's weird? What dad wouldn't care about his daughter?"

After moments of thinking about the weekend when Marcus Ange had left, Mariah realized that he only spoke about the dog, and he didn't seem worried about Serina, his daughter, one bit.

"Mariah, Serina's dad might be going through a tough time right now. He was most likely hiding his fear and sadness so he would not worry you," said the school counselor.

"I just can't help but think there might be a chance that Serina's dad is involved."

"Let's be real. Do you really think that somebody who loves her would pull her away from her life like this?" Mariah shook her head slowly. "Well alright then. That was the bell. You should get to class."

"Yeah, thanks." They both got up to leave the conference room, and went out into the cold abyss of the hallways that soon were filled with students.

"Yeah, my stupid brother thinks that he saw some kind of eyeball in a wall." While Mariah was walking to her class, a group of girls was talking, coincidently. When Mariah realized who was doing the talking, she thought she could learn more about the subject because they have English together.

So, she took this as an opportunity, not only because it might be related to Serina, but thinking it might just be something weird to look into. "An eye in the wall?" Mariah turned around with a little grin on her face. She didn't believe a thing that she heard, but she was interested in knowing more.

"That's what he said. Don't ask me." The older sister, Aliza Cornwall, continued to walk with her friends but shortly after, it was just the two of them.

"You think there might be a slight chance that he's telling the truth?"

"No way! Mariah, you're putting too much thought into this. No, no," she shook her head and sighed, "not trying to be rude, but I think you're involving yourself too much in Serina's situation. Ever since she went missing, you've been more talkative and detective-like. Kinda scares me." She tittered. "Look, do whatever you want. I'm not trying to judge, but just know other people are. I'll see ya later." Aliza turned in the opposite direction than the class they both were supposed to go to.

At first, Mariah was confused about why they did not head in the same direction, but then she noticed everyone was going to their homerooms. Turning around and trying her best to make it to class on time, Aliza's words repeated in her mind. "Am I really getting judged?" Mariah thought out loud. She hated the idea of people judging others. She was a nice girl, the type to help others out in that situation.

When she finally made it to her homeroom, Mariah apologized to the teacher for being late. "Sorry, I thought we were going to class, not homeroom." Her peers laughed as she made it to her seat.

After putting her English stuff on the desk, she looked around a bit, seeing most of the class looking at her, smirking, and giggling. Then, the teacher spoke, grabbing everybody's attention. "It's alright, Mariah," he pointed to the board, "as I was saying, next month is the homecoming."

Homecoming, now that would be a month to remember, especially with Mariah's birthday coming up. The last birthday Mariah had was quite special. It was celebrated back in her hometown where she was born, and where most of her family lived. Her birthday was filled with family, just family. Cousins that could be easily mistaken for friends, but it was all family.

At first, Mariah thought this would be the worst day ever to celebrate her birthday because she had no friends with her. Sure, she loved her family, but some alone time at her age with teenage friends would mean a lot.

The family wasn't what made that whole week special. It was because of a girl she met. Taking away all of her worries, being around this girl just made Mariah feel calm, safe. And when she was alone with her family, all she could think about was that girl she met down at the park. Mariah didn't get her name when they met though. They never exchanged names. Until the next day when she went down to the park again, and there she was. In Mariah's eyes, she was beautiful. The girl had long, brown-hair, was tall, and had amazing style, not to mention the greatest smile.

"Hey, again." Mariah walked up to her and she turned around, smiling brightly as always.

"Hi." Neither of them could think of what to say next. "Uh, have we met?"

"Oh!" This caught Mariah off guard. "Yes, we've met. Yesterday we were both at the park, and bumped into each other, then we hung out for like an hour?"

"That was you!" She laughed. "God, after you left I realized I never got your name."

Mariah laughed as well. "Same here. My name's Mariah."

"Angellica, but you can call me Angel."

"Angel," she said repeating it. "That's a wonderful name."

* * *

"No—" There was a dramatic pause between Mariah's words. "Way!" There was a reason for this.

Once she got home from school that Monday, she started scrolling through some news headlines online and something caught her eye. Serina Ange's name along with her dog, Ritz. "This is all lies!"

The document that she found online was an article in which Marcus talked about how Ritz had been found dead. They were making it go as public as it possibly could. The article also had the reporter's own reflection on why Marcus wanted this information to spread so far. But in the end, nothing could be made to a full conclusion.

As soon as Marcus Ange had taken Ritz back home, he had come up with a plan—faking Ritz's death to make Serina come home. Marcus thought that Serina had run away, just like the rumor some of her classmates spread around in school. She just ran away from home and fled.

There were many questions to be answered. "I have to figure out where Serina lives," Mariah said out loud.

She went to her parents' room. "Mom?"

Since somebody had called about the dog, she hoped her mom would still have the number, or even better, the address.

"Yes?" Nellie was just sitting on the couch playing some kind of candy game on her phone.

"By any chance do you have Marcus's number? Serina's dad?"

Mariah's mom looked bewildered at first, but she closed the game and opened up her recent call list. "Yeah, why?" She held her phone up so Mariah couldn't see the screen. She wouldn't let her daughter see the number before she answered her question.

"Why?" Mariah repeated, "because I'm interested in how Ritz is doing." It was partly true.

Nellie caved in, and she showed her daughter the phone screen. The number displayed. She put the number in her own phone and blessed her mom, quickly going back into her room to do more research.

"Where is Serina? Why would Serina's dad do this type of thing? Is he somehow involved?" Muttering the questions she wanted to find out the answers to, she wrote them down in four columns, one with each proposal. She then started to scribble down the information she had proof of so far, and the truth that she knew so far, then put some views of her own down at the bottom of the page.

"I'm making food. Come out of your room soon!" Joe, Mariah's father, called out from what sounded like the living room.

"Oh no, Dad's cooking? I better get rid of my taste buds now!" She replied from inside her room, shouting back with a laugh that followed. Then, went back to work.

- Went missing after school. Serina walks home.
- No traces of her disappearance.
- Serina seemed off before she left the day she went missing.
- Possibly in a different country, but most likely somewhere in this town.
- Marcus has something to do with this situation.
- Is Marcus trying to get Serina to come home by saying that Ritz had died?
- Terrible dad move.
- This is annoying. I can not think.

Mariah put down her pen after writing all the ideas she had down. The first three things were accurate; the rest speculation. Mariah just sat there as her head spun. What was going on in there was not satisfying. After researching the questions she had written down and finding no clues, she got frustrated Not many answers, but more so presuming.

Even after all those late nights online reading all those news articles, no answers. The time had come for Mariah to call Marcus. He ended up not picking up. So, instead of giving up, she sent him a text.

"Hey! It's Mariah. We met when you picked up your dog. I'm your daughter's friend and have an award that I picked up for her a while back. I was wondering if I could come to your house and drop it off for you?"

She was hopeful that her text would get a response, hopeful that she would get a chance to do some detective work.

A couple of hours later, there was still no reply. During the time she was waiting for a response, it was like the urge you get to hear the phone ring when waiting for a text back from your crush. The whole wait was worth it because sooner or later she knew she was going to get a text back, and she did. Although, it was late at night so Mariah would have to wait until the next day to do anything about it.

Marcus was stuck at work all day—not really stuck, but he was there all day. He did get home around 8 p.m. though, not that late but it was still dark outside, the stars shining. Then there was Ritz. He barked when Marcus came through the front door, and all he did was kick the poor dog out of the way. His phone rang and he picked up, passing by the empty food and water bowls meant for the dog. Serina was right. He wasn't taking care of Ritz. When he was on the phone, he kept on talking about work and what would be the plan for the week ahead of him. Then when one of his coworkers asked him about what he'd seen on the news, instantly Marcus hung up and said, "Forget about it."

The next thing on Marcus's list was to make some food. He wasn't a cook, so he just took a box of Kids Cuisine out of the freezer. There was a variety of these frozen meals packed into the freezer, and he pulled out one that had three separate sections. The main dish had some little chicken strips that looked like donut holes with fries. The meal also had corn, and chocolate dessert. He put it in the microwave with the time specified on the box and waited.

While Marcus was waiting, he leaned against the counter and scrolled through his phone. Something popped up on his screen. It was a phone call, but he denied it. Work was calling again and he didn't feel like answering it because he was hungry, not to mention he was sure the person was going to ask about the news again. The microwave beeped when the food was done. Then another phone call came in and without checking the phone, he just turned his phone off.

Getting the food out of the microwave, his next move was to go out into the living room and turn on the television as he ate. When it turned on, the first thing that popped up was his own face on the screen. He smiled to himself and continued to watch.

"Marcus Ange, also the boss of Limie, has reported his dog named Ritz is dead. The news comes just a few months after his daughter, Serina's, disappearance. We'll have the latest developments in the case after a short commercial break."

"Thank you, Sherran." Marcus switched the channels, already knowing what he'd said. He dialed in The Discovery Channel. Ritz then barked at his feet, trying to beg for food. Marcus groaned and put his foot on the nightstand next to the recliner he was sitting in. "Come on stupid dog." Leading him to his kennel, Marcus secured him in.

After a couple of hours had passed, maybe more, he finally decided to turn his phone back on again. He found thirteen missed calls and four messages. One call and one message from an unknown number. He looked to see who it was from. It was from Mariah.

He began to type on his phone, "Sorry for the late response. Of course, you can come over and drop off the award. You can also stay for lunch if you'd like. Here's my address. I'll see you tomorrow!" With the address attached below, he pressed send.

"Looks like I'll be doing something tomorrow." He looked at the dog. "Looks like I'll have to do something with you, too."

Chapter 13

Alliance

Angellica and Mariah had some great memories, eventually turning their friendship into an actual relationship. Sadly, since Mariah had to end her birthday vacation, they started a long-distance relationship. They became girlfriends. Mariah loved Angellica, but Angellica did not seem to love her back with the same amount of care and effort. She ended up cheating on Mariah with this guy named Charles. It was their two month anniversary, and Mariah wanted to do something special, so that night, she called her one and only, Angellica.

Of course, the lovely girlfriend picked up, but when Mariah started to hear the sounds coming from the other end she was absolutely disgusted. Charles and Angellica were having sex. Who knows if Angellica meant to answer the phone call or did it on purpose, just to break poor Mariah's heart.

She hung up, hearing enough, and immediately texted her, "Please tell me that was just porn you were watching?" No reply came until the next morning.

That's when everything went down. Mariah couldn't trust Angellica, and they got into a huge argument. The only one who shed tears was Mariah. She was completely heartbroken, empty. She didn't know how to feel because she thought that Angellica was the one. She thought they were meant to be soulmates. But without a flinch, Angellica ended it with Mariah that morning, not even face to face on a video call, but with just one text. "It's over."

Once Mariah read that message, their relationship wasn't the only thing that was over, but her life as well. Angellica was an actual angel in her eyes. She loved and cared for her so much that she wanted to spend the rest of her life with her. Go on adventures, travel around the world.

That week, Mariah had cut herself. She was suicidal, but her family saved her. Angellica heard of this, of her self-harm, and texted her after a month of ghosting Mariah. She tried to text her saying that she was sorry and that she wanted to get back together, but Mariah just ghosted her back. Giving her the payback she deserved. Unless it was all a lie, a second chance to break her heart again. Which was one of the reasons Mariah never replied to Angellica's text messages.

When Mariah's family tried to console her, she said one thing that her family would never forget because when Mariah said it, her tone was serious, and she meant it. "When you really love someone, you can never let go. Trust me on that."

Love to Mariah meant a lot. She was one of those people who gets too emotionally attached and sometimes not in a good way. She hurt so much. The pain wouldn't go away for months. Every single night she had dreams of the memories that she and Angellica had made together. All those late nights thinking of Angellica, wishing that she could turn back time. Wishing she could change her past. But if that happened, she wouldn't be where she is now. In Serina's life.

Meeting Serina was an open door, a door to escape from the heartbreak caused by Angellica. Meeting Serina had helped Mariah find her happiness again. It made her feel free, made her feel safe again. She realized that Angellica was just a moment in her life that taught her a lesson that she needed to learn, and because of this she now knew more about relationships and what not to do to mess things up. But, of course, there was always that fear of screwing up with Serina.

This is why Mariah was trying to take it slower than when she met Angellica, for a higher percentage of success of having Serina as her girlfriend. Being able to call Serina hers.

Now, she would not be able to do that for a while. Serina was gone from the surface of the earth, missing, taken hostage. Now, what Mariah was focusing on was not getting Serina as a girlfriend, but saving her. Then, just maybe, she would get back on track with her plan.

The whole eye in the wall thing that was mentioned at school kept on replaying in not only the child's mind—who saw it himself—but Mariah's as well. Little did she know, three other students in her grade and class were thinking the same thing. Serina's disappearance was not be only affecting Mariah anymore. Dean Parry, Steve Reynolds, and Mercy Cunningham were invested in it as well.

Dean was the athletic, typical football player. He and Serina were friends, or at least in his eyes. He thought they were close enough to be called friends and maybe even best friends. Dean had a dark secret that nobody knew about, and Serina was so close to hearing it. Until she went missing, of course.

Steve was one of the kids who had bullied Serina, used her for her money. Mercy was a totally different story. She was one of the popular students who joined dance because cheerleading wasn't her thing.

On the surface, Mercy appeared to hate Serina, despise her because of her money and the guys who hung around her. She appeared to be jealous, but on the inside, it was totally different. She loved Serina, not in a romantic way, but she admired her. Mercy loved how Serina had so many accomplishments.

One wish—Mercy has been keeping a hold on one wish for almost her whole life. That wish was ditching her toxic friends, and becoming friends with Serina. But with Serina gone that would never happen. So, she held on to what she had, thinking without the friends she had now her life would fall apart.

"Alright," Mariah looked into her bathroom mirror. She was getting ready to head over to Marcus's place. "This is good enough." After getting the award she promised to bring to the house, she said goodbye to her parents and left the house. Hoping for the best when she arrived at Marcus's house.

The weather was nice out that day. There were barely any clouds in the sky, and the sun was shining bright, getting warmer as the day progressed. A perfect moment to just lay on the grass and close your eyes, letting the heat touch your eyelids as you relax. Mariah's mind wandered as she walked down the sidewalk.

"Mariah! Welcome, come on inside. Hopefully, the place is clean enough for you. It's kind of a mess right now though." The place was spotless. Marcus did do some cleaning before Mariah arrived.

"Oh no, it's fine, Mr. Ange."

"Please, call me Marcus." He closed the front door after Mariah got inside.

"Yes, sorry, Marcus."

There was no dog when she arrived. It was a little suspicious to Mariah. But, maybe she thought wrong. Maybe Ritz was actually dead. But the information she had heard on the news was fake. It didn't make any sense.

Marcus was very welcoming. Shortly after her arrival, he made some food for her and him to eat. They sat down in his nice kitchen and had a fun conversation about Serina—how she acted—how Marcus was so proud of her.

He even shed some tears, breaking down in front of Mariah. "I'm so sorry—Marcus."

"It's quite alright. I mustn't cry in front of you anyway. It's not professional."

After a hour passed, Mariah headed off. There was nothing suspicious about Marcus that led him to be connected with Serina's disappearance. He seemed to really have loved her, and Ritz must really be dead. She walked home.

Unfortunately, that's not what happened at all. That was all the perfect plan that Mariah had thought of on her way over. The nice day got to her. When she arrived, her knees started to tremble and she thought of just leaving. She said to herself she couldn't give up, for Serina's sake. She knocked on the door, and to her surprise, things were not going as she planned.

"Who are you?" The man who opened the door was true Marcus. "I'm not going to buy your Girl Scout cookies. Get out of here." He was about to close the door.

"Wait!" Mariah was confused. She put up a hand to the door so that it wouldn't close. "It's Mariah, Marcus. I am here because of Serina's award?"

"Hold on." Marcus was holding a phone, talking to his work. He then nodded and opened the door, waiting for Mariah to come in. "Come in. Also, call me Mr. Ange. What are you, my friend?" He then walked off after Mariah went inside. She had to close the door herself.

A minute or two passed, then he returned to the foyer. "I'm back. What were you saying about the sales?" Marcus just went right back to the call.

Mariah was completely disgusted with how the things she imagined were so different than reality, but this just made her grin, her detective signs tingling. She looked around the house. It wasn't that clean. A lot of dust collection that looked a couple of weeks old. Since Serina wasn't home, it wasn't much of a surprise that the place wasn't spotless as usual.

"First thing's first." Mariah talked to herself while Marcus was out of her way. "Where's Ritz?" She looked around for any weird movement or secret passages. She laughed to herself, thinking it was crazy that would be a thing.

"What are you laughing about?" Marcus came around the corner. He was off the phone now.

"Oh! Nothing, Mr. Ange. Just admiring the place you got here. It's nice." She smiled, hoping to lighten the mood.

"Well, I have some food in the kitchen. Help yourself. Something came up down the block, and I have to take care of it. So, don't touch anything, and I will be back in like ten minutes." Without even wanting to hear a response from Mariah he left, dialing a number in his phone and bringing it up to his ear. "Where is it again?"

This worked splendidly for Mariah. It meant she didn't have to be quiet and could look around wherever she wanted for ten minutes. In a house as big as Serina's, that wouldn't get her too far though.

Mariah got started right away. "Ritz? Come here, buddy? You here?" She tried calling the dog to see if he would make any noise that she could go to. Thankfully, that worked.

A noise came from upstairs somewhere, so she went up the stairs quickly and called out his name again. More yips came from a closed-door, and it smelled terrible. It smelled like shit.

Mariah opened the door, and her senses were correct. There was a bunch of shit in the kennel that Ritz was locked inside. There was no food bowl, no water bowl, just a storage room with Ritz inside a cage.

"You poor baby! I knew you were still alive." She hastily went to the cage and unlocked it. Ritz jumped out onto her lap, licking her face, happy to be saved.

"I knew it." Marcus came walking into the bedroom. "Mariah, I want you to go downstairs."

She turned around and shook her head, disagreeing. "No, you can't just abuse this poor dog, Mr. Ange. It's not right and I won't allow it!"

"Then bring the damn dog with, I don't care. Just come downstairs." His phone rang, and he looked at the caller ID, ignoring it.

"I thought you had something to take care of?" Mariah was suspicious.

"I'm not going anywhere with you inside my house. What if you were some robber?" He paused, shaking his head, and he laughed a bit. "Plus, my whole plan was to see what you would do when you were alone at my house."

Mariah's face turned red out of embarrassment as she followed Marcus downstairs into the kitchen. There was some cheese and crackers on a plate on the counter. Marcus grabbed a few, and Mariah did the same, then they both sat down and spoke for a long time. Mariah asked him a bunch of her detective questions, which got her nowhere. She recorded the whole thing secretly on her phone, but ended up deleting it because everything Marcus said was the truth.

He didn't take care of the dog because he didn't know how to. The reason for the news reports, he was just trying to drag his daughter out. He knew how much the pup meant to her. He told Mariah that he was trying to be a good dad, but with work and trying to support the good life he was trying to provide for Serina, there wasn't much family time.

In Serina's eyes, and other people's eyes, this may be terrible parenting, but after Mariah heard the reasoning behind it all, she felt sympathy for the guy. It took a while for Marcus to convince Mariah to believe him. But, in the end, it worked. Despite Marcus being a cold-hearted guy on the outside with a lemony personality, he was a decent guy who was keeping up an act for the public.

"Will you help me?" Mariah needed help with finding Serina, and the answer was yes. Marcus nodded, and that was when they spoke a little about their truce.

Since Marcus was a higher-up, being the owner of Limie and all that, it would be easy for him to walk around town and look for answers without an issue. One, he had money to spend on searching for answers, and two, he had a way with the police and the detectives. So if they were to make any discoveries regarding Serina's disappearance, they could go to them right away. This seemed like a good plan. Mariah being the inside source with the school and the peers who had bullied Serina and spread rumors about her.

Marcus told Mariah to tell him all the rumors going around because one of the rumors might be true, and they could get a lead. On the other hand, Mariah asked something of Marcus, to be a better father for Serina when she came back home.

They shook on their plan and ideas. By then it had gotten a little later than what Mariah had anticipated. She put the award inside of Serina's room. After that, they both said their goodbyes.

Now having one another's number saved as contacts in their phones, Mariah had more help than she had started off with, which was a good thing.

However, there was one thing that would always be an obstacle—Marcus's work. He did agree to help Mariah find his daughter, but he didn't promise that work wouldn't get in the way. Mariah jotted down in her notes her concern about Marcus keeping his word about being a better dad to his daughter, and taking care of her dog.

"Will this all be a good thing?" Mariah jotted down more things in her notes, thinking out loud. "It's not like I'm an actual detective, but the rush going through my blood feels amazing—plus, I have to find Serina. She deserves so much more than to be in a terrible, cold, lonely place. Wherever she is, I hope she is not dying of blood loss and not going crazy by now."

Mariah thought the worst of Serina's kidnapping. She came to the conclusion that one of the rumors was just a lie, running away. She told herself that she wouldn't run away because of Ritz.

"Where would she go anyway if it's true what Marcus said?" There was a lot more depth to their conversation than what Mariah had imagined. Sure, he seemed like a total asshole, but he was caring and was just another person living among everyone else with their own problems. "He is so confusing," she said out loud to herself. She wrote down another bullet list of what she learned.

- Serina doesn't have a lot of money on her and Mr. Ange gives her money only when she needs it.
- It was a kidnapping/hostage-taking occurrence.
- Because he is rich, Mr. Ange has a higher advantage of getting local people to help.
- Serina is in town still, over eighty percent sure.

Mariah didn't write down much, but it was still something to keep her mind moving. After checking the latest news headlines for any stories about cars being stolen, fake IDs, or suspicious hostage-taking events, nothing of the sort showed up. That gave an answer to the last bullet point—Serina is still in her hometown, but where?

"You're still working on that assignment? Maybe you should call it quits for the evening. It seems like you've been working on this a lot." Joe was hovering over Mariah's work. As soon as he started talking, she closed her notes and turned around, smiling at her dad.

"It's a pretty hard assignment. Plus, we could've chosen partners, but I wanted to do it myself." She paused, then added, "And, I'm not feeling so well. I think I might be getting sick, dad."

He felt her forehead. "Maybe it's just because you're overworking yourself, sweetheart. Get some sleep, okay?" Mariah nodded and got up from her chair. She shut off the mini-lamp on her desk and stretched.

"Looks like I'll be getting a lot of sleep before school on Monday." She plopped down in her bed, and waited for the slumber to come.

Chapter 14

Trust broken, or has it just begun?

O nce I got out of the shower, I didn't feel like getting dressed right away. Instead, I went downstairs and fetched myself something to drink. I made some hot chocolate, which I was very excited about because I didn't think Jimmy had any lying around.

I remembered that Jimmy might be coming back home soon, and he would probably be kind of shocked to see me walking around with my hair shrouded up in a towel with just another sheet around my body. I would not like to see his face if that's how he found me when he came home.

So, I went back upstairs into my designated bedroom, and looked through the closet for some new clothing. Nothing in here was much my style, but it was something new, something clean. I grabbed a mustard yellow t-shirt that looked like it came from a fair, and some black athletic shorts. Satisfying enough. My skin felt the air blowing against it, and it was soothing. Sure, it gave me some chills, which was my fault. But as long as I didn't go down to the basement, I should be fine.

Humming to myself, I went to make some food, something

extraordinary. As I was looking through the drawers, there was a hand-written recipe for a cake. "Sure, let's do some baking," I said out loud. "Let's just hope I do not burn the house down by leaving the cake in the oven for too long."

I followed the instructions on the paper I found step by step. I thought it was going pretty well. When I pulled the cake out of the oven and finished making the frosting, it looked good. *But does it taste good?* I cut a slice off, and put it on a paper plate, ready to munch down on it with a spoon. I took a few bites and made two conclusions: "This isn't bad" as well as, "I could do better." It wasn't the best cake I'd ever made, but hey, I didn't know the recipe or who had come up with it. It could have been Jimmy. He is a home chef.

After just one slice, I was full. I wanted to make more food since there was nothing else to do, but I couldn't get myself to do it. Walking around with nothing coming to my mind regarding what to do, I plopped down on the carpet in the living room and just stared at the ceiling.

How long has Jimmy been gone? Probably awhile, probably doing his own thing.

"Television!" I shot up from the ground and picked up the remote. The sudden thought of watching TV came into my mind. Maybe there was something interesting on, like perhaps a romantic comedy movie.

When I first turned on the TV, it wasn't a cool movie, but the news that came on. Right at that moment, there was a story on about my dog. This day couldn't have gone a whole twenty-four hours without something going wrong, right? The information came to me through a screen. I learned that my dog had died.

My goddamn father didn't take care of him. I knew Ritz would starve to death because my father doesn't do shit around the house. I can't believe him.

I could not stand to watch that channel anymore. With anger building up inside me, the grasp on the remote was harder, and I switched to another channel. It was a kid's show, and I didn't feel like watching something animated. I switched the channel again, this time landing on some kind of adventure movie. I came upon a scene where a couple of characters were in a jungle. I shrugged, noticing how hard I was gripping the remote. I set it down after turning up the volume a bit, and I stared at the screen while the random movie played.

After a while, I thought my anger would calm down, but the more I thought about it the more it wouldn't leave my mind, the more fury got added to the ball growing inside me. I just needed to yell, to scream, to slap my father across the face. But I couldn't, I couldn't scream because I was alone in the house. I needed somebody to scream back. And then it came to me, Jimmy.

He wouldn't care if I screamed at him, right? He will understand everything I have to yell out and rant about anyway, plus he needs a girl in his life to yell at him sometimes.

And that's what I planned while watching the movie, trying to keep the ball of anger inside of my chest.

Soon enough, I knew my prayers would be answered, and I was right. As I looked out the window and saw Jimmy walking up to the front door, the ball of anger started to rise in my throat. It was ready to explode.

As soon as the door opened, my mouth opened. "Jimmy!" I half shouted.

As he came inside we made eye contact, and he gave me a confused look, probably questioning me standing there, giving him a pissed off expression. "Did you see the fucking news? If you haven't, my dog is dead and it's all my father's fault." Walking towards Jimmy, I put a finger up to his chest. He was speechless at first. "Do you know what I am thinking right now? Do you know how much I want to yell at someone?" Raising my voice a little at the second part of that sentence, I couldn't control myself seeing a face such as his in front of me, with that damned mask he always wears.

"Yell at me then," Jimmy responded to all my words, closing the door behind him and setting a bag he had down on the floor. "If you need someone to yell at, yell at me." He nodded his head, and his voice sounded so calm. Now I felt bad about yelling at him, but the red ball of anger was stronger than the tiny blue ball of sympathy.

"I hope he dies. My father, I really hope he perishes. I do not want him to stand on this earth any longer with his own legs!" I started to traverse around as words left my mouth. "I swear, I just wish he died. I don't care how or when. I just want him dead." My hands rolled into fists, and I walked up to Jimmy, who was standing there, taking it in. I hit him carelessly on the chest, not too solid. I thought I would be hurting him, but he just stood there with a bland face, looking down at me and his eyes were glossy. I shook my head to forget about silly details. "Do you know how much I'm hurting right now? How much I want to punch that guy in the face?" I kept on punching his chest, each punch getting weaker as time went by. "It isn't fair, Ritz didn't have to die. It's not fair. I loved him! This isn't fucking fair! This world is trash!" More and more words spat out of my mouth, most of them I was regretting, but I couldn't help myself.

I kept on yelling and lashing out at Jimmy until the ball inside of me ran out of energy, and I just stood there. In front of somebody who wasn't a stranger, but at the same time, wasn't a friend.

Who is he to me?

He then took my hands so I would stop hitting him. He used a light touch, and he proceeded to look down at me. His eyes looked like a dark ocean, like they always have. I could tell that he was listening. I could tell that he cared and that he didn't care that I hit him or anything. He took it in and shared my anger.

A couple of seconds after I stopped talking, he let go of my hands. They rested at my sides as he spoke. "I'll be right back, okay? I have some business I need to take care of." I heard that his voice had a tint of violence in it. I nodded in acknowledgment, not inquiring where he was running off to again.

Then he disappeared, without any words, nothing else. He left the house, and I was there all alone again. I really shouldn't complain. It didn't matter to me. But, there was this feeling inside of me, a feeling that made my chest clench up as I stood there. Did I not want him to leave? I shook my head. That could not be possible. As I have said before, we're not friends. But, we are not strangers. Asking myself again, what are we, what kind of relationship do we have?

And so, I walked upstairs. My mind raced, and I went to get a blanket from one of the bedrooms. It was a fuzzy red one. I wrapped it around me, on my shoulders, and I snuggled up into it. The warmth felt nice. After getting wrapped in the blanket, I stepped downstairs, careful not to tread on the blanket while I moved down. I got into the living room and sat, leaning my back into the couch and gazed at the front door, waiting for Jimmy to walk back in once he was done with whatever he was doing.

* * *

Without closing my eyes for more than one second for blinking, I kept on staring at the door. One hour passed. Another after that, and when I thought there was another hour coming, the doorknob twisted, and he walked inside.

"Jimmy!" I stood up instantly when I saw him, the blanket falling off of my shoulders, and I ran up to him. His clothes were covered in blood. His arms were bruised up, his shirt ripped. It looked like he had gotten into a fight. I looked up and down his body, taking in his appearance. "What happened to you?" To be honest, I was concerned.

Jimmy hacked into his elbow and locked the door. He looked at me. "It's nothing, don't worry about it, okay?" But I knew it wasn't nothing. He has never come home like this before. Just what did he do?

"Come on," I took Jimmy's hand, and I started to drag him with me. My body was moving. My mind seemed to be blank, but I knew exactly what I was doing. "You're coming with me, and we're going to get you fixed up, okay? What kind of injuries do you have, anything serious?" I brought him into the upstairs bathroom and urged him to sit down on the toilet after turning on the bathroom light.

"Serina, it's nothing. I swear." He said that, but he let me do whatever I wanted to him. So I kept going. I grabbed a rag and wet it. "It's just some scratches and bruises. There is really nothing wrong." Insisting, I still didn't stop.

"Take off your shirt, okay? Let's get these cuts cleaned up then." Why was I worrying so much? Why did I care? Is it because he was taking care of me? Is it because I feel like I have to do something in return for everything he has done for me? Or is it because I actually care about this guy? My abductor.

"What?" He didn't take off his shirt as I told him to, and

I stood in front of him, looking down at him. I repeated what I said but he shook his head. "I can't take off my shirt in front of you, Serina." Me being who I was, being in this caring mood for him, I kept my ground. Since he didn't take off his shirt, I started to do it for him without thinking. He complied and helped me a little. The mask got in the way, of course, but he made sure that the mask would stay on. Now, he was shirtless. My kidnapper was shirtless right in front of me. Who would have thought?

"Take your mask off too. It's best to clean that up too. It looks like you have a bruised eye." He shook his head at me, disagreeing with my comment. "Jimmy, just take off your mask. I won't leave when I see your face. I will stay here with you. I just need to know you're okay!" Persisting, even more, I put the rag down on the bathroom counter and then brought up my hands to the bottom of his mask. I started to take it off for him. Bringing it up from off his neck and above his lips, exposing the bottom part of his face.

"Serina!" He sternly spoke and took my wrists, squeezing them, which made my grip loosen up, making me let go of the mask. "Don't."

I didn't expect him to grab my wrists like that. He grabbed me so hard, my whole body tensed up and froze. I slowly nodded. "Okay—okay. I'll let you keep on your stupid mask. Let me go." After saying that, I saw the hesitation in his body before he let go of my wrists. I stepped back. "Okay," I repeated the word. "By the looks of what happened to your torso, it might hurt a little when I do this, just a little warning." My hand reached over and grabbed the rag. I wet it one more time before I stepped closer to Jimmy and pressed the rag on his chest lightly. "Is this okay?" I looked into his eyes, and to my surprise he was already staring at me. A small smile appeared on my face. He did not say anything, but by the way he was looking at me, it didn't hurt at all. I soon looked back down at what I was doing.

I pressed the rag against his skin, and for some reason I got into deep thought. I felt my heart skip a beat. This made me wonder, what was he thinking? What were his thoughts about all of this? Out of the corner of my eye, I still saw him looking at my face. It was embarrassing. But, I kept on doing what I was doing, helping clean up the dried blood on his body, and making sure there was nothing too serious.

A couple of minutes went by. The rag, by now, had been over every inch of his torso, and I cleaned everything up. I pulled my hand back with the rag and looked back at him. He was still looking at me. "Thank you." He finally spoke after all of that silence. Looking at him, I was speechless. No words coming out of my mouth. "I really appreciate it. You have no idea how much that meant to me. How much all of this means to me." Jimmy did sound like he was telling the truth, but his voice sounded—sad? That's when he suddenly hugged me. When I was caught up in my thoughts, he wrapped his arms around me and pulled me into a hug. I felt comfortable. The warmth from his body transferred to mine, and my arms moved. I squeezed him back.

"Jimmy, what happened to you anyway?" I was inquisitive. I did not leave the hug because he kept his arms around me, and some part of me wanted to stay in the hug. Something about being in this hug made me feel good, emotionally, and physically.

Thinking about it, having somebody hug me, someone who cares about me, and I—even though it is weird to think it— care about him too.

"I just had some business to take care of. You don't need to worry about it, okay?" There was a pause of silence. "I'll make sure you are happy and that you get everything you want. We can be with each other forever, be by each other's sides."

My eyes widened. What came out of his mouth troubled me. My mind got tied up into a nasty knot.

Forever?

Chapter 15

What we are

It had been about a week since the whole incident with Jimmy. It seemed like his wounds were healing up pretty well. For some reason, ever since I took care of him that night, it seemed like our relationship had grown from when we first met. Would it be normal to call him a friend?

That is basically what we've become. Scratch the whole keeping me a prisoner in his house thing. However, lately, I have felt as if I do not want to leave. I haven't thought about leaving in a long time. Sometimes that fact makes me wonder if I'm even in the right mind because it's usually not normal to feel safe and reassured in a situation like this.

Even if I feel safe, even if I don't want to leave anymore, things really have changed since that night. For example, Jimmy never lets me watch television without him here anymore, like he's hiding something. He won't let me get a snatch of news from the outside world, which just brings up the percentage that I think he's concealing something. He used to be perfectly fine with letting me use the television when he wasn't home, so why not anymore? Well, I guess he's been home a lot lately. He hasn't gone out for many errands, or many businesses type things. Maybe he is just on some vacation from his work, and I'm speculating too much about this.

These days, when Jimmy sits downstairs, and I'm upstairs in bed, I think about everything that has happened. When I first arrived here, to now. Walking home from school, and getting sedated. Waking up in a basement, getting my own very room. Looking at family photos, the photos disappearing. Having these weird dreams, seeing that boy, the warmth the boy gave me, the pain of that fire. The death of my dog, the anger of my kidnapper. The other victim from that room. The cops that were looking for me. The hatred for my father. The wounds Jimmy arrived with. The relationship we have. A lot has definitely happened, and it is a lot to take in. And so, I grab my journal, remaining in my bedroom as pretty much always, and I write. I write about everything.

New pages. New story.

My name is Serina Ange. I am a rich girl who seems to have a perfect life. The girl who went missing and got kidnapped. Walking home from a school day when I was supposed to stay after for this award ceremony thing, I got drugged by this strange male walking on the same side of the sidewalk as I was. It makes me wonder what would have happened if I stayed at school that day? If I said yes to the guy who asked me to the dance, would I have gone peacefully to the dance. Would I have had fun? Maybe I would have fallen in love, but I guess you can never know what'll happen in the future, and you can't turn back time, no matter how much you may or may not want to. Time passed. I woke up in my kidnapper's basement. It was cold. The stone floors and walls were transferring chills through my body. I remember trying to move past him, trying to run away. In the end, he didn't put me back into the basement, and he moved me into a room that I soon called my own. He prepared meals for me. I read books that were on the shelves. My kidnapper was taking care of me.

I thought about escaping and running away. But, I gained a fondness for this new lifestyle. That's when I had this first weird dream, a vision where it was peaceful, a dream where my abductor seemed to know what it was all about. I remember snooping around, finding the closet, and picking out some new clothes to wear. I looked around the house, ventured around, found the hatch in Jimmy's closet, got to see what everything looked like. Later on, I made myself comfortable, like there was nothing wrong. I was stupid because I cried about my deceased mom one night. I asked questions, never got any answers or at least clear answers from Jimmy, which was annoying. If you think about it, it's been a long time since I was kidnapped, strange.

Back on topic, Jimmy gave me a notebook when I asked for one. It was supposed to occupy my boredom. Jimmy said this weird thing about knowing him, but I've never met a guy named Jimmy before, and he doesn't seem familiar at all. I don't even have that many friends, or really any friends at all. That reminds me, we watched a movie together and I was so close to figuring out what he looked like. But he woke up like he wasn't even asleep unless he's a really light sleeper. Being a light sleeper must be nice, of course, if you want to wake up easily.

More time has passed, I don't even know how

long. I can't really tell the time here. Jimmy had some company over, and I was stuck downstairs until the meet and greet was over. What a surprise, I had another dream! It was a dream where I was hooked up with IV bags and everything. That is when I met the—scratch that. I don't want Jimmy to read and find out because it seemed like he was hiding something that day. HE KISSED ME! How could I leave that part out? Jimmy actually kissed me, and it was a surprise. Now that I think of it, he seems like a really nice guy to date. But not me, I will not date him, never.

The cops came, blah blah, I got stuck with the weird guy with chains in the room below the hatch in Jimmy's closet. I thought I would never get out of there, but I ended up getting saved—If you could even say I was saved. Apart from all these things that happened to me—I shared my life story. To him, to the guy who kidnapped me, who forced a kiss on me, who—seems like he actually cares. That's right—Jimmy, the very one who took me hostage, really seems to care about me. And I, to be honest, I care about him as well.

No, what am I writing? Whatever. I'm too lazy to erase it. I now have a sudden feeling to stop writing so, here is the end, future me.

Putting the notebook away, I sighed. I couldn't believe I just thought that and wrote it down for anyone to read. Talk about embarrassing! It's weird though. I never thought that I would think that in the first place. As every second went by, I wondered more and more, and there was this recurring question in my head, "Who is Jimmy to me?" I guess I would have to figure that out pretty quickly, especially now that we seemed closer. This gave me a huge chance to run away, or it gave me a huge chance to live a better life and completely change my life.

"Who wants lunch?" Jimmy came up behind me with a chuckle, his hands tickling my sides. When I said we got closer, I really do mean that we got closer.

I laughed along with him, my whole body squirming. "Stop, stop!" I turned around to look up at him. "You always do this to me, you big meanie."

"What else am I supposed to do, stand ten feet apart and never talk to you? How are we supposed to become closer?"

"Oh shut up."

In the end, this person who wanted to have our relationship grow let go of me and started to make some sandwiches. And I just leaned up against a kitchen counter, observing him. As I was watching—totally not a creep move—I thought about the same thing that had been on my mind for days. Sure, we got closer and everything, but he was still hiding stuff from me and I did not like that at all. Keeping secrets and keeping them in a way where it was clear that someone was hiding something, really pissed me off. For instance, who was that girl whose name I saw on the boxes after the encounter with the police? If I remember correctly, her name was Maya.

Maya, just who are you? Do I need to worry?

I shook those thoughts from my mind, and I tried to clear them. I told myself, the past is in the past. Correct?

"You okay? You seem to be spacing out." Jimmy got done with making sandwiches. I hadn't even realized. Nodding, I showed I'm fine. "Are you sure?"

Gosh, I really don't want to tell him the truth.

"I'm okay, don't worry about it."

Not like I want to disturb him anyway. What will he do if he finds out that I am thinking about us, thinking about him, thinking about Maya? I wonder if he will get irritated with me.

* * *

Another dream. How did I know? I knew exactly how it felt after having had a couple of them at least. It was not a typical dream, so it was not an atmosphere that I was used to. Everything around me was white. It was like I was in some different dimension. It was weird. At first, that was all I thought I would see until I heard what seemed to be a little kid's voice.

"I've been waiting for you, Serina." A pause. "That is your name, right?" I turned around, detecting the voice coming from behind me, and it was that same little boy who gave me warmth in the other illusion I had.

How did he get here? Why is he here? How does he know my name? Questions filled my brain and got tied up into a knot. I ended up not responding to the fellow.

I stepped back a little. To his eyes, I probably look terrified, confused.

I'm not going to lie, I am. More confused than scared though. I hope the kid doesn't get the wrong idea.
I blink.

It was just all white around us. It was silent too. Even if the boy spoke, he spoke in a quiet tone, and it didn't seem to echo at all. The sound was weird. We stared at each other. I could basically hear his breathing. One, he breathed in. Two, three, four, he breathed out. His body trembled.

Chilly, maybe? I spin my head around to try and figure this out. I feel tension build from just us staring, so I decide I might as well look like I am at least doing something.

I blinked. I saw a hospital bed. I hadn't seen it there before, but I knew it was the same bed that popped up in my dreams.

I blinked.

In a split second, without even wanting to, I was in the bed, laying down, as if I was there all along. The place I was in started to fill in with the darkness. It was coming towards me at a fast speed until it suddenly stopped. It was dark. I could barely see, or at least I was blind to a certain extent.

One, two, three. The number of hands I felt crawling up my body. I looked under the blanket that I was under. There were large, red hands. Four, five, six, seven. Just how many hands were there? My body got the chills. I moved, trying to get those nasty things off of me, but they kept on wriggling up. I saw more, eight, nine, ten—eighteen hands. There were red hands, large, red hands, crawling, touching my body. When most reached my shoulders, all of them froze. It was like they were communicating with each other.

Frozen, that's what they were. That's what I was. Suddenly, the kid came up. He had a completely different appearance. A couple of bruises were noticeable on his body. It made worry spark inside of me.

"This is what he did to me. That is why you have to leave, escape. Do not trust him."

The kid's voice—I never thought that it could sound like that. Stern, strong, scary.

"What?" My throat was dry. My speech sounded raspy.

A couple of swift moments later, I got pushed down. I looked to see how, and instead of seeing those eighteen hands, there was only one pair. Huge, bigger than my own body. They were pushing me down, keeping me pushed into the bed, like restraints.

Is this boy controlling these hands? Was he the one making me have these dreams all along?

It is useless to move. Even if I did, I would never get out of this. There is no way.

"What are you doing to me? Why are you doing this?" I started asking questions. He screamed, the bed shook, and my eyes widened.

What the actual hell is going on?

"You don't get it! You don't get it at all!" His voice got louder, deeper, scarier. "Jimmy is a bad person. He is a really bad person! You have no idea what he did. You have no idea what he has done. What he did to Maya."

Maya. A name I had heard before, the name from the boxes that I saw in the storage room in Jimmy's house. Before I could ask any more questions, he continued speaking, yelling at me. I winced at his voice.

"I can't tell you the details, but I know he still has everything you need to know in the red folder."

The red folder?

"That's just who he is. He can't let go of the past. He has to keep everything in check to make sure no one finds out."

Secrets?

"I loved Maya, and he just had to take her away from me." The hands that were pressing my body down started to give me intense pain. The boy chuckled. "I wonder what's so special about you. If I were alive, I would know. But I'm not."

My chest felt empty. My whole body felt empty. My mind was gaining more knots as seconds passed. Then there was a loud thump. I heard Jimmy's voice.

"Serina!"

Chapter 16

Murderer

Mariah got a text message from Marcus a couple of days after they met. It read, "Meet me at my place Friday night at 6:00 p.m." So, she told her parents that she had something after school that might not be done till late. Of course, they didn't question her and said that was fine.

"Hey mom, dad, is it okay if I stay after school tomorrow so that I can study and go to a club I joined?" Making up two defenses, she hoped they would believe her.

"That works out perfectly! Your father and I are going to be going on a date, so just come home safely afterward, okay honey?" Going on a date on a Friday night was something Mariah's parents did at least once or twice a month, or every few months, depending on how much money they had and depending what their schedule was.

"Awesome, thank you!" A wide smile crawling to her face, Mariah overflowed with happiness, with anticipation for the next day.

Now, it was Friday night. She was on her way to Serina's dad's house. Her parents thought she was still at school. Since her parents didn't know where she was, she hoped they wouldn't get too suspicious and figure it out. All that

was on her mind while she was on her way was Serina and
her parents. Being worried about how Serina was doing.
If she was okay. Falling for Serina more and more as she
thought about her.

When she arrived at Serina's house, she noticed the door
was open slightly. "Mr. Ange?" she called. There was no
response. She turned the knob and opened it up a crack.
But she discerned something off. "Mr. Ange, are you home?"
Looking through the crack of the door, she saw some red
paint on the floor. Is he painting something? She wondered.

Her hand pushed against the door, and it opened it up
more, giving her eyes a better view inside the house. Once
her ears started getting a better sound, she heard classical
music playing. Mariah stepped in, passing over some of
the red paint by the door. Since the tune was playing, she
thought Marcus could not hear her. She proceeded to let
herself in. The more she wandered into the house, down
the hallway, she seemed to see more drops of the red paint,
and then smelled a disgusting stench. The scent going up
her nostrils made her almost gag. It smelled like there was
a dead critter in the house.

Her automatic reaction was to think of Serina's dog.
"Ritz? Is Ritz okay?" Mariah began looking around more
frantically, but the thing she found was not Ritz, nor a
dead animal.

With haste, Mariah took her phone out of her pocket and
opened up her phone dial. Dialing a three-digit emergency
number everyone knows.

"9-1-1 what is your emergency?"

At first glance, it did look like paint, but it was actually
blood. Marcus' blood. "I found a dead body, oh lord, please
come help." Mariah's voice was squeaking on her end, her
hand shaking, her whole body trembling.

"Calm down. Can you tell me the address?"

Mariah ended up stuttering, but she told the 9-1-1 operator the address, a dog whimpered in the background.

The alliance between Mariah and Marcus had now ended.

* * *

While she was waiting for the police to arrive, she wandered around the house, mainly to get away from the stench that came off of Mr. Ange's body. That was when she found something that caught her eye, a paper the size of an ID card. It was someone's driver's license.

Sliding it in her pocket, she ended up keeping it for herself, and when she was about to tell the police about the piece of evidence she found, she changed her mind.

"I found—" There were people outside talking to Mariah, and there were also people investigating inside.

"You found what, honey?" As she was getting interviewed, her voice froze up. Mariah just stood there.

"Nothing."

"Are you sure?" They were suspicious. "It's okay. You can tell us anything. You will not get in any trouble, we promise."

Her parents were contacted, of course, since she was legally under-age. Nellie and Joe were not very happy to hear that their daughter was at someone's house, not only that but there was a dead body there. They were worried sick.

"Mariah! You're okay?" Her parents interrupted the conversation, which thankfully to Mariah meant she did not have to tell the police the truth.

"Why did you lie to us? We are going to have a real chat when we get home, young lady," said Nellie gently. It's a good thing he had started the conversation. Joe was furious and if he had been the one to speak first, he would not have been so nice to her.

Jameson Smith. Mariah was getting closer to figuring out

this whole thing about Serina. Or that's what she thought because when she found the ID, she knew it had to be connected somehow. Who else would try to kill Marcus than the person who had taken Serina? Suddenly, a scary thought came to her mind.

What if there are cameras and the bad guys are watching the house?

If there were, perhaps the killer knew who she was, and she would be next. Maybe the people around her were in danger as well.

"If they killed Serina's father, I'm sure they won't hesitate to kill me too, or anyone else who gets closer to Serina," she said quietly with a hum at the end. "I'll take that risk, if it means finding her and saving her. I'll do anything."

On the car ride home, Mariah leaned her head against the cold window and tried to link the clues together. Her parents were speaking in hushed tones in the front seats, but the more they spoke, the more their voices started to drift in Mariah's head. The words going through one ear and right out the other, starting to float around the car like distant fog. Her mind was too focused on Serina and her father. She couldn't pay attention to her surroundings.

Eventually, the car got parked in their driveway. They had returned home. Mariah quickly got out of the car and practically jogged to the front door. She wanted to avoid a conversation with her parents, so she reached into her purse, pulled out her house key and opened the door, then headed straight for the living room. Google was the first place she turned. She typed Jameson Smith's name in the search bar. There was nothing on the Internet about him. The picture that was on the driver's license didn't help at all. It seemed to have been burned out. Mariah knew what that meant.

"Good thing I paid attention in class," she said out loud.

The picture of Jameson Smith had been blinded out by a cigarette. Mariah had learned about this practice in History class. "People used to do this all the time to block their identity. I didn't know it was still a thing," she said softly.

There was more information on there that was unreadable. However, Mariah looked at an address that was on there and she smiled, getting one more piece of information. The address of where Serina might be; the address of the person who may have killed Serina's father; the address of a psychopath.

The investigation didn't get too far. Her parents walked into the room. "Tell me, why did you lie to us?" Joe didn't give Mariah a chance to explain herself. "We trusted you, and you went behind our backs to—what—" There was a pause, "go to some old guy's house?"

Her mother added on, "and the guy was murdered too! What if something happened to you?" She then was cut off by her husband. Nellie cowered back, watching the two talk back and forth.

"If I wasn't there, then he would have never been found! You guys don't get it. I'm trying to help a dear friend to me, someone I—" she hesitated but continued her sentence, "someone I fell in love with! How am I supposed to just sit back and do nothing?" She threw her hands in the air. Both of her parents were shocked.

"It was dangerous! Love is no excuse, Mariah!" Joe let out a deep sigh and rubbed his forehead. What his daughter said about love made him hesitate. "You can promise us you did not have anything to do with that man's death. You were not a part of this?"

Mariah was shaken to hear her father say this. Even more shocked when her mother didn't seem bothered by the question. "What?" She became speechless, which wasn't helping her case with the suspicions. "No! You guys think I would be involved with a *murder*?"

Neither of her parents said anything. They were waiting for a response to come out of her mouth, but nothing else came out. Mariah's eyebrows furrowed as she looked first at her mother, then her father. She crossed her arms. No explanation, no response, just a shake of her head before storming off to her bedroom, locking herself inside.

She talked to herself, grabbed a notebook, and started writing down her thoughts, along with the new information she had gained. "Why does nobody seem to believe me?" Thinking out loud she said, "The investigators didn't seem to either. But what surprises me most is my parents." Just like her father, she sighed. "Serina. When will this ever end? When will I get to see your beautiful face again? When will I?"

> "You have such a beautiful face, Mariah."
> Angellica smiled as her hand caressed Mariah's cheek. She blushed.
> "Are you being serious right now or just teasing me again?" asked Mariah with a giggle.
> "Just teasing," Angellica removed her hand and giggled. When she heard what Mariah said next, she could not help but smile.
> "You are such an angel from hell. My Angel."

"Get that out of your head, Mariah. That was all in the past. Focus on Serina," Mariah said out loud to herself. She didn't mean to blackout and think about the past. Mariah kept on beating herself up about it whenever Angellica crossed her mind. Saying that out loud didn't stop her thoughts from developing.

Mariah's crush on Serina had started after the heartbreak

she had with Angellica. One day she was off. Whenever she looked at food or thought about eating, she would feel sick to her stomach. It was a weird thing because she wasn't throwing up food after she ate, and she wasn't purposely not eating because she was insecure about her body. It was a different situation. That's when Serina came into her life, and the first time that she had laid eyes on her, the first thing she noticed was her looks. Mariah thought that she was absolutely stunning. The first time they spoke one day at lunch her heart fluttered. Mariah learned that she was a pretty nice girl. Her mind filled with the thoughts of Serina, a train that wouldn't stop. Not long after, she realized that she was falling in love again. This scared Mariah, but at the same time she was happy that she might have found someone better than her, someone who could make her feel again. One thing Mariah hoped was that her and Serina's relationship would end up better than her and Angellica's relationship.

"I'm not hungry," said Mariah one day at school. She had started getting hungry the hour before, and when lunchtime came around she was eagerly waiting in line for the food. However, when she got closer to what was being served, the scent entered her nose. When she got even closer, her eyes examined the food.

As the lunch ladies were putting the food on the plates, that is when it suddenly hit her. The sensation of being sick. The feeling you get when you are about to throw up. That's never a good feeling.

Instantly, her arm crossed over her stomach, and her hand wrapped around her side. Her eyes wouldn't move away from the food. The more she looked at the food, the closer she got, the faster her heart raced.

I can't do this. I can't eat. If I eat, I'm going to puke.

When it was her turn to get a plate, rather than grabbing the tray held out to her, she squinted her eyes shut for a couple of seconds. The students behind her were getting irritated. They ordered her to move, and when she didn't, they eventually skipped ahead of her in line. Mariah just stood there like a statue, frozen and unable to move.

The only person in the world who would have asked if she was okay rather than forsaking her, Mariah would never forget. "Are you okay? Hello?" Mariah's eyes opened. The feeling of someone's hand was on her shoulder, and when she turned to see who it was, it was one of the most beautiful girls she had ever seen.

She had long, brown hair, straight as ever. At first glance, her eyes looked like a shade of blue. But when her eyes adjusted, she realized they were a hazel color. Her body shape was between an hourglass and a top hourglass, but Mariah would never know the exact answer without little to no clothing. Her hips and bust were the same measurements, complimenting well with a well-defined waist which was narrower than both. Every inch of her body seemed to be proportionate. Nothing seemed to be too out of shape. She was very appealing to the eye.

"Hi," was the first word that came out of Mariah's mouth. "Yeah, I'm okay, don't worry!" Seeing this gorgeous girl, she didn't want to seem weird or make a fool out of herself. Then, without recognizing it, Mariah took a glance at the back of her body, slightly curious about what she would see. The girl's shoulders were rounded perfectly. The shirt she was wearing showed her skin and it seemed so smooth. Eyes wandering lower, she took one more click glance. Rounded buttocks, mainly girls with the hourglass figure have them, and yet again, it was appealing.

"Are you sure you don't need to go to the nurse or any-thing?" The brown-haired girl's hand tightened a little on

Mariah's shoulder. Her heart couldn't help but skip a beat.

"I'm sure!" said Mariah with a stutter. "Thank you, I appreciate it, Serina."

"No problem!" Smiling, Serina did not realize that the new girl knew her name. "Want to eat lunch together?"

And that's when Mariah officially talked to the girl she fawned over from afar, though Serina didn't remember that moment at all. That day, the feeling of sickness went away. It all started with Angel, the anxiety of having her gone. The problems Mariah went through are what most likely caused her to feel like she could not eat. What caused her to feel sick. But when Serina came around, it was like she got rid of that feeling, those feelings. Serina became the new angel to Mariah.

As days went by, Mariah tried to talk to her little crush. However, whenever she got the chance, it seemed like Serina was ignoring her. Being hurt by this, she stopped trying to get in contact with Serina. She watched from the shadows. Until, of course, the award ceremony.

"I wonder if Serina will be there. She must be. She'll get the most important prize! I'm so excited for her. I can't wait!" Fantasizing from backstage, you could almost feel the energy coming off of Mariah. You could almost see the figurative shrine that Mariah had created in Serina's honor anytime she talked about her.

In the end, Serina didn't show up, and Mariah was heartbroken. She got angry.

What the hell. I didn't even need to come to this ceremony. This was a waste of time.

Gritting her teeth, and standing up from her chair, Mariah was about to storm off, but then a teacher called her name. She turned around and smiled. "Yes?" Acting like the pure girl she seemed to be, she ended up accepting Serina's prize on her behalf. "I'll be sure to get this to her!"

When she got home that night, she couldn't seem to eat. It had started up again. Her stomach started to hurt like crazy. Sitting up, her back arched. She hunched around the room, grunting in discomfort. She knew she had to go to the bathroom or something, maybe get some fresh air. So, Mariah held her stomach as she walked out of the room and started heading towards the bathroom. On her way to the bathroom though, her movement was tense, and her body ended up leaning up against the wall because she lost sensation in her legs.

"Dammit!" Spoken with a sting, eyes squinted. Mariah thought to herself, "What the hell? I thought I could withstand this longer."

Mariah did not want to be weak and have to depend on someone else. She thought she could handle herself, be strong, but the pain was too intense. "I need to get someone."

Before Mariah could move any further, she felt the pain intensify. Thankfully, her mom walked out into the hallway and saw her daughter in this condition. Not saying anything at first, she just gasped at what she saw, seeing her baby in pain.

"Mariah," Nellie reached her hand out to only get snapped at.

"Shut up." A little truth of Mariah's personality came out. She knew she shouldn't have done that, showing her true self, but she also knew she couldn't act like someone she wasn't at that moment. Act like the innocent girl. "Shit." Mumbling under her breath, then falling to the floor, her legs giving up on her.

Her mother instantly bent down to her knees and got by her side, putting a hand on Mariah's back. Mariah didn't accept the help though. She just pushed her mother's hand away and stood up, using the last bit of strength she had left, and walked over to the bathroom. She felt like she could walk more and stand, her mind tricking her thoughts. Mariah thought it was getting better. But it wasn't.

"Mariah, let me help you." Nellie followed her into the bathroom and let out another gasp when she saw her daughter collapse to the floor and grasp the toilet with her hands. "Oh dear," the mother started to worry, seeing her child like this, seeing her hurl into the bowl.

Mariah's mother didn't want to leave Mariah alone like that, so the best thing she could think of to do was to be there for her, hold her hair back and console her with a hand on her back. Nellie knew that Mariah needed to eat something, so she suggested it, but of course after Mariah was finished with the toilet, she hesitated to answer her mother. Unsure of what to do because every time she looked at food, she got sicker. In the end, she gave in and they both went downstairs.

"Just a little strawberry, okay?" Nellie took the time to cut strawberries into small pieces, handing over a piece to Mariah. The hesitation was even greater now, seeing the food in front of her. The smell going up to her nose, nausea already getting to her, more than ever.

Mariah thought she looked dumb, hesitating like this, not eating the small strawberry. She felt like a fool, but still, she ended up trying. Taking the strawberry from her mother's hand, she put it up to her mouth. The smell got worse and her head started spinning. She gulped, looking at the strawberry for long moments until finally putting it in her mouth and chewing. It looked like things were going well at first, up till she gagged. Pushing Nellie out of the way, she spit the chewed strawberry into the sink, not swallowing a single bit of it.

"Dammit!" Mariah slammed her right fist onto the

counter, making a bang. Her mind tricked her even more, thinking she was going somewhere, thinking that this was helping, that her mother was helping. Only to end up in a disaster.

Nellie stumbled back, not expecting the push from Mariah and she hit her spine against the handle of a cupboard, which hurt a lot. The second gasp of the hour left her mouth. She knew her daughter didn't mean to hurt her, so she tried to act like everything was fine. She knew she couldn't worry Mariah or make her feel guilty at all. "Hey, it's okay, it's okay," she repeated as she walked back up to Mariah, yet again putting a hand onto her back to try and console her. She was trying her best, though she was clueless about what to do in this situation.

Just like the push Mariah gave to Nellie, she turned around and raised her voice at her too. "No, it's not okay! None of this is okay! I told you I couldn't eat but you still fucking forced me to anyway! I can't do this! I'm too god damn scared!" Mariah ended up slamming her fist against something again, only this time it was the cupboard that was under the sink. But then she felt bad, started to feel guilty, and pulled her mother into a hug, lowering her voice and whispering, "I can't do this."

Nellie flinched when her daughter yelled at her but when she hugged her, she relaxed a little, just a little. But her body was still tense, maybe a little too tense, a little too noticeable. "I'm sorry." That's all that could leave her mouth as they hugged, but Mariah backed away with her eyes wide.

"Were you just scared of me?"

Mariah's mother knew she was tensed up. She knew her reaction wasn't the best and now that Mariah figured it out, she became speechless but knew she had to reply. "No! Of course not!"

Mariah let go of Nellie. "I need to be alone right now, mom."

"Wait, I'm not, I promise! It was just a reflex, baby." She felt like a failure of a mother. Nellie needed to do something. She couldn't just watch her daughter walk away thinking that she didn't love her or something. So, when she saw her legs starting to move, she reached out and grabbed Mariah's arm.

Mariah snapped at her, harshly moving her body to get away from Nellie's grasp. "Mom!"

There was nothing else to be done. Mariah walked off to go to her room. Nellie called out, "If you need anything, I am always here for you, Mariah." Now Nellie was just standing alone in the kitchen, feeling terrible. Both of them were feeling terrible, feeling guilty of something, but not knowing what. And with their family traits, neither of them would confront the other.

Mariah knew she had to do something before it was too late. She didn't want anything to happen to Serina. If Serina got hurt or is hurt, maybe even near death when Mariah arrived—if Serina would even be at the address on the card—Mariah would go into rage mode.

The perfect, innocent girl. Everyone thinks that Mariah is just the shy, new kid, the shy new and weird kid. This is why people don't talk to Mariah that much, but Mariah didn't mind that. She was doing such a good job keeping it on the low, keeping her emotions intact, until Serina, of course.

Slowly, as time went on, Mariah was getting closer to breaking. Every second that went by, every thought that crossed her mind added to the anxiety that was about to overflow. Whether that was going to happen tomorrow, or in a week, it depended on how well Mariah kept it in, kept it to herself.

Now, there was a path drawn into her head. After thinking and thinking, after her mind being all unorganized, there was finally a path drawn for her. Finding and saving Serina was her number one priority, and she knew that this Jameson guy had something to do with it. Closing her eyes, she thought of how to start the plan. She reviewed the bullet points that were in her head, ready to follow the green path.

1. Research more at the library about Jameson Smith to see if it gives any leads.
2. If there was something found out, or nothing found out at all, the next step is to go to the house, investigate there.
3. If it is the right house, try to be independent, try to be quiet, and go inside to save her.
4. If all goes well, they will leave the house. If the person chases after them, call the police and run. If it comes to it, steal your mom's car.
5. Serina thanks Mariah so much, and in the end— Mariah's happy ending—a kiss. The romantic scene where the knight saves the princess.

That is how Mariah had everything planned. That's how she hoped it would all go. She did not want the plan to go haywire and go in the wrong direction. She didn't want anyone to get hurt. She only wanted to save the one she fell in love with. She wanted the happy movie ending where her love falls in love with her because of the saving. If this didn't happen that way, Mariah wouldn't know what to do. If she didn't save Serina, if she didn't get any leads, she would scream. Scream at the top of her lungs, feel hopeless, feel useless, feel stupid.

One step forward. Mariah's feet stepped towards the beginning of the green path. The journey began.

Chapter 17

Get ready

It was another school day. Mariah's parents wouldn't let her stay after school or anything, especially after the incident that happened with Marcus. So, because of this, Mariah couldn't think of a way to go to the library to search more on who Jameson Smith is. She tried to plead so that her parents would agree to let her stay at the library after school, but nothing worked.

Until one class period when luck was on her side. "Alright class, we're going to go down to the library for the hour. Grab your stuff, and let's head down." Once inside, Mariah cheered, and her eyes lit up. The only problem was that the ID she had of Jameson was not on her.

"Teach, can I go to my locker real quick?"

"Why?" Of course, like a lot of teachers, they were suspicious of a student wanting to go to their locker right after the bell rang.

"I have the wrong notebook, I'm sorry." As almost always, a lie was created, and the student was allowed to go in the end. When Mariah returned with a notebook and the card, she intended to take a spot at the computers. The good luck went to waste though. There were no open spots for Mariah to sit.

"Are you serious?" Setting her things down at a table, she pulled the chair out to sit down.

"Mariah, come here!" Mariah's ears perked hearing her name, and she looked over to see somebody who she didn't like very much, Aliza Cornwell. She was about to pretend she didn't see the person who called her name, but then saw that there was an open spot next to her. "Come sit next to me girl!"

She knew she had to take this chance, even if it was someone she disliked. Coincidentally, it was also the sister of the little boy who went to get the red ball that rolled into the weird house's yard—where an eyeball was suspected to have been seen. Mariah rolled her eyes at the thought of recognizing her. But, in the end, she sat down and turned on the computer.

It was silent for a while. Mariah was happy that she didn't have to make conversation with her computer neighbor. She started typing "Jameson Smith" into Google, but nothing popped up. The next thing she wanted to try was searching for the address that was on the ID. The house did pop up. A smile crawled onto Mariah's face. The girl next to her noticed.

"What are you smiling about? Some kind of—" Aliza's sentence was cut off as she looked at Mariah's screen. "Ew, no way." Her voice got louder. The whole class could hear her. She was that one student who raised her voice in class without noticing and thought it was cool. "That's the stupid house my little brother said he saw an eyeball in." Her voice told everyone that she thought the whole eyeball thing was stupid.

"What?" That one word was the only response Mariah gave. She couldn't help but keep on listening.

A finger flew in front of Mariah's face, and it poked the screen. "There. That was the window my brother said he saw the gross, fucking thing."

"Ms. Cornwell! Language!" The teacher spoke.

Two students who were in the same class as Mariah, sitting a row behind them on the computers, were eavesdropping. Dean Parry and Mercy Cunningham. Similar to Mariah, they were interested in the topic, in the house, in Serina. So, they waited.

Dean and Mercy waited until class would end, not working on their schoolwork in the meantime. They just watched Mariah's screen. They watched as Mariah wrote down things in her notebook. They noticed how deeply focused she was. Her eyes locked, her mind locked onto her goal.

Mariah had no idea that two kids were watching her. She only knew that the girl she was sitting next to her was watching her. As the class went on, Mariah was wary, but that did not stop her from investigating.

The bell rang, and Mariah had to close all the tabs, though she did save them just in case she needed to go back to them at all. She didn't learn much about Jameson because he was wiped off the Internet. No social media, no photos, only the location of where he lives.

"Mariah, wait up!" She was already zooming out of the library once she'd gathered all of her stuff. She wanted to keep walking, but she couldn't just ignore whoever wanted her to wait for them. She turned around.

"Who are you?" An unfamiliar face popped up, along with another face she didn't know. Two strangers.

"My name is Dean." He looked over to the side and saw Mercy beside him. "This is Mercy."

While Dean and Mercy were watching Mariah, they conversed with each other, learning that they kind of had the same goal, the same suspicions. A guy like Dean and a girl like Mercy would be the perfect couple. The athletic popular boy with the hot, popular girl. What a set-up.

"We just wanted to talk to you for a little bit."

Dean didn't know what to say, so Mercy took over. "It's about the house you called up in your search, and the whole thing with the eyeball that keeps on going around. We want to help you with whatever you are doing. What are you doing?" All three of them started to walk side by side in the hallway. Both Dean's and Mercy's eyes set on Mariah.

"I was—" Mariah hesitated before answering them. She was wondering why they were interested, people like them. She knew that these two were popular, and she did not want to mess with them. "Researching something, a project I'm doing. I guess." The intensity that the two had with their eyes gave Mariah the chills.

"A project?" Dean jumped in. "What kind of project? Are you looking into the eye? Do you think there's something larger going on just like we do?"

"Just like you do?" Mariah finally looked over and made eye contact with Dean. This caught her attention. "What—do you mean?"

"I think you know exactly what we mean." Mercy rolled her eyes and let out a small, cute laugh. "There is something weird going on in that house and I want to figure it out. So—" Mariah stopped at her locker, but Mercy stood in front of her so she couldn't get to her lock. "What information do you have so far?"

"Can we help?" Dean just stood off to the side respectfully.

"I don't think you want to know. It's weird. And don't you guys have classes to get to or something? The warning bell is going to ring soon."

"Oh come on, you big baby. Just answer the question and I'll get out of your way so that you can get to your class."

"Fine." Little did she know when Mariah started speaking, there was another eavesdropper. Mariah continued, "I suspect that Serina is in that house. Serina Ange, the girl who went missing from our school. Don't ask how I found out the address, I just did. Do you guys want to help? Come over to my house after school and we can talk about it." Mariah sighed, trying to make this conversation go as fast as it could. "That's all I'm telling you right now. Can you get out of my way?"

Mercy's mouth dropped, so did Dean's. "*The* Serina Ange? Dude, she's like one of my best friends!" Now Dean just needed to help out. "You bet. I will come over to your place. Give me your number." Dean handed Mariah his phone, and she put her number into it.

Handing Dean's phone back to him, she spoke again, getting a little more annoyed. The warning bell had rang already. "Okay, okay, just message me. Get out of my way, and let's talk later."

The two finally left, so did the third person who was hovering around a corner.

Mariah didn't expect this to happen today. Getting the house onto her phone on the maps, getting the location, getting two people who were interested and willing to help her with her investigation. She did wonder though, why would people like them be worried for Serina and the eye-ball in the house? Why would they be smart enough to be thinking deeply about the situation in the first place?

Shrugging all of those thoughts off, Mariah thought that ignoring those questions be would be the best idea. "It's better to not go alone anyway," she told herself, walking in the hallway and hearing the bell ring again. "Great, because of those two idiots I'm late for class." A pause, "God I hope Serina is okay."

* * *

One new notification. A text message from an unknown

number. "I wonder who this might be," Mariah said in a sarcastic tone. Of course, it was Dean.

"Hey Mariah, it's Dean from school! Give me your address, and Mercy and I will head over there right after school!" Mariah's address was sent to Dean, and she sent another message right after it warning Dean that if they made fun of her small house and cheap living, she would end their truce in an instant.

"Whoa. Whoa, okay, man."

"I promise."

"We promise."

Dean replied in an instant by sending three different text messages.

By the time school ended, Mariah was already home. She decided to skip the last class of the day since it was just a study-hall, and sometimes they would let their students leave school an hour early. She made sure to let her parents know that two of her friends were coming over after school. She also made sure that the house at least looked presentable. Nellie and Joe agreed to have their daughter's friends over, only if they would meet them first. They had become more strict parents since the incident. Mariah was thankful that they even allowed this to happen. She was happy that she was allowed to let people come over, only she had lied about what they were going to do.

Mariah's parents thought that they would hang out just as friends, laughing, making fun of each other and all that fun stuff teenagers do. But little did they know that they would do something unexpected, something weird, like investigating a girl who had gone missing. Not an everyday thing kids their age do. Some people go home and fall asleep right away. Some play video games all night. Some are little goody-two-shoes, and some party all night.

"You ready to go to Mariah's place?" Dean asked Mercy as

they walked out the school doors together, both of them not having anything on them but their cellphones and maybe some money.

"You know I am. I thought it would just be some kind of paranormal joke she was doing research about, but it's actually a real investigation! It feels like I'm in some kind of movie or book." Laughter surrounded them. "Being in a book, wouldn't that be interesting?" Mercy suggested. "We would never know either. We'd just be characters in a book but never know. It's strange to think about."

"You're weird!"

The athletic pretty boy walking next to her nudged her shoulder lightly and chuckled. They both continued to walk and talk. That is until they noticed that someone was following them, and Mercy got scared. "That guy behind us has been following us ever since we left the school. Do you know who he is?" They made sure to whisper so they wouldn't get caught by whoever was following them.

Dean took a quick look behind them, acting as if nothing was suspicious and he shook his head, no. Their legs started to move them faster and Dean took Mercy's hand, interlinking their fingers for support to console her. "It'll be okay. If they try to mess with us then I'll beat them up, don't worry."

"Okay." And so, they held hands, continuing the walk to Mariah's house with a stranger behind them.

Time passed. The two got closer to their destination and the person who had been following them was still there, still following. If Dean and Mercy stopped, the person would stop. If they walked faster, the person matched their pace. Dean couldn't handle it anymore and decided to say something.

"Hey, you got a problem or something man?" Mercy stayed behind Dean as he turned around to face the student, who didn't say anything, only looked a bit startled. "Answer me, you creep. Why are you following us around?"

"Add me in." His voice was deep. It matched his appearance. He had dark brown hair that almost looked like it was jet black; brown eyes that looked like they matched the darkness of his pupils. He was wearing a white t-shirt with a baggy jean jacket over it, complimenting the black jeans he was wearing that had a couple of rips in them.

"Add you in? Are you on something? Speak English before I start throwing punches!" Dean took steps towards the male standing ahead of him.

"My name is Steve. Steve Reynolds. I want to be a part of whatever you guys are going to do involving Serina Ange."

Mercy stepped in. "What do you want with Serina, huh? You don't look or sound like you're her friend. Oh wait, you're Stevie, the person who made jokes about Serina's disappearance. You asshole." She growled.

"Hey, hey, Mercy. Let's see what Mariah says about it. He's followed us this far, right?" Dean looked at Mercy and gave her a confident look, a look that convinced Mercy to trust him. He looked back at Steve. "Okay, Stevie, you can come with us. But that doesn't mean we like you or trust you just yet. You could have just talked to us like a normal human being dude."

A third person was added. Three teenagers walking down a sidewalk on a sunny day, the wind picking up as minutes went by. Before they knew it, they all arrived and Mariah was ready for them.

"Dean, Mercy, and—" Mariah was confused about the new face, but she instantly knew who he was when she got a better look at him. "Steve." She hastily went beside Mercy and Dean and started freaking out a little. "Why is Steve here? Do you know who he is?"

"What? What do you mean, Mariah? He was following

us and said he wanted to help us so we let him tag along, I guess." Mercy didn't know what was the problem. She did know that Mariah knew something though.

"He hurt Serina!"

"What? No, I didn't!"

"Uh, yeah you did. I watched you!"

"I never once hurt her in my life! Sure, I made fun of her and stuff, but I NEVER hurt her." Steve scoffed.

"You're not helping us out." Mariah said just like that. "Now go away and forget about this whole thing—" she stopped her sentence. "No wait, actually, you'd be useful." That was correct. Also, she didn't want him to go telling people about their little plan. "You can help us out, but we will have rules."

Once everything was situated with the drama outside, Mariah let them in. "I thought you'd have a bigger house. What are you, poor?" As soon as the words left Steve's mouth, Mariah's hands clenched into fists.

Dean remembered the warning she had given him before the arrival. "Uh oh, you messed up dude."

But to everyone's surprise, Mariah didn't do anything and she just continued. "Let's go into my room and talk about this. Make yourself at home. Just don't make a mess and don't eat all my food."

"Yes ma'am." Steve rolled his eyes and spoke in a sarcastic tone. His attitude was not the greatest, which the others didn't like about him. But nothing could be changed. That's just the person he was.

"Okay." Mariah laid down on her bed and made herself comfortable. Mercy sat down in a chair at Mariah's desk that she had in the corner of her room. Dean just leaned up against the wall and put his hands in his pockets. Steve, however, went and joined Mariah on the bed.

Everyone looked at him strangely. "What? You said to make yourself comfortable so I did."

Mariah continued. "As all of you know, Serina went missing a while ago, and the news has nothing about her whereabouts. Her father, Marcus, just died, and the dog that was out in my living room is her dog, Ritz."

"Whoa, how do you know her dad died?" Mercy's arms were crossed. She leaned back into the chair and looked at Mariah, deeply listening to what she was saying.

"I was the one who found the body." Before she let anyone say anything about that, she kept talking and did not let anyone interrupt her. "Don't tell ANYONE this, but while I was there, I found a driver's license with the name Jameson Smith on it, and an address. But sadly, the photo of him was too crossed out to know what he looks like." After a small pause, Mariah looked from one person to the next, to the next. No one was not saying anything. Silence filled the atmosphere.

"I found the card, and I didn't turn it in to the police because I knew they would be useless. I did some research as Mercy and Dean saw in the library at school today, and we learned that it was the same house where some girl in our grade had spread a rumor about her little brother seeing an eyeball there. Some creepy stuff."

"Gross! I heard about that before, and it creeped me the hell out." Steve winced hearing about it again.

"I know right! So creepy," Dean added on.

"Anyway, continuing on. I want to do some research. I deeply care about Serina, and if you guys at least have some decency, you'll help me save her if she is actually at the house on this card. It just makes sense. I'm sure the killer was the person who took Serina because we were getting leads onto where she was, and boom, Marcus died!" Mariah continued to ramble on, but she became inaudible.

Mercy had to stop her. "Mariah! Calm down, we can't understand a single thing you're saying. Slow down."

"Yeah, Mercy is right. If what you say is true, then we will save Serina. No doubt about it."

"Then she'll give us a huge paycheck because we saved the precious, rich girl!"

"Steve!" Mariah, Dean, and Mercy all said at once, locking their eyes on him.

"Right, right. Sorry."

"We're not going to do anything dramatic, that's all I know for sure. We're just going to check out the house, knock on the door, look through the windows, maybe ask to use the restroom, just something, anything to get us anywhere near more answers. You get me?"

"I can record it all with my phone." Serina's bully, Steve, raised a hand in the air with his phone in his palm.

"Alright, that's good. If we find something, we can have evidence." The leader of this whole scheme, which of course was Mariah, nodded. "If we know Serina is there, some-one will call the cops, and then if all goes well, Serina will be saved."

"And we get lots of cash!" Everyone glared at Steve again. "Oh right, yeah. No money, yep."

Mariah went into more detail about the plan, but she mainly left it short and simple for the people to under-stand. Somewhere in the back of her mind, she thought to herself as she spoke, "I need to make it sound like an elementary school direction packet." In the end, everyone nodded when she was done speaking. The plan stuck in everyone's heads.

"Awesome. Then this weekend? Will that work out for everyone?"

"I have football practice, but I am sure I can skip it." Dean yawned. After all of this talking, he seemed tired out, but pumped up at the same time.

"I can go." Mercy clapped her hands together. "I'll be

with Dean the whole time, and we'll come here together to meet up with you two."

"I'm never busy, so I'm free to do whatever, whenever."

"Alright. This weekend it is. Friday night we pack up what we need, and we text each other any questions and all that. And remember, we are just teenagers who are deeply involved with a rumor that may or may not be true. We are just stupid teenagers."

Stupid teenagers they were. That was the one thing that Mariah was one hundred percent sure about.

Chapter 18

Maya

Hearing Jimmy's voice scared me. The whole thing that happened with the kid I once thought was innocent and sweet and warm scared me. I sat up in the bed, eyes wide, as I looked at the person who took me into his home.

"What? What is it? Why are you freaking out?"

Though he should probably be the one who is asking me that because I'm shaking in my boots right now.

"You—just come here—I just—come on." He grabbed my hand and I stood up. We walked out of the bedroom and went downstairs into the living room.

"Why are we out here, Jimmy?"

"I know something happened. I know it. Just tell me the truth, please." I knew what he was talking about and he seemed to know what I dreamed about, but how? Can I really trust him with the truth when he doesn't confide in me about things I ask?

"I just had a bad dream, that's all. It was only a bad dream."

"Stop lying!" Jimmy squeezed my hand harder and he

179

looked at me with those eyes, those beautiful yet dangerous eyes. "What was it about?"

I hesitated. He probably noticed this. "My father, it was about my father." Hanging my head low, that's the only excuse that I could come up with. Hopefully, he believed me.

He did. "I'm sorry." Finally, he let go of me and I stood up from the couch that he had set me down at.

Please don't ask about it.

"You can talk to me, you know. I'm here for you and I want to let you know that."

"Well duh, you're the only person that I can talk to."

"That's not what I mean." I could hear Jimmy's voice struggling. "I care about you. That's why I want you to know that I am here for you."

We looked at each other in silence after that. I ended up sitting back down on the couch. Suddenly, he raised his arms and grabbed me, pulling me into a hug, not just any normal hug. The hug was tight and his face was basically buried within my hair.

There's no other explanation for Jimmy saying this to me. He likes me, a lot.

I tried to pull away from the hug that we were in, but he just held me tighter to not give me a chance to leave. "Jimmy, I have a question. Let go." Once I said that he let go and looked at me. The anger and the danger in his eyes had disappeared. Now it looked like he was just a normal caring person—without seeing the rest of his face due to the mask of course.

"Why do you like me? When did you start liking me?"

Before asking the question that's been on my mind, I looked away from him. "Do you love me?"

I know I shouldn't be asking, but there's no other way that he could just think of me as a sister, right? The tension that builds up, but the way it fades away quickly is abnormal.

I was in my own thoughts, thinking, not giving Jimmy a second look. I avoided eye contact. What would I reply with if he said yes? Would I be creeped out, happy, maybe confused? My hands pulsed, going into a fist and coming back out. I could feel the warmth go into my fingertips as they hit my palm.

I didn't hear an answer yet. It felt like ten minutes had already gone by, but I was wrong. It had only been ten seconds, but it felt like so much longer.

Then, something unexpected happened. Without hearing a yes, or a no, I felt something. My eyes met his. He was holding his hand on my chin and he moved his other hand to his mask. Was he going to show me his face? Was he going to reveal his identity?

Yes, I think he was. He started to pull his mask up, revealing his jawline, the part of his neck I'd never seen before. He had a pretty sharp jawline. On the right, there was a mark. It looked like some kind of birthmark that he had and, to be honest, it was kind of cute.

The mask moved more, revealing his lips, the soft-toned red lips that were begging for attention. I stared at them before looking back up into his eyes, only to see that he was staring down at mine.

A couple of seconds later, even though it was obvious from how slow it was going, from how fast my heart started beating, he leaned in and kissed me.

I kissed back.

I guess he loves me.

* * *

"I'm going to take a nap, there are leftovers in the fridge from the other night."

"Alright, goodnight." I waved to him as I watched Jimmy walk up the stairs, going to his bedroom to sleep.

What happened earlier, it was still on my mind. We kissed and it felt like time stopped. I saw half of his face and I just anticipated seeing more.

I can't believe we did that. I can't believe I did that.

During the kiss, it got a little more intimate. He pulled me in closer by the waist. Minutes later, I could still feel his touch latched onto me, melted into my brain. My heart was still beating just as fast as before.

I responded, putting a hand on his neck, sliding it to go behind his head.

You don't know how badly I wanted to touch his hair, but I couldn't reach it because the mask was in the way.

When Jimmy was out of sight and I heard his bedroom door squeak, I put my elbows on the kitchen counter and hid my face in my hands. My skin felt so hot.

I can't imagine how red my face is.

I need to calm down. Why am I acting like this? There's no way that there's even a possibility that I have feelings for him too, right? That wouldn't make sense, falling in love with the person who took you away from your home, away from your life. But I guess it's not that bad.

What am I saying?

I can't stop thinking about it. I can't stop thinking about him. I can't stop thinking about what his face looks like, how handsome he is under that mask of his. Deep breaths, Serina. In and out. I breathed and I looked up from my hands, around the house. I saw it in a different color than when I first arrived here.

When I first came to this house, everything around me was unusual, weird. It was cold and I was scared. But now when I look around, I notice things that I hadn't seen before. The warm tint that surrounded me, giving me a safe feeling, if that makes sense? It was quiet, but peaceful that way. It was like I lived here, like it was my own house, like we were a couple. A couple living peacefully in this house.

A couple?

Okay, now I need to stop. I need to occupy myself with something, anything.

That reminds me, the door that was locked down here by the kitchen, the room where I got the ladder from. I can look through there while he's asleep. It's not a very nice guest thing to do, but what's the worst that can happen?

A tint of jealousy. Is that what I'm feeling? No way, I can't believe it.

I walked closer to the door that I found locked when I first came here and I put my hand on the doorknob. I remembered seeing boxes with the name, "Maya", on them and I needed to know who she was. If she was his girlfriend, or wife, maybe.

Maybe I'm just thinking too much about it, overthinking like I usually do. They're probably just friends. But I guess there's no other way of finding out if I don't go check it out. So,

*I opened the door. Good thing I didn't have to go get the key
again. I wonder why it's not locked?*

The one-room that made me feel cold again, maybe
because I hadn't been in there much, and I just felt a weird
vibe coming from it. I left the door open. The light from
the kitchen and the hallway had entered the room, lighting
it up slightly. The carpet was soft, at least.

That's always a plus.

"Maya, just who are you?" I said out loud to myself, sitting
down on the floor and grabbing the biggest box that had
the name on it.

Time to open it.

Opening it, I saw a bunch of papers, envelopes, photos.
When I pulled the envelopes out of the box, most of them
were empty. The others just held lists of stuff to get from
the store or notes about what this person liked. Or I'm
assuming they liked.

I read through what this Maya person may like. As I was
reading, I learned that Maya was female.

This only stirs up more jealousy even though I don't know why.

All of the things that I read from the paper I was surprised by. Everything that she liked and was interested in
I liked. I never thought that someone else's favorite dessert
would be an Île flottante. Or as most people know it by the
name, floating island. The dessert consisted of meringues
poached in vanilla custard and topped with caramel sauce
and toasted almonds.

God just thinking about it makes my stomach growl. I haven't had Île flottante in such a long time!

Moving on, the papers were kind of boring. Next were the pictures. Those would have been pretty nice to look at. I hoped to finally get to see what Jimmy's mystery face looks like.

Of course, I have bad luck though. All of the pictures were of the girl, Maya. They had to be her. Who else would it be? This person didn't look familiar at all so they can't be from this town. I basically knew everyone.

Maya was kind of cute though. She had blonde hair that extended down to almost her waist.

Who would grow out their hair that long? Isn't it annoying to brush and take care of?

In the photo I was looking at, she had a cute, pink floral crown on. I was starting to get more jealous of how stunning she was. Blue eyes, just like Jimmy. They went well with her hair. Don't even get me started on her skin. If this picture was a filter or some shit, it would be so fake. Her skin looked like she just came out of the womb!

More and more photos of her were what I pulled out of the box.

Maybe she really is Jimmy's girlfriend. But then why would he kiss me? Why would he take me? I'll find out sooner or later, the more we get closer I bet. The next photo was of her. Her again, and again. Until I pulled out a folded rectangular picture. I unfolded it and a man was standing next to her. He looked strangely familiar. The eyes, the face. Where have I seen him before?

Something in my mind clicked. I brought the picture closer to my face. Those eyes, the chubby looking cheeks. He definitely had some kind of glow up, but this whole situation didn't make sense at all.

Then a realization came to me.

It's the boy. He is the boy who pops up in my dreams all the time, only about ten years older. I just know it. The eyes are the same, the way they curve. The kind of face shape he has, it's definitely the same boy who pops up in my dreams but older. Does that mean he's still alive? I look closer at the photo. I know I'm right, but there's something inside of my brain telling me that I'm wrong and that I'm believing nonsensical things.

If there was this photo, there must be a photo with Jimmy included in it too, right? I already had so many pictures out of the box though. I was doubtful there would be more.

As I continued to look through the box for pictures, I was right, there were no more pictures in there. I wouldn't know what Jimmy looks like until he took off his mask if he trusted me enough.

All that was left in the box were some envelopes and a couple of folders. I assumed the envelopes were supposed to be sent somewhere, but it appeared they had never been opened, so maybe he wrote them but never sent them.

I wonder if these were love letters he never gave to Maya.

I ended up opening one. I read through the paragraph that was on the paper. It almost filled up one whole side. It was not a love letter, but more of a friendly letter. Reading this, I learned that they were just friends—thankfully—and that they lived really far from each other.

I think Maya lives in Australia?

It's kind of a relief that she's not his girlfriend though. Not because I want him as a boyfriend, no way. But because he kissed me and that would mean that he would be cheating on Maya, and that's not a good thing to do.

I was in class one day and I was minding my own business getting my work done. Let me tell you that there were only three girls in that classroom and the rest were boys. A couple of the boys totally fawned over the two girls and I was just there as an extra. Anyway, while I was working I overheard a group of the boys talking in the corner of the room. They were not being quiet at all, and I don't think they were even trying to be. One of them said something about cheating, saying that it is allowed if they don't get caught. His friends agreed.

I spoke up when I heard that. "If you really love someone, you don't cheat on them. When you love someone that means you care for them and when you care for them, you don't want to hurt them. Or at least that's how I see love. It's just an asshole thing to cheat, being heartbroken is not fun at all."

I decided not to go through any more of the letters. I think I got all the information that I was really worried about. I had reached the bottom of the box. There were just a couple more things to look through: a bunch of folders. Although, one thing popped out, a bright red folder. That was when I remembered that the boy in my dream had said something about the truth being in a red folder.

This might be what I am looking for. My hand goes for the red folder and I pull it out of the box.

I opened the folder and I saw something that I wasn't expecting. It was a tape. "A tape?"

Okay, that's kind of weird, not going to lie. Why would there be a tape recording in this folder? Why would this tape be important? I guess I have to go watch it, but I don't want to wake up Jimmy.

My mind was torn between two decisions. I ended up taking the risk. I kept the tape in my hands and stood up, leaving the room and going to the living room. Good thing there was a slot for a tape to go into. So old fashioned.

From what the boy in my dream said, it seemed like this tape was a bad thing.

I can't remember exactly what he said but I think he said something bad about Jimmy, that Jimmy did something bad and that this was the truth. Can I trust him though? I guess I'll find out the truth. Maybe something Jimmy has been hiding from me. Maybe this will make me realize whether I want to stay in this place or to leave.

A loading screen is what I saw, well not like a YouTube loading screen or a screen that you'd expect to pop up these days. It was just a black screen.

A couple of seconds later it started to play and for some reason, the volume was all the way up. It was extremely loud. I jumped for the remote before the video could wake up Jimmy and I turned down the volume. I looked behind me warily to make sure that he wasn't coming down the stairs. I didn't see him so I turned back around and continued to play the video.

It was a person. It looked like Jimmy, but of course, his face was not shown on the camera. It only showed his chest down to his waist. I saw his hands. They were shaking. They must have been shaking a lot to be able to be seen by the video. This fact made me feel bad for him, that something bad happened to him and I was worried about him—about what happened.

"It's November 13th, and I just wanted to say I'm sorry. I'm sorry. I'm sorry." That's definitely Jimmy speaking. A shaky voice, shaky hands, stuffy too.

Is he crying? Is that why he didn't show his face on camera?

The talking continued. I listened. "I killed her. I know I did. I know I made a mistake. I didn't mean to kill her though. I promise I didn't mean to kill you. I know you're not listening to this. I know that you're dead because your blood was on my hands." He was talking fast, a couple of words here and there were hard to understand. But this, just the beginning of the clip, made my eyes open, made my chest drop but at the same time. I wanted to keep listening.

"Maya, this is for you. This is an apology video. This is me saying that I'm sorry for killing you, Maya. I really didn't mean to. You have to trust me. It's just that you got too close to my research. You got too close to my goal, what I am working so hard for." He laughed for a couple of seconds quietly. "I'm afraid that the cops are going to find me, but I'm pretty sure I hid your body well. No one is going to find your body. By the time someone finds your body, it's going to be just bones. Fuck. I'm sorry. I'm running. If I don't run the police will catch me. If I don't run then your boyfriend might just capture me to get revenge. I'm sorry. I killed you. I killed Maya. Oh my god, I actually killed you." One of Jimmy's hands clenched his shirt where his chest was, his voice cracked saying the next thing.

"You got too close to figuring out my plan. I just need to find her, Maya. You know all about her. I know you know how much she means to me. It's just you didn't know what I was going to do with her. She was my first love, my first friend. She is the moon and the stars, I swear. She shines brighter than any shooting star seen in the sky. I'm so cheesy." Another laugh, this time it was longer than the first one. "You always said that about me, Maya. How cheesy I was. But now I'm in deep trouble. I killed someone. I killed you. I have to run. The police are after me, aren't they? They'll find some kind of clue—" his sentence stopped, and Jimmy turned around.

By now, I was staring at the screen with a hand over my mouth. I listened, I watched. "Ian? Ian, what are you doing here? Ian what the hell." He stood up. Now I could see what he was looking at. The boy, the grown man, I mean. The boy, but ten years older. The guy I saw in the photo back in the boxes, he was standing in the same room as Jimmy.

"What the hell did you do?"

Ian, that's the boy's name. Interesting. He sounded pretty pissed. I guess he found out that Jimmy killed someone.

"You found out, didn't you?"

"You know I did." The two males got closer to each other. I saw the back of Jimmy's head. He had brown hair.

I thought that there would be more talking, but I heard a loud bang. A gunshot. At first, I thought Jimmy shot Ian but he didn't. Jimmy moved out of the camera's way just a bit and I saw him holding onto both of Ian's hands. Ian was holding the gun and he tried to shoot but missed.

I can't believe that Jimmy went through something like that.

"You asked for it, Ian. I'm so sorry. But at least you'll get to meet your lover again soon, right?" With a swift movement, Jimmy turned the tables and took the gun away from the boy from my dreams and he shot him instead. Ian fell to the floor. Jimmy killed two people.

"What are you doing?" I heard Jimmy's voice again only this time it was more clear.

Shit.

I turned around and there he was. I removed my hand from my mouth and spoke.

"Wait, it's not what it looks like. I didn't mean to—"

"Serina." He looked at the screen. His eyes had that look of danger again.

Shit.

"How much did you fucking see? How much did you find out? Why the hell did you go through my stuff?" He raised his voice at me and walked up to me, taking my arm and forcing me up from the ground. His grip hurt and I winced in pain, letting out a small whimper.

"Please, Jimmy, I'll tell you everything just let me go!"

"Why? Are you scared? Are you scared of me, Serina?" His grip just got tighter and something slipped out of my mouth. It was half true.

"Yes!"

"I'll show you how scary I can be." He stepped forward, making me go backward. He raised his voice more, yelling. "Am I scary to you Serina? How much do I scare you? Huh?" He pushed me up against a wall, my back hitting up against it. I squinted my eyes for a couple of seconds before looking at him. He raised his fist like he was going to punch me and instinctively I put both of my arms in front of my face for protection. He punched the wall behind me. "You thought I was really going to hurt you? Do I look like that kind of person? Do I act like it? Do you think I'll hurt you? Serina, I'll NEVER hurt you. You KNOW that!"

I kept my arms in front of my face. I didn't know what to do. I felt my whole body shaking. He was scaring me, pinning me up against the wall like this, punching the wall behind me, yelling at me.

He moved my arms and pinned them up against the wall above my head and used his other hand to grab my chin. He forced me to look at him. "Look at me. LOOK AT ME!" I looked at him like he said. I blinked. Before I could do something he leaned forward and kissed me then leaned back. "After everything, you're scared of me? Do you want to leave? Do you think I'm crazy? Do you think I'm a psychopath?" He leaned forward again, giving me another kiss, this time it was deeper. I tried to push away. He wouldn't give me a chance to talk. With his hand pinning my hands above my head, I couldn't move them.

How is his grip so tight?

He backed away again. I coughed and spoke. "STOP!" Yelling back at him I squirmed more, trying to get out of his grip but nothing was working. A couple of more seconds later, his free hand went to my neck and he squeezed his fingers on the sides—not entirely choking me. I could still breathe, but he had reduced my blood flow and I felt light-headed. I couldn't talk.

"Fuck, Serina! If you watched the beginning, you know I didn't mean to kill her. I didn't mean to kill anyone. It was just an accident, and Ian was just self-defense! You don't know anything so please you have to believe me! I'm not a bad guy, please."

What he was doing right now didn't make it so believable. Pinning my arms, keeping me against the wall, a hand up to my throat. It scared me even more.

"God damnit." He finally let go of my hands and of my

throat. I coughed more. "FUCK! I swore to myself I would never touch you like that. Shit, I'm such a terrible person! I made another mistake." He backed away, turned around, and put his hands on the top of his head, taking deep breaths. Even though I could, I didn't speak. I just leaned up against the wall and felt myself slowly fall down to the ground. Everything around me was blurry because of the tears that filled up in my eyes.

"I would never hurt you. I said I would never hurt you. I promised myself; but look what I just did!" Jimmy threw his hands in the air and out of anger or regret, I can't tell which one, he pushed a glass vase onto the ground, making it shatter.

With my glossy eyes, I saw him coming towards me again. He kneeled down in front of me and put a hand on my cheek. He rubbed his thumb softly. "I'm sorry." His voice calmed down now, but he still scared me. "Just tell me how much you saw. How much you know."

"Why can't you just tell me the truth?" I whispered, my eyes giving up and creating waterfalls.

"I'm scared."

"Why are you scared?" I shook my head. "What are you scared of?"

"You leaving!" He raised his voice again. I jumped. The next time he spoke, his voice got quiet again. "I don't want you to leave me. Please don't leave me. I need you, Serina."

"I won't. If you just tell me the truth, I promise I won't leave. I care about you too, you know. You don't know how much jealousy I felt when I saw Maya's name. I thought she was your girlfriend or something!" Without realizing it, without wanting to, I started saying what was in my head. "I don't know why I felt like that but I did. Once I knew she was just a friend, I calmed down; but now I know that you KILLED two people!"

"I didn't mean to—"

I cut him off. "The second one is understandable. I don't know why you killed Maya, but I'm sure it was understandable too! If you just talked to me, told me the truth, I'm sure I would have listened! Why don't you just tell me the truth rather than lie to me all the time? What's that going to do, huh? You love me, don't you?"

"I do. But—"

I cut him off again. "Then act like it, you asshole! Tell me that you love me. Tell me that you won't hurt anyone else. Promise me that you'll be here for me. Promise me that you will tell me EVERYTHING!"

"I promise. I love you. Okay? Is that good enough?" I'm sure he was just going along with everything I was saying to end this faster. I'm sure he was lying just to get rid of me, just to shut me up.

Before I could say anything else—before I could cut him off again—he pulled me into a hug and I gave in, wrapping my arms around him. We hugged there on the floor together. Me sobbing like a huge baby, but I didn't feel that self-conscious after I heard he was doing the same thing.

He kept on whispering to me that he loved me as I asked of him. He kept on whispering in my ear that he was sorry and that he'll tell me everything just not tonight or not now because it was too soon. And my sad self nodded, agreeing with him, saying that I'll give him all the time he needs.

I can't help but think to myself, has he killed anyone else? Will he continue to kill? Who is this person that he kept on talking about in the video? Who is the person he killed for?

This is too much. I can't handle it. Why can't things just be normal? Why does life have to be such a crazy and dangerous roller coaster?

* * *

When I calmed down—when we both calmed down—
we just stood in the kitchen holding mugs filled with hot
chocolate. We hadn't said anything to each other in a while.
He decided to make both of us a cup of something warm
to drink and we just stood there, drinking it in silence.
We were probably thinking about the same thing, about
what had just happened. I leaned up against the counter
and glanced at him a couple of times. He wasn't saying
anything. He wasn't looking up from his mug at all. I had
to say something. I needed to. I couldn't just let things end
like this. There had to be something I could do, right? Or
would it always stay like this? Silent.

"I'm not scared of you." There I said something, looking
at him as I said it but looking away instantly after. I took
a sip of the hot chocolate. Thankfully it had cooled down,
otherwise I would have totally burned my whole tongue by
now. He didn't reply. I got worried. "Jimmy?"

He replied right away after I said his name. "Yeah, yeah.
I heard you. I know. It's just—you know—I don't know
how to explain it."

"It's okay. It's alright." Just as I thought things were beyond
awkward.

"What you saw, what you now know, are you not going
to leave? Do you *want* to leave?" I heard him sigh. Clearly,
you could tell that he had given up. "I'll let you walk out
that door right now if you want." He closed his eyes. "If
you do, I don't want to see you leave. I don't want to hear
you say anything. Just walk out." He waited a couple of
seconds before saying goodbye. "Goodbye, Serina."

I was frozen, standing there, looking at him. "I'm not
leaving." Leaning off the counter, I walked to be in front of
him, my feet sliding across the tile floor. "You cared about

me in a way that I thought no one would have cared about me and it's strangely comforting. I want to feel more of what I feel when I'm with you. It's strange."

"What?" Jimmy opened his eyes and made eye contact with me. He seemed to be speechless, not believing what I was saying. I guess he actually thought that I would leave.

No words, that's what I'm thinking. Using no words to tell him the truth. When he opened his eyes and looked at me, I knew that he didn't believe me. I needed to show him, not tell him. The only way that I could do that is to kiss him. It's not like we haven't kissed before. We have mutual feelings, right?

I lean in. He knows exactly what I'm doing as I see his eyes move down to look at my lips. I look back at his. We kiss again. I told him my answer and he replied.

I still don't know much about him, his past, and everything. But everyone has done something bad in their past, right? Not everyone has killed someone though, so that's a little different. I'm sure he had a reason. I'm sure he'll open up to me one day. I'm sure.

Breaking the kiss I spoke. "Are you going to stop overthinking now? I'm not leaving, Jimmy."

"I always overthink." Of course, he came up with that type of response.

"Let's just move on from what happened, okay? I know what it must feel like, what having secrets is like. What it feels like to hold back and hide stuff. I get it. I understand." My hand reached down and held Jimmy's. I started leading him upstairs. I know both he and I needed sleep. "But I do want to know one thing about Maya."

"Depends." I could tell that he got a bit nervous. I don't know if it was because I was holding his hand or because of the question.

"Why did you do it? How did it happen?"

"I was—" Anticipating an answer, I let go of his hand and stood at his bedroom door beside him, looking up at him. I saw his eyes wander around the hallway. "Doing a personal project and she started to figure out what I was getting into and I didn't want to get into trouble so I had—I needed—I accidentally—you know. I couldn't take the chance. I didn't hide it well enough, and that's why Ian found out. I had to cut him off too. Otherwise I would be in more trouble." Without letting me butt in, he continued. "I know I made a mistake, but please, Serina, don't think badly of me. If you did, if you hated me, I don't know what I would do."

"It's okay," I tried to reassure him. "Just get some rest and drink some water. Self-care is important. I want you to take care of yourself and I want you to not make any more mistakes again, from here on out. Just leave it be in the past and let it go, live a normal life, live for a better future. Everything will be alright."

I hoped I was saying the right words. I hoped I wasn't giving him some kind of hope to do more bad things. I'd really hate it if he killed someone again. If he killed someone again, I don't know what I would do.

"Goodnight, Serina."

"Goodnight, Jimmy."

Chapter 19

Careful now

It was now the weekend, early in the morning, but Mariah was already alert. She barely slept the night before. She wasn't going to bring a bag with her or anything because they might need to escape. If they needed to run, she felt like the bag would get in the way. She was expecting the worst to happen—who wouldn't.

Out of boredom, Mariah decided to text Steve. "Hey, Stevie," she typed, using the nickname most of the students in the school called him to tease him, "do you think you can come over to my place earlier? Like way earlier? Like hours earlier? Like soon?"

To her surprise, she got a text back almost right away. "Why? You scared princess?"

"Oh shut up and just come over, alright?"

"Sure, whatever you say."

The conversation ended there. Steve was now on his way to Mariah's house.

Steve used to be the smart, nice quiet kid. The one who was made fun of for wearing nerdy glasses. In middle school, he was bullied to the extent of gaining bruises and even breaking an arm. Something no kid should have to go through at that time of life.

His parents eventually decided to move out of the neighborhood so he could switch schools. That was how he got into a school where the students worried more about riches than looks. These days instead of wearing long white socks that came up to his knees, tan jeans with suspenders connected, a white, long sleeved button down shirt and thick, black glasses, he wore jeans without the suspenders, usually black jeans with rips in them. He also wore jean jackets, hoodies, and the shoes that students say are trending, such as Converse or Vans.

Being bullied in middle school had not only formed the way Steve looked, but how he acted too. He made a major transformation, going from being the school's nerd to the school bully.

"I'm here." Mariah's phone dinged, and she went to get the door for him, only to see that he had let himself inside.

"Sorry, I didn't think you would mind." He made himself at home pretty quickly, taking off his shoes and setting down the backpack filled with supplies he had brought. He leaned it against the wall by the door.

"No, it's alright." Mariah let it slide. "Let's go into my room. I kind of want to be in there right now."

"Sure."

The two walked down the hallway and into Mariah's room. Steve again sat down and made himself comfortable in Mariah's bed. They were sitting next to each other. The only discrepancy was that Mariah was under the covers. It was silent.

"So, why did you bring me here?" Turning his head to look at Mariah, tilting it a bit in confusion, he did have some theories in mind.

"I was bored, I guess." There was a short moment of silence. "Didn't I already tell you why over text?"

"No, you told me to shut up." Laughter filled the room.

Hours passed. Mariah and Steve hung out in her room the whole time and bonded in a way. A new friendship being sculptured.

"Time's coming close, isn't it?"

"Yeah, the other two should be coming soon. I should probably wait in my living room to open the door for them."

"Wait, Mariah." She let out a quiet hum as she twirled around, about to walk out the door but stopped at the sound of Steve's voice.

A second later, he leaned in and kissed her. Hastily, Mariah pushed him back and wiped her mouth. "What do you think you're doing!?"

"I'm sorry, I just thought—I mean—" It was obvious that Steve didn't know what he was doing.

"You know I like girls, right? Why would you ever, UGH!" An overreaction came from Mariah. She turned around and went out into the hallway bumping into the one and only Dean with a small screech.

"Whoa, are you guys okay?" Dean put his hands on Mariah's shoulders and looked down at her.

Mercy continued Dean's sentence. "We let ourselves in because we heard your voice, and we thought the worst."

"I'm fine, thanks." Still annoyed by what Steve did, she walked off into the kitchen to get a glass of water.

"What happened dude?" Dean whispered, walking over to the school bully.

"Nothing, don't fucking worry about it." Now he was in a bad mood too.

Mercy laughed a little and crossed her arms. "Well, we better be a pretty good team to be acting like this right before a mission!"

* * *

Out the door they went, heading to the address that was on the card Mariah had found, the address where creepy stuff had been seen by students in their school.

"This is it." Reaching their destination, they looked at the residence. It was a small, rectangular home with faded yellow walls. It looked like an older house. The white shutters that were attached to the sides of the windows were not fully painted like they used to be. Some of the paint had fallen off, and the brown wood was showing. Below the yellow paint were stone bricks, moss being their best friend.

The windows were clean though, spic and span, giving the four teenagers a clear view of the inside. The glass complimented the bushes that were surrounding the house. Some had Annabelle hydrangea flowers on them. Some were just plain old green plants.

"Some kind of house," Steve scoffed. Mercy agreed with him. Standing right next to Dean, Mercy planned on sticking with him the whole time. Mariah was ahead of the group, standing in front of all of them, and she started to walk into Jameson's yard.

Steve was the first to follow behind her, but the kiss was still on his mind, and he felt a bit awkward being near her. Thinking to himself, thinking that she was disgusted by him.

He started to feel that level of anxiety that he once felt in middle school. He did not like the feeling at all. So, the best he could do was keep his distance and pretend that everything was okay between them. Because if he had to do something, he would rather keep her as a friend rather than a stranger. He would do anything to keep her in his life. That was how much he cared about her.

Steve looked around. Through the windows his eyes saw what looked like a normal-looking household. It was clean and tidy. It looked like no one was home. None of the lights were on. He didn't see anyone walking around at all. The shadows were normal. He looked over at Mariah for confirmation that she was seeing the same thing.

What Steve thought about Mariah was the complete opposite of what she was thinking. The kiss was on her mind just a little bit, but she was focused more on their mission, their goal, on Serina.

"We should go inside," Mariah said, breaking the silence, looking at Steve as if there was nothing wrong. As if nothing ever happened. This hurt Steve a little, but he understood.

"What? Are you joking with me, dude?" Mariah then looked over at Dean once he spoke.

"Well, we can't figure out anything from the outside."

For some reason, Mercy agreed with Mariah, nodding. "I think we should go in. What do we have to lose, right?"

"See, Mercy is on my side."

"But, I don't want to go inside. I can uh—" She seemed to be hesitating, fiddling with the phone she had in her hands. "I'll stay out and keep watch." A slight glimpse of a phone number was on her screen. But because of the protective mode she had on her phone, no one could see what she was doing.

"What's the saying, all words yet no bark or some shit?"

"Hey, Steve, be nice. If Mercy wants to stay out here, then she can."

"Yeah, whatever. She's just scared."

"Am not!" Mercy argued, but Mariah ended their conversation.

"Alright! Listen up." She spoke quietly so that only the three teens around her could hear, being the leader that she meant to be on this execution. "I want Steve to continue recording. Mercy is going to stay out here and keep watch, Dean and I will go inside and look around just like Steve. Deal? If we find something, we clap three times and we meet up in front. If you see someone, just be careful. We don't want to get caught breaking into the place."

Everyone nodded, thinking that this was just going to be a quick look inside followed by an even quicker exit. Thinking that nothing bad was going to happen, they had confidence.

Steve held on tight to the camera that he was holding. Mercy was still messing with her phone in her hands, acting a little suspicious about it as her eyes glanced down at the phone a bunch, whispering words that the others didn't hear. Yet, no one paid attention to that.

Mariah twisted the doorknob on the front door, but when it didn't open, she dropped her head in defeat. The door was locked from the inside. "Of course it's locked. What was I thinking?"

"You weren't thinking," Steve said, standing shoulder to shoulder with Mariah. Before she had the chance to yell at him because of what he said, more words escaped his mouth. "I know how to lock pick doors, so if you could just hold the camera then I can get this door open."

She listened to him, taking the camera from out of his hands so that he could kneel on the porch. Once at the doorknob, he got something out of his pocket and put it inside of the doorknob. He worked it precisely until there was a click, and he smiled. Twisting the knob, the door creaked as it slowly opened up, cold air escaping.

"I got it." Steve's smile stayed on his face as turned around, standing up straight to take the camera back. Mariah's and his hands brushed up against each other during the exchange. "Let's go on in."

They walked into the house. One step after the other, taking quiet steps. Dean headed in after Mariah, who walked inside first after handing the camera to Steve. Steve followed behind with the camera starting to record their every move.

Right when they walked in, they saw a closet to the right

of them, and a door that seemed to go into a basement in front of them. To the left was a living room. Past that was a kitchen. It was a cozy space.

"Imagine we're in some grandma's place," Steve laughed under his breath as he said that, but made sure to whisper. Although the others didn't like that he spoke at all, and they shushed him.

The house smelled like a grandma's place, so Steve wasn't that wrong. As everyone's eyes looked around and scanned the rooms that they walked into, they noticed how dark it seemed to be in the house. The curtains in the living room were opened, and some sunlight shined through, but there was something off. The shadows in the corners expanded as far as they could. The dark energy the house had just in general gave everyone goosebumps. It was too normal of a house, which made everyone get tensed up. If they were right about who lived here and what happened here, it made it even more creepy.

There was a second floor, upstairs being even darker. You couldn't see what was past the top step. Dean motioned that he was going to go take a peek upstairs. Mariah saw this and nodded as she headed for the kitchen. Steve was focused on the camera when Dean started carefully walking up the stairs, and he recorded him. Then he turned to Mariah, deciding to follow her. Everything was going well so far. Mariah did not see anything suspicious. She didn't see anyone in the house, so she felt somewhat relieved; but at the same time that made her think there was going to be something upstairs. She started to really worry about her friend who may be up there.

A snap was heard. It was Mariah trying to get Steve's attention. When they made eye contact, Steve gave her a look as if to day, "Don't scare me like that." She couldn't help but smile a little at the look that was given to her. Mariah shook her head and then pointed at the door, which was connected to the kitchen. Walking up to it, she put her hand on the knob, the camera getting a close up of her twisting it and opening the door. Inside were a bunch of boxes.

"Maya?" Mariah whispered to herself and Steve, seeing boxes that had that name on them, seeing that there was some stuff laying around that wasn't in boxes. But thankfully yet scarily, she found no one.

Meanwhile, Dean was upstairs looking around. At first, there seemed to be nothing wrong. As he continued further down the hallway that was upstairs, there was one last door he hadn't checked. He had already opened a door that led to a bedroom. After that, he opened a door that led to a bathroom, and he assumed that this was another bedroom. Opening the door slowly, he let out a shaky breath then a sigh of relief when all he saw was darkness in there. His body untensed, thinking that the house was clear.

But, a couple of seconds later, a person came into his view. He clapped three times, but it only echoed through the hallway. The other two didn't hear a thing. Dean started to back away slowly. The male that was in that bedroom walked through the doorway and came towards him.

"What are you doing in my house?"

"Serina." Not answering the stranger's question, another person came into view, coming out of the same bedroom the other one came out of.

"Shit. Serina get back into the room, now!"

To Dean's surprise, Serina turned around and quickly went into the room. "Wait, Serina!" He stopped walking backward and held his stance knowing he had to do something. Learning that they were correct, he wanted to save Serina. He needed to. "You'll pay for this. You're going to get locked up behind bars!" Dean acted tough. Some part of him was thinking that he could take this stranger down. They were about the same height.

Taking steps forward, he was about to make a move but was stopped. A swing to the head is what Dean got. The stranger raised his hand quickly after getting something from his back pocket, smashing the object he had into Dean's dead. Red liquid appeared.

Suddenly, a thud was heard, coming from the upstairs. It made Mariah jump. The two downstairs looked at each other, telepathically telling each other that they should check on Dean. So, they quickly walked out of the room that they were in, closing the door and looking as if nothing happened, that they'd never gone into that room.

They tried not to make a sound, but they knew they had to hurry up just in case something had happened. Something didn't feel right. It felt like their bodies were being crushed by an anvil as they got closer and closer to the stairs. Somehow they are using their strength to keep them from getting completely crushed.

Running up the stairs now, there was something that definitely didn't feel right. The camera view got a little blurry since Steve was too busy running up the stairs and following Mariah to keep it in focus. Once they reached the top step and were now standing in the hallway upstairs, they saw two people. One of them was Dean, and the other was a stranger wearing a black mask with blood all over his hands. The hallway light was turned on and the scene was shown better.

Dean was on the floor with the tall male standing over him with what looked like a hammer in his hand. Clear as day, there was more blood. Mariah screamed.

When she saw the person, she knew who he was: Jameson Smith. She knew that he had to be the one with that name, the one who must have killed Marcus. It all came to Mariah now, it had to be true. Because now, another death might have happened. Another body was right in front of her, and so was the murderer. Connecting the pieces, she was happy that she was correct, but quickly that happiness got drenched with fear.

"Jameson Smith," Mariah said confidently.

"How do you know that name?" He was not denying it. "How the hell do you know my name?" His voice shook as he spoke. He had been caught.

Steve was freaking out, his breath picking up and his head feeling fuzzy. He knew he had to get this on the footage so he turned the camera towards Dean and Jameson. Then, Mariah moved without even thinking. She took steps towards the male with the bloody hammer in his hands. She held a hand out in a protective way, making sure that Jameson had no way to get to Steve. Good thing she did because when he saw that Steve was recording everything, all he wanted was to get that camera out of his hands. He wanted to get rid of the evidence.

"Is he still alive?" Mariah asked Steve, staring down Jameson, not taking her eyes off of him. Noticing that the murderer stumbled backward a bit.

"He's still breathing, yes." That was a relief. Next thing you know, right before Mariah said something else, Serina walked out of the room again. Both of the girls' eyes widened. They made eye contact for a split second before Serina looked down and saw the body on the floor.

"You said you'd never do this again!" She seemed angry, scared. Mariah thought that Serina was being held captive against her will.

"Serina! Thank God you're safe! Thank God!" But she would have never thought that Serina was on his side. "Come with us. We need to get out of here!"

Serina didn't move. "Serina! What are you doing?" Mariah was dumbfounded when she realized Serina had no intention of leaving. Instead, Serina just grabbed onto the murderer's arm and whispered something that only he could have heard.

"Mariah, watch out!"

"No, Jimmy!" Serina screeched.

Jameson Smith raised his hand again, raising it above Mariah's head. Because of the height difference, he could have easily killed her in one blow. He had the advantage. The hand held the hammer. Letting gravity do its thing, the hand and the hammer started to fall, and it was about to hit Mariah. He was losing control. He was scared. Jameson thought to himself, telling himself that he needed to kill everyone here and run away, far away.

"Mariah, we need to get out of here, now! Let's go!" Steve took Mariah's hand, and he turned around. On his other hand, he still kept a hold of the camera, not letting it go. He started to run for the stairs, and Mariah couldn't get out of his grip.

"Wait, Serina, but Serina is back there! And Dean!" But Steve still wouldn't stop. They almost tripped and fell down the stairs. When they were at the bottom of the stairs, Mariah looked behind them just to see if she could get one last glance at Serina, only to see Jameson coming down the stairs behind them. Steve pulled Mariah along, leading her to the front door and quickly out to the front of the house. Mercy was there freaking out.

"What happened? Where's Dean?" Her voice got louder with each question she asked. "Who is that?" All Steve could say was one word. "Run!" Mercy's chest dropped. She knew something bad had happened.

So, the three of them started running away from the house, running away from the male who was chasing them. Thankfully, there were sirens in the distance, red and blue lights flashing, cop cars speeding down the road. The cops were heading towards Jameson's house, all thanks to Mercy.

"9-1-1 what's your emergency?"

"Hi, my friends and I are at someone's house right now, and we—"

Mercy had called the police shortly after they arrived at the house. That allowed the cops to arrive at the house at the perfect time, or at least in time so there wouldn't be any more deaths.

"They're planning to go inside of the house. And there might be a murderer in there and—" the girl on the other end of the phone call told her to calm down. After talking over the phone and staying connected, Mercy kept the girl updated.

"Okay, Mercy darling, we are going to send people over there. If what you are saying is true you guys might be in danger. We're on our way, okay? Tell me anything that happens. Keep me updated."

Once Jameson saw that the cops were coming, he knew someone had summoned the police. He knew that he was in even more trouble than before. He stopped running after them and turned around, running as fast as he could back toward the house, and he slammed the front door shut once he got inside.

Chapter 20

Don't go

The next day things were pretty tense in the morning. All because of last night when I argued with him a little about the tape I had watched. But, as the day went on the atmosphere casually lifted. We were perfect like nothing had happened the other day. Throughout the day, it was casual. It felt like I had forgotten everything about my old life. It felt like I had already graduated from high school and was now living with my fiancé. Crazy, huh?

That morning when I got up, Jimmy was still asleep in his room, so I decided to take a shower. After I got out, he was still asleep.

He has never slept in this late before. I wonder if he did something last night after I went to bed. Oh well. If he was still tired, I will respect that and let him get his beauty rest. Now, we all know he needs that.

I'm kidding. From what I have seen so far, his face is just fine.

Walking into my bedroom, or the bedroom, I picked out a new outfit. Looking through the closet, I chose a tiffany blue sweatshirt. It had words on the back of it that said,

"BROKEN PROMISES". The letters were glitchy with a picture that was in between the two words.

I wonder whose clothes these are and where they came from—probably the mall.

I didn't want to make breakfast without him being awake, so I just sat down and looked out the window, watching the sunrise and the cars as they drove by.

"Good Morning." Finally, a voice that I knew. Jimmy.

Turning around, I smiled. "Good Morning sleepy-head!" Since I was crouched down by the window, I stood up and walked over to him. "How did you sleep?"

"Why didn't you wake me up?"

Of course, he didn't answer my question. I'm trying to be polite here.

"You looked peaceful while you slept, and I didn't want to bother you. I thought you needed the sleep."

He didn't say anything at first. He just nodded. "Did you eat?"

"No, I was waiting for you to wake up."

What is this, some kind of business boss and worker sort of talk? Why does it feel so weird?

That's basically how the morning went. Jimmy made breakfast for me, insisting he should, and he wouldn't let me touch anything. He would only allow me to sit down at the kitchen table. Once he was done, he brought the food to the table and sat down himself, barely making any eye contact with me. We both ate and finished our food, and that was when the conversation picked up again.

"How'd you sleep?"

"Good, good. I actually got up this morning pretty early and took a shower!" I tried to lift the mood, smiling and my voice giving a little giggle. Thank God he reacted, rather than being bland.

He smiled back. I could tell by the way he was looking at me—I hope—he was thinking I was cute. "That's great. I'm happy you're taking care of yourself and that you're healthy."

What are you, my mother?

"Well, what are we going to do today?" Kicking my feet under the table, I kept on staring into his eyes, even if they drifted away from mine. "Maybe you should give me a good morning kiss. We're basically a married couple." Teasingly, I giggled.

"I'm not sure. Whatever you want to do, I guess. I got nothing planned for the next week." He answered my question for one of the first times ever, and I smiled at him real big, then took a step towards him. "What?" he said, sounding kind of flustered.

I knew he got flustered from hearing me say that.

"Does that mean you want me to kiss you?" Quickly that nervousness went away. From what I could tell, he became a lot more confident as he stood up.

"Maybe yeah, maybe not." I didn't give him a straight answer. I knew it wouldn't matter. Being a brat wouldn't hurt.

That morning, his lips touched mine again. Just a little quick peck though, nothing special. "You definitely like me back, Serina."

"And what if I do? It's not like you took me hostage and took care of me."

He laughed. "Don't make it so evil. I'm happy." Jimmy then pat my head, continuing to talk. "Let's celebrate tonight. You have feelings for me. Our feelings becoming mutual, so let's celebrate it. You don't know how much it means to me. You don't."

"Maybe if you told me—" I stopped talking and switched up my sentence, standing up. "Okay, let's celebrate tonight."

It really does feel like we're living the perfect life, without jobs of course; but we have a sustainable life, a calm life, a loving life, a nice house, great chemistry. If only it planned out normally. If only it didn't start with me being scared only because I didn't know where the hell I am. I wonder how it would have gone if it went normally.

Thinking about what has happened before, how this all began, it's crazy. Thinking about when I started developing feelings for the person who kidnapped me. I couldn't imagine a certain time when I did. It made me feel loved. I could also name the times where I cared for him and took care of him. I really can't believe it.

Too much thinking. That is what I do. Way too much, and I need to stop. We are going to celebrate soon anyway.

I had no idea what he had planned, but he was taking way too long. I decided to take another shower to pass the time.

Once I got out of the shower, I wrapped a towel around my body and was about to dry myself off and put on the same clothes I just had on, but then something I remembered popped into my mind. In the bedroom, there was a white robe, a soft one at that. It would be so relaxing to be in a robe. I wanted to try it out.

I peeked out the door, opening it just a crack to see if Jimmy was anywhere upstairs. I didn't want him to see my body, or at least not yet. I wasn't ready. Once I saw the coast was clear, I quickly got out and shut the bathroom door behind me and then went into my room, closing that door once I got in. It was still there, the white robe. I let my towel drop to the floor while I walked up to it, my hands reaching out and feeling the softness of the material. It was made of terry cloth, maybe fleece. I'm not entirely sure. I'm not good at remembering those kinds of details.

I put my arms into the sleeves and wrapped the robe around my body, tying it up around my waist, and then I turned around in a circle like a little kid. I was right. It was relaxing. I loved robes.

Ah, Jimmy, I forgot about him for a second. I should probably go check on what he's doing or what he's planning.

"Jimmy?" Leaving my room I looked around, going down-stairs first because I thought he was downstairs but to my surprise, he wasn't there. Maybe in his room? "Jimmy, where are you, when are we going to celebrate?"

Sometimes I hate stairs, especially right after you walk down them, you have to go walk back up them. It's like forgetting your phone upstairs when you go downstairs, or the other way around. Or sometimes when you walk into a room, realizing you forgot why you're in there, so you leave, but then walk back in and suddenly remember what you needed to get.

"Is he in his bedroom?" Being who I was, I talked out loud to myself when I got upstairs, walking down the hallway to the door at the end of the hallway, walking on inside his room. I was right. "Hey, did you not hear me?"

"What are you wearing?" It looked like he had just had his mask off. When I walked in it looked like he had just put it back on. He looked up at me, his eyes going up and down my body. To be honest, I felt myself blush.

"What, it's just a robe?" After I said that, I looked at myself and saw that my chest was wide open, almost showing *something* if you know what I mean. My hands went to the robe and covered my chest with the robe quickly and I apologized.

Jimmy went silent. I watched him walk closer to me, looking down at me. He looked intimidating. When we were inches apart, his eyes were saying something, but I couldn't tell what they were saying. I couldn't read them. I guess his actions told me instead. He leaned in and kissed me again. Ever since we kissed that one day, it felt like we kissed a lot more, and it's crazy. We weren't even a thing yet, but we were now kissing intensely.

Next, something I wasn't expecting at all happened. He hoisted me up and carried me to the bed, setting me down on it while he got onto it himself. His mouth was on my mouth still, and I sucked in my gut as my robe spread wide, but he only kissed me harder, down my neck, and to my chest.

I let out a soft moan. I didn't know what to do, so I let him take over, my fingers brushing his chest.

* * *

That wasn't the kind of celebration I was thinking of at all. "I don't know if I should apologize or not," he said to me. I was voiceless. But before I could do anything about it, he stopped me, putting a hand over my mouth as he looked like he was focusing, listening to something.

"There's someone in the house." I didn't hear a thing. This made me confused, but I nodded and pushed his hand off of my mouth.

I whispered, "What do we do?"

This time I heard it. I heard someone walking up the stairs. I heard the stairs creak.

Someone is in the house, but why? Who?

Jimmy and I looked at each other. I was practically naked, and so was he. He turned around, both of us staying quiet, and he went to his closet, putting on a random shirt and some sweatpants that looked like they had stains on them.

If this person comes into the room then I would not want them to see me like this. Without asking, I walked over to his closet. It's not like he would mind anyway. Maybe he would even find it cute.

I grabbed one of his shirts and put it on, letting the robe I put on after he took it off me earlier slip down to the floor. I stood there naked until I put the shirt on, the bottom of the shirt reaching down to the top of my thighs. I looked through his drawers a little, still staying as quiet as I could. There were jeans, other pants, but I didn't want to wear jeans. I was kind of unlucky there until I opened up another drawer, and there was another pair of sweatpants, a black pair. I slipped them on, turning my head around to see what Jimmy was doing, but he was gone, and the door was cracked open a bit.

I should hurry up.

With a swift movement, I also grabbed a sweatshirt from the closet. It was bright orange, like neon orange, but it was comfortable. Taking it off the hanger and putting it on, getting my hair out of it, and situating the clothing, I heard three claps. Did Jimmy just clap now?

I turned around and walked to the door cautiously.

He better not be pulling a prank on me, I swear.

When I got to the door, I peeked out, seeing something I never thought I would see. Another person, and I knew him. It was a guy who went to my school, Dean. I came out of the bedroom and stood behind Jimmy. Dean and I made eye contact, and I heard his voice. After not hearing someone else's voice in so long, it felt so weird that it gave my body goosebumps.

"Shit, Serina. Go back into the room, now!" Jimmy freaked out a bit. I jumped. Why was he so on guard?

Is it because a kid from my school is here? How did they even find me? How did this all happen?

The way Jimmy sounded, I turned around as fast as I could. Him being angry, I don't want to see that side of him. I got back into the room, hearing Dean's voice out in the hallway with Jimmy, and I made sure to listen in on what was happening. I made sure to stand close to the bedroom door, careful not to get caught snooping. There was no more talking to be heard. I was kind of hoping to hear more of what would happen but I didn't, so I took the initiative to peek out of the door again. This time I saw something I really did not like. Dean was on the floor and what's worse is that I saw blood. As soon as I saw the blood, my heart rate sped up, and I didn't know what to do.

I think Jimmy just killed another person. He promised me he wouldn't do it! I made him promise, but he did it. Why did he do it? It was unnecessary!

I was freaking out, leaning up against a wall. My chest ached and my mind was racing. I tilted my head back so it was up against the wall as well, and I stared up at the ceiling. I could hear my heart yelling to get some fresh air.

Next, I heard a scream, and I looked over at the bedroom door. It sounded like a girl's scream unless it was a boy with a very girly scream. Why were there more people in the house?

Is the person who just screamed also from my school? Why are they here?

So many questions popped into my head, and it was getting overwhelming. I wanted to see, I needed to see what would happen next. I started to tip-toe to the door. "Jameson Smith."

That name. I know it from somewhere. I swear I know that name, but who is this Jameson Smith?

"How do you know that name?"

He's not denying it.

"How the hell do you know my name?"

It is Jimmy saying that. Jimmy is Jameson Smith? Why does that name sound so familiar?

Jimmy did say to me that we know each other, that I know him. Then it clicked. Jameson is my childhood friend! Jameson Smith, the little boy I hung out with in the tree house, the little boy who suddenly moved away, my best friend when I was a kid!

This can't be real. That can't be him. But he just admitted it. Holy shit! I mean, Holy Shit! I don't know how to react in this situation. I never knew he would lie to be this much. Why couldn't he just tell me the truth? This doesn't make any sense.

Whatever happened to you, Jameson, to make you turn out like this? Whatever happened to the sweet little boy I once knew?

"Is he still alive?"

The person who said Jimmy's real name spoke again. The more I hear her talk, the more I feel like I know her but I just don't know where I have heard her voice before. I don't remember. All of this is killing me. I should show myself. I should get out of this room.

"He's still breathing, yes."

There's another person? A male? No way, just how many people are inside of Jimmy's house? Just how many more people have to die?

I have to show myself. I have to. I don't care what Jimmy says or if he yells at me. I need to get out, and that's exactly what I'm doing.

Opening the door, I walked out again and I saw four people. One person on the ground, one person kneeling by them, one person standing up and another who was towering over all of them.

Dean.

Stevie.

Mariah.

Jimmy.

I know all of these people. They are students from my school, and my childhood friend. Everyone in the same room. I made clear eye contact with Mariah before I looked down, not wanting to look into her eyes.

Mariah, I know her. She is the girl who last saw me before

I went missing, the girl who had never asked me for my money, the girl who probably was heartbroken when I lied to her. Why is she here? Dean, he's still alive on the floor, thank God. Please don't die, Dean. Seeing you on your last breaths, if you die soon, seeing you like this, me standing here like this. It makes me feel so guilty, and if I had to say one thing to you, Dean, I would say that you were always a friend to me. It's just I didn't know how to be friends with someone at school with what I have been through. So I have to apologize, and I have to thank you.

Jimmy betrayed me. I couldn't believe it. My mouth moved before my mind could even process what was going on. I looked up at Jimmy, raising my voice without meaning to. "You said you'd never do this again!"

"Serina! Thank God you're safe! Thank God!" I turned to look at Mariah again. She sounded like she was working hard to find me. I wanted to know all of the details, how she did all of this, why she did all of this. It just didn't make any sense. "Come with us, we need to get out of here!"

Get me out of here? Why? Is this what your plan was? Was it to find me and then drag me out of here? What if I want to stay? What if I don't want to leave? You don't know anything. You're here, and you being here is just endangering yourself. I'm sorry, Mariah.

"Serina! What are you doing?"

I'm not moving. I can't move.

I noticed that Jimmy tensed up. I looked back up at him and the look he gave me was scary, really scary. It looked as if he was getting out of control.

I need to do something. I need to.

I can't let him kill another person. I can't let him hurt someone ever again. I need to help him, or at least I try to by grabbing onto his arm and whispering to him, hoping the kids in my school wouldn't hear.

"Jameson, please stop." Using his real name, I hoped he would calm down a bit. But it did the complete opposite.

"Mariah, watch out!" Stevie yelled.

I made a mistake. Was it my fault? Oh my God.

"No, Jimmy!"

"Mariah, we need to get out of here, now! Let's go!"

"Wait, Serina, but Serina is back there! And Dean!"

Jimmy almost just killed another person. Jimmy just almost hit Mariah over the head with what I'm assuming he hit Dean with. I saw Stevie pull Mariah away, and I noticed how hard she was trying to stay here, for me and Dean. She shrugged to get out of his grip but it didn't work out so well and they started to disappear down the stairs.

Then, I saw Jimmy go after them. "Wait, no! Stop, please!" I guess my grip wasn't strong enough. He harshly shifted his shoulder and got his arm out of my grasp and he went to the stairs. Staring down them, I could see the expression he was making with his eyes from where I was. I froze up. I just stood there frozen as I watched Jimmy go down the stairs. I was useless.

There was one thing that I could do. I crouched down next to Dean's body. They said he was alive. I shook him. His eyes were closed. "Dean, Dean wake up. Come on, open your eyes. I'm here, it's Serina." He never opened his eyes. My heart was pounding so much.

I checked his pulse.

Dean was dead.

I can't let him kill any more people. I need to move. Come on legs, don't fail on me now.

I got up, leaving Dean's body there, whispering an apology as I walked down the hallway. I went down the stairs. The front door was open.

I have to go outside. I haven't been outside in forever.

"Jimmy!" Once I was down the stairs I walked outside. The fresh air pressing up again on my face felt so nice and my body got chills. My body was asking me, "What the hell is this feeling again?"

Looking around, I saw no one at first until down the sidewalk a little to the left, I saw Jimmy running after the students. "Jimmy stop!" It was useless. I was useless.

Then, this is the part where my heart completely stopped. Hearing the sirens of the police, looking down the street, and seeing the lights. Oh no, oh no, the police are coming. They're going to get Jimmy.

I didn't want to think of all the possibilities. I never thought this would happen, not like this at least. The cars speeding down the street, I saw Jimmy freeze up. It felt like his heart had stopped too. I needed to do something, something deep down inside of me was telling me to help him. So, I turned around and walked back inside. Shortly after I walked into the living room, silently freaking out to myself, the front door slammed and I jumped. Jimmy was in the house with me and he walked into the living room.

"Serina, is he alive? Is he really alive?"

"Yes, I mean no. Dear God, Jimmy! You, you're Jameson!"
I wanted to say a lot more, but couldn't find the words.

"You just said that he was alive!"

"I did? Shit, Jimmy, I'm not thinking straight. How can
I act calmly in a situation like this?"

As the police cars pulled into the driveway, their lights
flickered through the living room window, flashing red
and blue lights, and when I looked at Jimmy, I could see
his face, his eyes, as they lit up in the colorful lights. The
only thing that I could see right now was him.

He put a hand on my shoulder and squeezed it lightly.
I looked at him worriedly, yelling at him with my eyes, but
my expression showed fear, and without actually speaking
I asked him what I should do. A couple of seconds later,
banging was heard at the door. I jumped again. They were
trying to get inside the house. The banging rang in my ears,
and the yelling too. The yelling that they did while they tried
to get inside echoed in my head. We both started freaking
out more. No words would come out of my mouth anymore.
My body was stiff. I just stood there and looked at the male
in front of me, looking at someone who I had feelings for.

He didn't speak either, which was understandable. But the
next thing he did surprised me. He let go of my shoulder,
and I saw his hands go to his neck. At the bottom of his
mask, and I saw that he was pulling off his mask. He was
taking off his mask.

The cloth being removed, I saw the part of the face that
I had already seen before. His red-toned lips, his birthmark
on the side of his cheek. Subconsciously I paid more attention when the mask started to go above his nose. It wasn't
too big, but it wasn't too small. Yet again, in this lighting
it was really hard to notice the small details.

Red and blue flashed on his skin. The cops were still trying
to break in. It felt like time was going as slow as it could.

Everything was in slow motion. The mask got pulled up above his eyes, above his eyebrows, until eventually his mask was off of his head, and for the first time ever, I saw my kidnapper's face. He edged closer, the red and blue lights flashing in his face. It gave me a decent view in that dark living room.

I could tell that his neck was a thick, powerful, short neck. Jimmy's jawline matched up with that perfectly—from what I could tell—it was on point. His eyebrows looked thick. Not too thick, not the kind of thick where people would call him ugly for having them, or people wouldn't bother him for plucking them.

If only I could see your face up close, Jimmy. If only I could see your face in bright light so that I could take in all of your features. If only I could stare at your face for so long that the image in my head would be unable to fade away.

His hair was slicked back, and it had that hat hair sort of thing going on, but it looked like he usually split it in the middle as it fell down, maybe by his eyes? Maybe I was wrong.

When our eyes met, I could tell that he was scared, and I was too.

Don't worry.

With the lights that were reflecting off his body, it looked like his hair was almost black. Or was it dark brown?

The banging got louder, and the door made a weird noise. I knew at that moment it was about to break. They were about to get into the house. Jimmy noticed this too. I wanted to look at him more, so I would never forget what he looked like, but our time together had run out.

"Goodbye, Serina."

Those words bolted right into my chest like a stab wound. It hurt hearing them, and it hurt even more when I saw his arms raise to put his mask back on. Then he ran for it. He ran for the back of the house. Where was he going? I wanted to follow him, but was frozen in place.

The door broke down. Jimmy was gone, and people started to flood in. The lights of the house turned on, and I got blinded for a good couple of seconds. I couldn't see. Everything around me was so bright. It was hard to notice what was happening around me. I barely heard a thing now, only the ringing in my ears, and I felt numb.

Someone touched me. I looked to see who it was and it was the police, two of them. They each grabbed one of my arms, and they started to pull me back towards the front of the house, and that's when I finally did something.

"Jimmy!" I yelled his name, I cried out his name so many times. "Jimmy please! Jameson! Jimmy! Jimmy!" A mix of using the name he told me and the name that I knew him by when we were kids all those years ago.

"It's going to be okay now. You're safe with us, ma'am please calm down."

"Are you Serina Ange? We need to get you to safety immediately."

I didn't even bother answering their questions. I just let them take me away. I saw people go after Jimmy, but I heard nothing. I heard nothing of him being found. Part of me wishes that he stays safe. Part of me wants him to run off and get away with all of this, to not get caught.

I'm outside again. I feel like passing out. They brought me to one of the cars that was still flashing the lights and got a blanket for me. They consoled me like I was some lost puppy. They thought the worst had happened. I could tell by their voices and how over the top nice they were being to me. I didn't want to be treated like this.

How many months have gone by?

I don't even know. But now I'm outside again. I'm in a car. I'm free.

Is that the right word to use?

Don't go, Jimmy.

Chapter 21

Red string

There's this deep feeling in my chest when I think of him. I don't know how to explain it. There are heavy chains on my chest, making it sink into my stomach. My mind becomes blank. I'm speechless. Then, once that happens all that I can turn my mind to think about is him. Always him. Sometimes when the smallest thought comes through my head, I feel like passing out. My head gets so lightheaded, and I can't stop overthinking. One of these days, I wouldn't be surprised if that happened.

I want to do stuff with him. I plan to do stuff with him. But I always turn it down after all the planning because I know deep down, he will never accept my offer. Even if that one day, that one moment when our eyes meet something is different. Maybe that's why I can't let go of him now. The look he gave me with his eyes, that one look, at that one moment, it felt like he was looking into my soul. Our souls were connecting.

Every other time we had looked at each other before that, it was normal. Like I was looking at a friend or something out of my reach. But now, when I think about looking into his eyes, I feel more of a connection. I felt my heart skip a beat at that one moment. I said in my mind, "This is different, this look—" I don't want to lose this feeling.

Sometimes I do feel that with him. Whenever we look at each other. Especially that one moment, that one day. What was different? Was it because I knew deep down when I saw his back turn the corner, him running—I knew it would be the last time I'd see him?

The thing is, I forgot all of the bad moments, how he kidnapped me. I paid more attention to him instead of being a wuss and backing out. I didn't have any nerves at that point. Nothing was pulling me away from him. There was no anxiety coming off of me. There weren't any ropes on my hands pulling me back. I got free.

But now they are strings, red strings pulling me back. They're easier to break through than the rope I once had. That makes sense. But it's difficult. The red string is more durable than the rope. The rope that was once chains. The chains that were once a broken heart. The red string is the most difficult. It plays with your emotional state all of the time, which makes it even harder to break. It seems as if the broken heart is Stage five, but it's Stage two. Stage one, now that's a different story. It's strange. Nothing is holding you back. Nothing around your wrists. Nothing that your heart has to deal with. You are free. You don't have to deal with all of the problems and shit you have to deal with at Stage five. Is there a reason for that?

If we go back to the beginning and track our steps, would we find our answer? Stage one, nothing. You feel free, flying in the wind. Stage two, broken heart. Your first love, your first heartbreak. It hurts, but you can still move on. There is still nothing holding you back by the wrists. Stage three, the chains. Chains are metal, or any other material if you think about it. But these are made of hard steel. They're hard to separate, stronger to pull you back, but you still have your mental state to back you up. You still have this sense of freedom, but now there's something strong pulling you back.

Stage four, rope. Rope can mess with your head, but not as much as the next stage. Not only does it mess with your head, but your wrists a lot more as well. The rope focuses on pulling you back as the chains did, only they leave red marks on your wrists, making them bleed if you try to move forward too much. They sting. Like the feeling of rejection that you get when you were hoping for a better answer.

Stage five, the red string. Why is it red? Red is the connection between hearts. The red string also seemed to be the invisible string that you have when two people—two soulmates—share that string. Of course, the string that is around your wrist is not the string that brings two soulmates together. It pulls them apart. If you're at this stage, this means you got past the other stages. Good for you. But can you get past the last stage and achieve your dream?

The red string is hard to break, even if it's a string. It doesn't pull you back so hard that you have marks on your wrists or make them bleed, but it takes a toll on your mind and your emotions. The mental state is the control center. It controls your mind, your emotions, your physical abilities, everything. So when something messes with the control center—a virus—it messes everything up. The red string blends in with your veins on your wrist, leading everywhere to your body, to your brain. It gives you thoughts that you might have never had before. It tells you things that might be wrong, but you tell yourself it's right—all because of that red string. Imagine planning to do something with the person you love, for example, the red string did not allow you to do that because it makes your actions deny it and cancel the whole thing after working on it just to be true.

Bad analogy, but it might make sense.

There's no exact way you can explain the red string that holds you back because, in my opinion, it's different for everybody because it depends on people's weaknesses. That is self-explanatory.

What stage am I on now you ask? Stage 5. And I can't complete the level. I don't know what happens at Stage 6, or Stage 7, or where the stages stop, where you meet the goal and meet the end of your dream. Who knows. It may differ for everyone else as well, just like the red string.

Chapter 22

My new family

F ar away, somewhere I haven't been to in a while. A long-distance I haven't gone in months. I arrived at the police station. Out of Jimmy's house, out of his yard, out into the road. It was scary at first. I felt like a puppy riding in a car for the first time.

When I was at the station, they brought me into a room, got me sweet treats and something warm to drink. I could tell they were being gentle with me. They thought the worst. They assumed Jimmy had hurt me, but he isn't the monster they think he is.

Asking me questions back and forth, I only gave short answers. I probably gave at most ten words. They were getting nowhere with me. They didn't believe me. They thought I was lying about him because I was scared, but I was telling the truth. They just didn't want to listen to me.

"Since your father died—"

Please don't mention that. I don't want to think about that. I'd rather not answer any more questions.

"Someone you're friends with told us—" The person talking to me looked down at a piece of paper. One of the many pieces in a pile of papers that were on the steel table that we were both sitting at. "Do you know Mariah Jarolds?"

My ears perked, I know that name. It was the girl I met back before the ceremony. It was the girl who came to rescue me from Jimmy.

I hate her.

If it weren't for her, I would be with Jimmy. If it weren't for her, things would have probably gone well.

I would say that I was a runaway because of my father because I was lost in my mind. I would say that Jimmy, my childhood friend, offered to take me in. I would say that Jimmy did nothing wrong, that it was all me, and everything would have been fine. Or at least I think.

I couldn't have done anything, though.

Mariah and her family had offered to take me in. That's what they told me. They said I had a choice, but I know I don't. It's either go with a family that I somewhat know and hate, or go into a random family I don't know—that I might hate even more—that might make me move out of state. I chose the first option of course, thinking that it might be better than some random chance of a family.

I could tell that the investigators were tired of hearing the same answers over and over. I was getting tired from hearing similar questions over and over. So, eventually they let me leave the station, and now I was on my way to Mariah's house.

I hope Mariah and Stevie are okay. I still can't believe that Jimmy did that to Dean. I wonder if he would have reacted differently if he knew that he was my friend? That's all in the past now. I can't change anything. I just need to stop thinking

*about it and think about what is going to happen when I arrive
at my new home, and meet my new family.*

When I got there, they didn't look like they had much
money. It was a small, yet cute house that they lived in.
I didn't know if I should be scared or excited that I got to
live another new life. I wondered if I would like it better
than Jimmy's place. It was smaller than his house, and there
would be more people, and I was sure they wouldn't act the
same way Jimmy did. I was sure they wouldn't care about
me as he does.

Getting out of the car, I was escorted to the front door,
and without us knocking it opened up. There was a mother,
a father, and a kid standing in the threshold. I learned their
names right then and there. Nellie was the mom. Joe was
the dad, and the kid was Mariah, an only child from what
I know so far.

"Welcome, Serina!" The parents' faces were filled with
sympathy for me. I knew they believed all of the rumors that
went around, and I'm sure they believed whatever the investigators or police told them too—if they told them anything.

"Serina, I have too much to talk to you about. You have
no idea." Mariah had that same face. The face of being sorry
and scared for me. The face of trying to be someone who
would make me feel better because of what I had just gone
through. But she also had a different face. Not going to lie.
When I looked at her, she had so many faces on I couldn't
tell which was her real one.

"Hi." One simple word, two letters. I stepped inside of
the house, and eventually me and Mariah's family were the
only ones there.

"I'll show her around. Do you guys want to start with
dinner?" Mariah took the initiative. What was she, the leader
of the household or something?

Looking around the house, it was small, just like the out-side of it. The living room had a brown couch. It was soft but not too soft, and when I ran my hand across it the couch didn't seem that comfortable. The walls of the house had paint coming off. Overall, the place just looked really old.

I wonder when this house was built.

There was one cool thing though. In the living room, there was a small fireplace. It looked like it hadn't been used in years. Family photos were hanging around the house in frames. They looked happy.

The kitchen was small but clean. Since her parents were in there, we didn't have a long look at it. Down a hallway, to the left of the living room, were the bedrooms and a bathroom. It was easy to remember where everything was since there were no stairs to walk up or down.

I guess that could be a plus.

We skipped going inside of her parent's room. She gave me a quick peek into the bathroom, but I could tell that she was just in a hurry to show me her room. I followed her, saying nothing, not touching anything, just letting my eyes wander and take in my surroundings. Into the room. It was cute, but small. She didn't have much in it. Mariah turned around and shut the door behind me, and smiled.

I guess we're staying in here until the food is ready.

"Can I ask you something?"
"What?" Just like how I was with the investigators and everything, I kept my talking to a minimum.

I haven't forgotten what happened. I don't think I ever will. It's engraved in my mind, engraved in my heart, impossible to get rid of. Mold has grown inside of me.

"What happened over the months you were gone? If you don't want to talk about it then that's completely understandable."

Once she asked that, I started to get a little moody. "If you want to know the truth, it's a lot, and it's completely different than what everyone is saying."

"It is? How so?"

"You're right, I don't want to talk about it." I saw Mariah sit down on her bed, and I decided to make myself a little bit comfortable and lean up against her wall, even though that wasn't very comfortable. "Long story short, I didn't want to get found, and I never wanted to leave."

I imagined she would have nothing to say about that, but I was wrong. She snapped back.

"I worked so hard to try and find you and save you and bring you back home. To hear you say that you never wanted to be saved in the first place—that hurts."

"Yeah?" I questioned. From the tone in her voice I sensed she not only felt hurt, but betrayed.

"That's crazy. You don't know how much you impacted people when you disappeared!"

"Impacted people?" This made me laugh, crossing my arms I continued to talk. "Who missed me? The people who used me for my money? The now-dead father who only cared about work and had blamed me for my mother's death?"

"That's not true!" She stood up from her bed and walked up to me. She wasn't intimidating at all. "You impacted me. Who cares about all those losers. You do not know how much of an impact you have been in my life and when you just—whatever. Your father, Marcus, he did care for you."

"No, he didn't!"

"Yes, he did. I talked to him and everything! He was trying to look for you too until he and I got too close to finding you, and he got murdered!"

"Lies!" I didn't want to talk about him. I didn't want to talk at all. "Mariah," I said her name, "I don't want to talk about that. Anything but that."

"Anything?"

"Anything," I repeated.

"Serina," she said. Her face looked just as serious as her words sounded. "Be my date to the homecoming dance."

"You want me to come to the homecoming dance with you? After I haven't gone to school in so long?"

"Yes." She was serious. I didn't know what to respond with. She was asking me to go as a friend, right?

Nothing wrong with girls who like girls, but I don't like girls. Do I? Oh well, what do I have to lose?

"Sure, I guess I can be your date." I did have to add this though. "Only as friends."

"Not as friends." Wow, that response was quick. "I want to go with you to the homecoming dance, as a person I am interested in. As my date."

"I don't—" I was stopped by the expression that was given to me. It was scary.

Is that the right word to explain what I am seeing right now? The manipulative look that she is giving me is twisting my words, changing my choice.

"Fine. I will. I'll be your date to homecoming."

That's how it all started.

* * *

I didn't expect the dance to come so soon. Monday and Tuesday rolled around. Mariah made me go to school for a couple of days. Everything was just overwhelming. Everyone around me kept on staring, kept on asking me a bunch of questions. I couldn't handle it.

"Where did you go?"

"What happened?"

"Is it true that you ran away from home?"

"Didn't you go on a vacation? How was it?"

"How did you go missing?"

Thousands of questions from tons of students, but that doesn't scratch out all of my peers that have a different attack.

"Bitch. I bet you just wanted to show off your money."

"You're such an attention seeker."

"I never thought of you as my friend."

"Nobody even cared or noticed."

Words filling up my head.

I would so rather continue being kidnapped than coming back to this on my first day back at school.

Because I kept on getting overwhelmed, I went home. Of course, Mariah came with me.

She was the worst. She was like a leech, but it was also kind of nice to have someone by my side. Even if she didn't know the full truth about what I was thinking. What I have been through.

Monday, Tuesday, Wednesday, Thursday, and Friday. The days of the week. Monday and Tuesday, Mariah and I stayed home together in her room. I tried to sleep those days for as long as I could. It didn't work out so much. Every ten seconds, Mariah would speak, ask me a question or she would try to get some kind of physical contact with me. Whether that being holding my hand, hugging me, playing with my hair. I just couldn't get rid of her. She was a virus.

When Friday, the night of the dance, arrived, we didn't go to school. Instead, Mariah spent practically all day getting us ready for our date. The date I didn't want to go on. I was sure I was going to see lots of classmates there, and sure they would all act the exact same way they had when I went to school back at the beginning of the week.

Mariah picked out our outfits to wear, and they matched. The one thing that weirded me out the most was when her outfit was a whole tuxedo. She was the man of whatever relationship we had going on. I was the woman. A normal black tux, complimenting well with a scarlet red, silky dress.

The dress wasn't that bad though. It definitely looked good on me. My favorite part about the dress was that it had a slit running up the side of it so that it would give room for my leg to pop out.

Apparently, that's the style that a lot of people tend to go with these days.

After hours and hours of planning everything and getting ready, it happened. We left the house and were on the way to the school dance. The stupid homecoming party that the school put together.

From my experiences with school dances, they are boring. They play music, have a bunch of junk food, and way too much drama happens. Way too much unnecessary drama.

"No way, is that Serina Ange? You got her to come?" Mercy and Steve came up to Mariah and me. Of course, Steve was the one to be more friendly. Mercy just seemed to be scared of me or angry with me. I shouldn't be surprised. I was the one who got Dean killed, wasn't I? It was my fault.

"It is! She's my date to the dance!"

"Date?" Mercy and I made eye contact. From the look she gave me, it was clear she hated me. Yet again, I was not surprised after all that has happened.

One thing that I was surprised about was Steve's reaction. "That's right, you are—"

He didn't finish that sentence, but I'm sure he was going to say lesbian. "I'm happy for you." He's not happy, I could tell by the tone of his voice. "Well, Mercy is my date!" As he said that it seemed like his eyes were glaring right at Mariah. Did something happen between them?

"I am?" What Mercy said made me laugh.

"Yep! You are." Steve put his arm around Mercy, but she pushed him away with disgust on her face. I just stood there, standing next to Mariah.

"I'm out of here. Dances are for losers anyway." The energy that Mercy had before, the happy, cheery dancer was now out of business. She stayed by her word. Mercy headed for the door and she walked right out of it.

"I'll uh—I'll go too." Steve followed her tracks, out the same door.

"Well, that was interesting. Are you ready to dance, Serina?"

Well, Mariah's mood doesn't seem to have changed. She just looks happy that she's with me. Overly happy.

She took my hand and dragged me onto the dance floor. The over students stared at us and many of the expressions changed. They were all having fun, dancing with their friends or their significant others. When we came onto the dance floor, I saw that a lot of those looks turn into looks of disgust. Was it because we were two girls? Was it because they all knew that we were on a date, or that Mariah is a lesbian?

This made me feel uncomfortable, maybe worse than just being overwhelmed by questions. It was all too much. I just wanted to be home, home with Jimmy.

Is that too much to ask? Right now, everyone thinks that I went through a really tough time. Everyone thinks that he's a bad guy. He's really not. I miss him.

Thinking about a guy while dancing with a girl isn't too fun, is it? Especially when a slow-dance song came on. Of course, I couldn't escape her now. I don't even know how to slow-dance but Mariah, being the male of the relationship, took the lead and helped me dance. We swayed to the beat, and she got closer to me. I felt weird, this whole thing was weird. No offense, Mariah.

I want it to be over. I want to go home. I want to sleep. I want Jimmy. I want this dance to end.

My wishes came true. After hours of the terror of being at the homecoming dance, it ended. People started to come up to me when their partners started to leave, but Mariah just dragged me out of there as fast as she could. Now we were going home. Or should I say, now we were going to Mariah's home, not mine? Not mine at all.

"Hey Serina," sitting with Mariah in the back seat of the car as we drove us to her place, Mariah set her hand on my thigh, giving me a smile that curled up to a smirk. "Did I tell you that it is my birthday today?"

Chapter 23

Just a dream?

Her actions at the end of the night were weird, and they only got weirder. It was like being her birthday was something special. Mariah acted as if her birthday was a day where she could do whatever she wanted with no consequences.

In the car, her hand on my thigh was doing awkward things. At first I thought it was just a friendly motion, but it slid to my inner thigh and I had to move it away. I don't know what she was doing, or if she was secretly drunk. I didn't smell any alcohol though. Either way, I wanted her to stop whatever she was doing.

Luckily she did. When we got to her place she backed off. When we got inside though, it started to get weird again.

"What do you want to do?" she asked me, and I just shrugged. "Can we talk about what happened when you got taken away then? When you got kidnapped? Or do you still want to talk about something else?"

Did she really ask that? Does she think that my answer is going to change? It hasn't been that long since I got out of that place. Since the last time I saw Jimmy.

"I don't want to talk about it. Like I said before, anything. Anything else."

That was a dangerous sentence. It was too late to take anything back. After relaxing what I just started, I made sure to keep my distance just in case she would try something.

"Okay, then, Serina. I like you."

"You what?" I was not expecting that. I was expecting her to do something. Maybe she really does just want to talk.

"You heard me. I like you. That is why I tried so hard to find you. It was because I fell in love with you." I don't know what was in the air, but the atmosphere changed dramatically. Why did she have to choose that topic out of everything?

"That's a pretty harsh word. Love. Saying that you fell in love with me when you don't even know me."

"Oh trust me, I know a lot more than you think." I assumed she let that spill out because she covered her mouth afterward. "You know what?"

"What is it this time?" I didn't want to hear her voice anymore.

"Since we're talking about this, I just have to. I'm sorry, but I've waited way too long."

"Waited too long?" Before I could say anything else, something predictable happened.

She kissed me. Well, I was expecting her to kiss me right then and there, and I imagined pushing her back and everything. But it didn't happen like that.

It felt like she was training for this moment her whole life. Mariah was a lot stronger than I thought she would be. Or maybe, I was letting it happen just so I could get my mind off of him. Maybe I was letting her take control of me at that moment, but I can't really say because my mind was all over the place, and it felt like I couldn't feel my own body. I felt numb.

Is that the right thing to say, is that a good way to explain it? I have no idea. So many things are clouding my head right now.

Mariah ended up breaking the kiss, but it didn't stop there. She leaned in close to me. My body was frozen, and I just stayed there. My arms uncrossed slowly as we kept eye contact. Her voice echoed through my head again. "I can't hold back anymore. I can't resist. It's so hard for me to just let other people try to take you from me. The thought of that hurts me and makes me so angry. You don't even know it, Serina. You are mine and only mine. Nobody else can have you."

I was surprised to hear these words come out of someone who I thought was just an innocent girl. Who was good at school, someone who I perceived didn't want me for my money. I was right. She didn't want me for my money. She just wanted me because she is in love.

Mariah put our faces just inches apart, and I could hear my mind yelling at me to do something, and yet I did nothing. I saw her hand raise, coming up to my face. She pressed her thumb against my lips. Feeling her soft touch, the brushing of her thumb against my lips, my face couldn't help but heat up.

I saw her mouth arch up into a grin, and that was when she spoke again. "I can't believe I'm this close to my dearest beloved. I love you so much. I would do anything for you. Anything to make you mine." This was way unexpected. This was creepy. I never knew someone like this would exist in real life, I thought it was just some video game stereotype. "Forever."

Forever? Now that's a little long. Sorry to tell you this Mariah, but you're not the one I want.

Though those words wouldn't leave my mouth and just

like what I did the night with Jimmy before everything went down, I let her have her way with me.

My body flinched when I felt something. It was her knee sliding in between my legs. She kept me up against the wall, grabbing my wrists even though I wasn't resisting and she pinned them against the cold wall. It gave me shivers. "Wait." I was just expecting a kiss, but nothing like that happened.

The first word I said she didn't listen to. "I don't want to stop. Your body is so delicate. The sight of you always makes my mind wander. It makes me wonder what else you could be hiding underneath all of this fabric." All I wanted to do was push her away now and call her a creep, that she was a psycho, but I did nothing. "You are everything to me. How could I not love every inch of you?"

My body flinched again as I felt the girl's hand on my thigh, messing with the waistband of my pants.

How can her parents trust her this much? Do they even know that she's into girls? Not that it matters. People can like whoever they want to. Still, some part of me was hoping that her parents would walk right in and see this and give her a good beating.

"Wait." That one word I repeated again, my head leaning up against the wall. I refused to look at her now. I felt her still touching me, sticking a hand up my shirt. Her hand grazed against my skin with a delicate touch. She was being gentle, but there was still that feeling of aggressiveness.

"I can't."

* * *

All four of us were sitting down at a table, forks in our hands, eating our food respectfully. I hadn't looked at Mariah once, but I could tell that she was staring me down. I can't believe that just happened. But at least it did one good thing. It made me forget.

Sitting there, laying there, standing there, the other person touches you, and you freeze up and let them do whatever they want. It gives them confidence. It makes the other person think that nothing is wrong and that they can keep going, am I right?

It's even worse when you're fake sleeping. Some people just think that it takes five minutes—not even—to fall asleep. And that's when they strike, making their moves when you're asleep, but you're really awake.

Still, the body freezes up, and there's nothing you can do until they start to go too far, and you have to pretend you woke up from the touch, acting like you're tired, making your voice sound like you just woke up. It's a pain, let me tell you that.

So many people get taken advantage of. Usually, the person who did it, they brag about it to their friends and literally tell everyone and anyone without the person's consent at all. It really does suck, but all you can do is let life move on, am I right? Try to avoid it and get it out of your mind. But you know that is never going to happen. You know there is nothing you can do about it.

What's worse is that I can relate to such things. Not just Mariah, but things that have happened in my past. I've got a bad reputation for freezing up in the worst times.

Moving on, I didn't have an appetite. After eating a couple of bites of my food, I stood up and excused myself. They let me leave. I just made up a lame excuse, saying that I needed some time alone after what just happened with the whole me disappearing thing.

That was somewhat true. I did need some alone time after everything that had happened between Jimmy and me. Also with what happened with Mariah. It makes it even worse because of what Mariah did. It brought up some bad memories of my past, and it made it a whole lot worse.

Instead of going into Mariah's room, I found the bathroom and went in there. Once the door was closed, it felt like my body just shattered. The wall that was keeping a hold of all of my emotions finally broke. My chest hurt. The tightening in my chest made it feel like I was suffocating. My whole body fell back against the door, and I slowly lowered myself, ending up on the floor. My eyes were open, but all I could see was a blurry screen. I didn't know what was happening around me. Every sense was focusing on what was happening to me, what I was feeling.

I don't like this feeling. I want to be in Jimmy's arms, but that won't happen anytime soon.

So, the only thing that I could do was bring my knees up to my chest, clicking like two puzzle pieces, and hide my face in them as my eyes became waterfalls.

I don't even know how much time had passed. I had been crying on Mariah's bathroom floor the whole time. I was surprised that no one had come to check on me or find me, unless they knew exactly what I was doing and decided to just leave me alone.

I guess this is my life from now on. This is how I am going to live. Jimmy is always on my mind as I remember all of the good memories we've made with each other, the bad as well. Just everything flashing in my mind, regretting things and dreaming to meet him again. Only to wake up every day in a bedroom with a girl that fell in love with me. Going back to school with students that use me. I don't want to live like this, but I have no other choice.

Right?

This is the end. I don't want it to be, but I don't see any other way of this ending, so this has to be the end. I tell myself that, but there's this huge gut feeling that I don't want to believe is true. This little orange orb inside of my stomach is saying that there is hope for me to meet Jimmy again. Maybe that's the small hope that's keeping me from stopping. That's the one thing that is pushing me to continue forward.

There was a knock on the door. Someone was finally trying to make contact with me. My legs were wobbly, but I decided to stand up and turn around, glancing at myself through the mirror. My eyes were still pink from sobbing. It's not like I cared about how I looked right now. Opening the door, I expected to see Mariah or her parents.

When I opened up the door though, the place has changed. I wasn't in Mariah's house anymore. The hallway looked familiar. A couple more glances around and I knew where I was. Jimmy's house.

How did I get here? This can't be real. This has to be some kind of dream.

I stepped out. It felt real. It felt like one of those dreams that I always used to have when I was at his house before I got taken away from it. Somehow, because it felt like one of those dreams, I felt like it was connected with him. That has to be the reason, unless I just missed him so much that my mind was tricking itself again.

"Hello?" I called out. Everything was dark and it seemed like none of the lights worked in the house. None of the doors would open up, so I went downstairs, looking around. The living room curtains were closed. Everything was dark. "Jimmy?"

The second time I said something lights flickered on. The living room light turned on and I saw a figure sitting down on the couch. The hair—it couldn't have been Jimmy, right? Out of excitement, fear, and confusion, I went up to the figure from behind, opening my mouth to say something but nothing would come out. Words would no longer work so I walked around the couch and looked at the person. It was Jimmy, but he seemed emotionless. He seemed frozen. It was like I was playing a video game and the game was bugging up on my half. My ping striking to an unreasonable number.

"Serina, is that really you? Or am I imagining things?"

I wanted to reply with, "Are you real? I thought this was a dream." But I couldn't.

When he spoke, his expression changed to how he was feeling. His words seemed real. It made me feel like we were in our own dimension, but I knew it couldn't be real because that only happens in fiction books.

"Can you not talk? Can you not understand me?" He stood up and walked towards me, reaching out to take my hand, but his hand went right through mine. We couldn't make any physical contact. "If you can, if this is somehow working, I need to tell you something. I need to tell you a lot of things, but there's no time. I just hope you are okay right now and I want to tell you that I'm okay. I'll be fine. I won't get caught, and I can promise you that."

Was he reading my mind at some point? How would he know that I cared? Is it because I screamed his name—wanted to scream his name? Is it because during our last look at each other, he saw the fear and pain in my eyes?

I probably have that same painful look on my face right now.

"Soon, we will see each other. I promise."

I'm sure those were just words that my mind wanted me

to hear. I'm sure this was all a big misunderstanding. There's no possible way that this could be real, not in the slightest. If it was, I have no idea what I would think, what I would say. Jimmy saying those words. I wanted them to be true, but deep down I knew this was just some kind of dream that I was having on Mariah's bathroom floor.

I was right. I had to have been. A moment later when I blinked inside of the dream everything went dark, and I felt like I had passed out. There was wind. It felt like I was falling from the roof of a tall building, only there was pure blackness around me. And when I hit the bottom, I woke up with a startle. Deep breaths I told myself. Looking around, I was in Mariah's bathroom. The confusion I was feeling was overbearing. I had to know that I was still in the same house. I had to know that once I opened the door, I'd be seeing Mariah's hallway and not Jimmy's.

I stood up, turned around, and opened the door in haste. I did see Mariah's hallway. I also saw Mariah standing there. "Are you okay, Serina?" I shook my head in response, stepping out of the bathroom and pushing the girl out of my way. I didn't know where I was going. I didn't know where I should go. In the end, I went into Mariah's room with the one and only Mariah behind me.

"I need to be alone right now. I need to have a big nice sleep. So please, Mariah, leave me the fuck alone for a while."

"Okay, I will leave you alone." The sadness in her voice didn't make me feel bad for her at all. Probably because she had so many sides to her that I didn't know what to think.

Once I was left alone, I still felt like someone was watching me, and she probably was. Peeking through that door of hers, I wouldn't be surprised if she was watching me sleep. I guess that's what someone would do if they were in love with someone, right? Or at least someone as crazy as her.

This is my new story, and I hate it.

Chapter 24

Clouded thoughts

What he said repeated in my mind. When I heard it, I felt my chest drop. How could he say that? What does he mean? Does he mean forever? Is he saying goodbye forever? I was paranoid. I didn't know what to do.

"GOD DAMNIT, FUUUUUCK!!"

I imagined myself outside, in the grass as the cold breeze washed over. "I can't take it anymore," I said, collapsing to my knees, my voice cracking while tears left my eyes. I was wailing.

I hadn't realized how much of a toll the ordeal I had been through created. We had known each other for less than a year. I don't even know how long it had been. Half a year, maybe? But in that short amount of time that seemed like it was going to last forever, how could someone like me end up worrying for someone like him so much?

The way his eyes creased when he seemed happy, the little chuckle he made, his caring personality, his lovely eyes, the color, the way they looked in the sunlight.

I couldn't take it anymore. I couldn't hold back. All this time, I thought that was just my character. Acting like everything was fine, smiling all the time, laughing all the time.

But the more I thought about it, the more I came to the realization that I laugh more and act more energetic when I'm nervous, when I'm scared, or when someone around me I like or either got hurt by is near me. Why? I guess I think to myself without even realizing it. "If I speak louder and act like I'm having a good time, they'll notice me." What a crazy thing to think, right?

Faking emotions. A sign of silent depression, I guess it can connect to me. I always imagined myself freaking out, or breaking down, telling people what I was thinking and what was going through my head. But instead, I didn't do that. I faked my emotions, and I realized now that I did that subconsciously all the time. When I had anxiety attacks, I could see them as the only times I let loose—putting a name on it—but I was actually just taking too much on my shoulders, and I needed to get rid of it all at once to be able to start all over again.

I'm thinking too much into this. I don't want people to think I'm crazy, self-diagnosing, or anything else. The human mind can assume many things about people.

Getting back on track, hearing Jimmy say those words made me neurotic as fuck. I thought they didn't care about me. I thought I did something wrong based on the tone of their voice. Did I do something wrong? Should I have done something differently? I'm sorry if I did something wrong.

I guess I don't fully grasp the situation until after it happens. Because then, I think about it a lot and overthink, leading to telling myself that I made all the mistakes when maybe, that's not the truth.

Thinking about the past can be a tough thing. I think about it now, now that you're gone and we haven't talked for God knows how long. We had so much time together when I could've kissed you more, when I could've bonded with you more, talked to you more, learned more about you. Now it's too late. I realize how childish I was with you sometimes, or how rude, how scared I was in the beginning, how skeptical I was being.

I'm sorry, Jimmy.

What is going through your head? What are you thinking? Throughout the whole thing, what have you been thinking? What were your true motives? Why did you do it in this way? Did something happen in your past?

I miss you. Is that too much already? For the short time we've known each other, I miss you. I can't believe that. I miss you.

I didn't think it would end up like this. I was by your side for months, and all I could think about was the weird stuff that was happening. Everything that was going through my mind was bad things. Well, not all of them. But you get what I mean. I regret not talking to you more. Even though it was awkward at some points, I couldn't just force myself, force some fake emotions to become vigorous and sparkling. You seemed to like that part of me.

I'm completely freaking out. I can't form words properly. I stand there, frozen, feeling my chest drop so much it hurts.

When you said your goodbye, thousands of thoughts went through my head, and all I wanted to do at that moment was cry. But I didn't, I didn't cry. I stood there while my whole body hurt. Why didn't I cry, Jimmy?

I know you'll be in contact with me soon, right? Hopefully

soon? What do I do when it's been a week, maybe a month, maybe even past my birthday? Do I try to look for you, or are you trying your best to look for me again, to not get caught?

Questions. Over and over, a bunch of problems clouding in my mind with all the thoughts, making it a whirlpool. I hope you're okay. I hope everything is going okay. I hope you don't get caught, even though the things you did were kind of illegal. I really hope we can talk again soon. I hope we can talk to each other soon, and maybe, just maybe, I hope we can kiss again. Getting to know each other, trying to live a normal life. That's such a dream, isn't it? After what you did. After what I've been through. What both of our positions are right now, it's just a dream. There's no way in hell that it could end with a happy ending.

No happy ending here, only endless thoughts of what's going to happen next. Waiting until you reach out to me. Waiting for a chance to strike.

I want to know about your family, your siblings, your hobbies. I want to know what kind of a person you are, even if I did know you during our childhood. How much did you change as a person, you know?

When I first met you, I would have never imagined that months later we could kiss. I would have never imagined that our relationship would get this far. It's crazy. Did you have it all planned out?

Please, let me see you again.

Am I really begging?

I'll say it again. Please.

If I come across your dead body or news report on the television, I wonder how much it will affect me if just seeing your back when you ran away affected me this much already.

I guess I should reply to what you said, right? Because the only thing I did was stand there, frozen.

Goodbye, Jimmy.

You will forever be in my mind, my memory. I will never forget you like I did before. I will never resent you, I assure you. So, if we ever meet again, let's introduce ourselves and say hello, okay? If we ever meet again—I really hope that day comes.

Those words make me cringe, saying goodbye, or bye. Reading it, saying it, anything. Saying those words without any context on why or where, or at least when it's not in the right moment. When you say goodbye out of nowhere, it's scary. I've seen and read way too many things where a "goodbye" means goodbye forever. Either they are dying, or they regret everything and are running away.

That's what I thought you meant when you said that to me, that you were regretting everything that happened between us recently, that you were regretting our childhood, our friendship—if you would even call it one. You're going to leave and never come back with that guilt and regret in your head, right? Regretting you ever met me, regretting you kissed me, regretting everything. And that's heartbreaking to think about, spending time with someone, kissing them, slowly falling for them, learning you like them, and it's too late. It's so heartbreaking.

It reminds me though of something involving love. It reminds me of one of my longest relationships that I've had. It was a silly relationship I think back in middle school or the beginning of high school. The way that they ended things with me, and the way you are ending things with me, they're way too similar. It hurts. I've been heartbroken, and I never thought I would feel the same feeling again, but with a different person. I never thought that I would fall in love with someone the same way I fell in love with someone in the past. It hurts. But what can you do about it, huh?

Unless some magical thing happens and this was all a dream, then I'd forget about you and everything. Wait, what am I saying? I don't want to forget about you. Even if you did intend to hurt me, even if we never meet again, I'm glad that you were a part of my life. Over time, I think I'm going to blame myself, blame myself more every single day after your departure because I cared for you so much. I guess that's just how the mind works. You blame yourself for a bunch of things that you may not need to blame yourself for, but you do it anyway because you're self-conscious and you have nothing else to blame it on. No one else to blame it on, so you blame yourself because you're not confident, and you don't trust yourself.

Do you really like me? When you kissed me, was that a sign of affection? Do you really care for me? Or were you just pretending this whole time and you wanted me for my money and my body? Should I even bother thinking about you every day? Should I bother to even try looking for you if you haven't tried looking for me?

I guess we won't be able to talk to each other for a while. I hope that's not a long time. I wish I get to see you again— how many times have I said that now? It feels like I'm a record player on repeat.

Though, some part of me is confident. Otherwise, why would you have tried so hard to keep me in your house? To capture me, take me hostage? If you didn't care about me, why would you feed me every day and everything, everything you did for me? So, some part of me is confident that you will look for me again and find me. Some part of me wants to believe that. I need patience, and I might be able to say we both need patience. I can't say so for sure though because we haven't talked about our actual feelings or what we were thinking yet, have we? Some part of me has confidence, and I'll try to keep that in mind. I'll try to keep a positive mind. Nobody likes someone who is always negative. Right? I guess that's another reason to keep a fake face on and do some fake emotions.

> *Jimmy.*
> *Please obtain me again.*
> *I'll be waiting for you.*
> *Evermore.*
> *However long it will take.*
> *I will be here.*
> *Waiting.*

Chapter 25

I love you

When I first saw you, I was scared to death. But now the more I think about it, I love that I met you. I would never go back in time and change the fact that you took me, that you took my heart. Your eyes seemed so evil, but kind. When I looked into your eyes, I could tell that they were staring into my soul, not because you wanted to kill me, but because you were in love with me. I still have no idea how long you have been in love with me, how long you have known me.

Wait, I lied. You are my one, and only. You were my one and only, but I didn't realize it when we were kids—when we were sitting up in that tree house all those days. Sometimes I think to myself I can't believe that I didn't recognize you, that I forgot about you. I didn't forget about you, necessarily. You were always a part of my life, a part of my mind. But, after the years passed, I thought I'd never see you again. I guess you made the effort to make that a lie too. Huh?

Meeting you, not going to lie, has been one of the best things to happen in my life. I am telling the truth! You coming into my life made it brighter. Not only because I had someone who was by my side, who cared for me, who cooked for me, despite the situation we were both in.

I guess over time, my mind decided to trust you, and due to that my heart began to fall.

I'm at a loss for words, to be honest. What do I say to someone as sweet as you? Though you do have secrets I don't know about, I'm confident I'll be the one to find you next and make you speak the truth.

That's crazy. Isn't it? I never thought how the tables would turn. I never thought that I would be the one chasing after you when you were the first one to chase me in the first place. I guess I fell for you hard. I mean, you are a good kisser. That one day when we were in your room and you decided to bring me in, and I subconsciously leaned closer as our lips met moments later, it made my heart skip a beat. And just maybe that move that you did made me lose my balance. I wonder what would have happened if you never kissed me, Jimmy. Or if you just never came up to me that one day. If you never took me. If you never looked at me in the eyes and spoke to me. If you treated me differently. I wonder.

But wondering is just for fools, right? All these "what if" questions that we ask ourselves. Is it really worth it?

I just want to see you again. Is that too much to ask? I know I'm sitting here in my room, but when do I get to see you again? Every time I close my eyes I think of you. Every time I sleep I have dreams about you. I just can't get you out of my head. The images of you on top of me and the other way around. The images of us kissing, of you going at my neck when we both got too carried away. Goosebumps, let me tell you that.

My father died. I don't know if you knew that already or not, but when I got taken away from your house by the cops, they gave me the news. What am I supposed to do, Jameson? Without you, I have no one.

The detectives and everything still haven't found any

leads on the killer. There were a couple of clues, but they won't bring a certain answer to someone. So, my father's killer is still out there. Am I happy though? I've told you before how much I hated my father. How I wanted him to die, to not be a part of my life anymore because of how he treated me. Sometimes I think it's my fault though. It's my fault that he is dead and it's my fault I will never get to hear his voice again. Although, at the same time I feel like this is a good thing, that he's dead. I did hate him, after all. I always thought of the bad times when he was alive, but now when I think of him, I think about all the happy times we had together when he was an actual father to me. When he seemed like he cared.

You're the only one for me. The only family—at least I would call it that—I have left. That's why I have to wonder. I have to think about that moment all the time. When I first saw your face, I couldn't even look at it closely. I couldn't even touch it. I couldn't do anything because you ran away.

The sirens booming in my head. The lights shining through the windows in the midst of the night. I can still see it vividly. You were freaking out. I had no idea what to do because you freaking out made me freak out. This made my mind race. I didn't know what to do. I didn't know if I should go out to the cops or run away with you. The only time I would go back in time to was that moment. I should have run away with you.

Your face, it wasn't how I imagined it at all. Your blue eyes don't match with your hair. That makes me wonder. Was it dyed? It had to have been because I remember Jameson being this little boy with dirty blonde hair, am I right? Unless I am wrong. It was such a long time ago anyway.

Your hair style, your facial features, they just match up with the rest of your body. They all compliment each other. When I look at you, in my eyes, you could be a model. If you

had a better life, would you have been a model? I wonder
what career you would have chosen. I wonder how your
grades would have been in school. You were bull-necked.
Your jaw, strictly defined. It matched with your toned chest,
your well-built arms, your lean, muscular legs. But your face.
Oh my god, your face. I never really saw your eyebrows
because of the mask you had on all the time, but your eyebrows. You had beautiful angled brows. Maybe even soft
angled brows. Having them with a high arch makes your
face look a lot more youthful. It makes you more attractive, or at least in my eyes—everything about you I find
attractive. Is that weird?

The height that you have. Towering above me when you
first took off your mask. Your eyes looking down at me.
Your hair getting in your face. It made me feel sorry for you.
Now that I could see the expression you were fully making,
I realize you made that expression a lot. That makes me feel
even worse for how I treated you. Why didn't you just tell
me how you felt in the first place? How were you feeling?
I thought it was pretty obvious that I cared about you when
you came home that one night with blood all over your
body, all those bruises.

It's flattering, your face. Like I said before, I never imagined it like this. Your teeth—they are perfect. Lined up
in almost a complete horizon, but not actually because
nobody's teeth are like that, right? No one can be perfect. Your sexy and symmetrical figure, I can't get it out
of my head.

Your hair was long, but not that long—at least long
enough to reach your eyes. Maybe reaching a little lower.
It looked like you usually split it in the middle because
the hairs on your head just seemed to fall like that. But
I guess that's not true. You were freaking out. I could
hear your heart whining to get out of your chest. Maybe

you were sweating too much. Maybe your mask gave you bad hat hair or something. I guess I'll never know what you normally look like if I don't see you normally. Maybe at a café we'll be sitting there at a table, looking at each other as we drink from our mugs, whatever drink that we were drinking that morning. Smiling at each other, laughing at each other, getting embarrassed. Catching up on the good old days. What happened when you left, what happened when we were separated. If things went that way, would I feel the same way I do now?

When our eyes met, when my eyes ventured your body, explored your face, when they took in your physique, I just wanted to kiss you. I wanted to scream at you, to let me call you mine, to let you call me yours. Is that weird? Am I overthinking things?

We've known each other for a long time, and I hate myself for being so dense. At that moment when our eyes met, when we both looked at each other with that fear in our eyes when the knocking was heard at the door, the loud masculine voices yelling at us to let them in or they would break the door down. I wanted you to look at me more. I wanted you to want me. I wanted you to notice me, to LOVE me. I wanted you to love me.

I love you.

I love you, I love you, I love you. I wish I would have said that. But I was too late. The door was knocked down, and my ears rang. Everything became foggy at that moment I saw you turn and run. I called out for you so many times. I should've said that I loved you. I should've said that I didn't hate you. I can't even imagine what you're thinking right now. What you think of me now. Do you still care for me, Jimmy?

I don't even know what to call you. Do I call you Jameson from when we were kids? Or Jimmy, the name you introduced to me when we first met in your house. I still can't get over the fact that I was so dense. The name you gave me was so similar, the hints you gave me were so obvious. I am sorry.

You turned around, I watched your arms as they raised, and I saw your hair disappear, along with your neck. The blackness of the mask camouflaged with the darkness in the room. You fled. You ran away. I couldn't do anything. The men grabbed my arms and pulled me back, saying that it was going to be alright, saying that I was saved.

I yelled your name so many times. I didn't want you to leave, but at the same time, I knew you had to. If you got caught, you probably would have been locked up for life, maybe even worse. I don't want to think about that. I don't want to think about your death.

I don't know where you went, but I was so happy, so relieved when I heard that you weren't found. That you had gotten away. My voice by then was gone.

You were long gone when they turned on the lights in your living room, but everything still looked foggy to me. It looked like there was just some kind of rock concert in here where they used special effect fog that spread across the room. My eyes didn't adjust to the light, or were the tears just covering up my vision?

Tears. Can you believe that? Can you believe that I cried for my kidnapper? The person who took me away from my home, my school, my life? The person who I thought I hated so much, the person who I wanted to get away from the whole time. I'm crying because of you, my heart aches because of you.

I want to see you again, and when I do all I want to do is stare at your face—without that ridiculous mask on. I want to admire you, your face, your body, your everything. I want to hear your voice. I want to see you. I want to hold you. I want to feel your touch, but you're gone.

Will this be my final goodbye, Jameson Smith?

Sitting in my bed, thinking about what happened the night before, sitting in my bed thinking I was alone. My knees scrunched up to my chest. I hid my face as I thought and cried more to myself. More tears, just for you. Does that make you happy?

"Dear, you need to stop crying. It's okay, you're safe now, you're home." They sent this girl into my room. I didn't like her at all. She seemed so fucking fake.

I wanted to push her away, scream. Tell her that this is not what I want. What I wanted was to be with you.

Thinking, over and over, for days, hours. How long have I been in my bedroom now? It must have been a while. When I came in here, it was daylight, and now it is dark.

Dark.

Reminds me of you. The darkness does. The darkness of your room. The darkness of your house. The darkness of the basement room I woke up in. The darkness of the room your brother was in.

Everything reminds me of you, and I can't stop myself from thinking that. My mind just goes automatically to you.

"We need to go. We cannot let you stay here, Serina. We have a house you can stay at. A lovely family would love to take you in."

No, no, no, no. I don't want to leave. Just leave me alone. Just let me be. Leave so that I can get up and find someone I love.

I want to find you. I need you.

My body moved. I stood up. I was being taken by the girl, going to this house, going somewhere strange. Yet again, it reminded me of you.

Jameson Smith

"One more time, this has to work."

Eighteen-year-old Jameson, or in other words, me, has been running away from authorities for months. In that time, I have been trying my best to get in contact with someone I have been in love with for my whole life, Serina Ange. The last thing I heard from her was when she screamed my name when the police broke down my front door. I regretted it so much, not bringing her with me, not being careful enough. Her voice, as beautiful as it is, won't stop echoing through my head. Over and over. And for once, I want it to stop—but at the same time, all I want to hear are her sweet words.

"I didn't do all of this for nothing. This can't be the end."

This isn't the end.

* * *

"Jameson!" A little girl laughed, saying my name. That little girl was Serina Ange. When we were about nine years old, we were sitting up in the tree house in my backyard.

The tree house wasn't special. It was just sitting in between three trees in a triangle form. It wasn't high off the ground either. A full-grown adult could stand there and their head would see over the platform. Being as young and small as we were, the place looked way bigger than it is. The first time I saw it, I was so happy. I had dreamed of getting a tree house my whole life, and when I finally got one, I got to spend time with my only friend. My first love.

I watched Serina as she climbed up the wide ladder, coming up and into the tree house with me. I greeted her with a smile. I was so happy to see her. "Hey!"

If only times were like that. If only I could go back in time. If only I could hang out with her in the tree house one more time. All of the memories that we've created are stuck in my mind, or at least most of them that I remember. After growing up and near graduation, it's hard to remember those times. Especially after all that's happened since I disappeared.

"Where are we going?" I remember being a little boy, ten years old. Finally, I reached double digits. But that saying doesn't come happy with me when I think of it.

One morning my mom woke me up. She scared me because she seemed to be in a rush to go somewhere. I saw my stuff all packed up, my clothes were emptied out of my closet, and everything was either in a black garbage bag or a big black suitcase.

"What's going on, mom?" She didn't explain anything to me. She just dragged me out of the house. "Where's dad?"

My father was a different story. I always loved him, and I always thought he loved us. Until one night I couldn't sleep. Stepping quietly, I went to tell my parents that I had a nightmare and that I wanted to sleep with them. When I got to the crack of the door, I peeked inside. My body froze as soon as I saw it happen. My father hit her. He hit my mother. When that happened, I remember being so scared. I remember seeing my mom being brave.

"I didn't sleep with him!" In their conversation, they were arguing. "It's not my fault that you drink all of the time and don't do shit around the house! So what if I need to get relieved sometimes."

"You're a druggie too so don't even come at me for that!" I was too young to know what all of this meant.

One thing that will never leave my mind from that night is when my mom's eyes and mine met. After that, well—it's a hard story to tell.

I kind of put the puzzle pieces together when she still didn't reply to me that night. In the end, we left the house, just me and my mom. I looked out the car window, watching all the houses go by as we drove. The really big horses that one of our neighbors had. They were always fun to look at. Our neighbor would sometimes let me and Serina go over there and pat their heads. It was nice.

I never saw that tree house that my childhood best friend and I created so many good memories in again. I abandoned her with no warning. I never got to say goodbye. I'm sorry, Serina.

There was this picture that I always kept on me at all times. A small photo of me, and her, smiling. Our small little fingers intertwined as we held hands. That moment, there was no care in the world. I was so happy. She was the one who made all my worries go away. She was the one who made me forget about all of my parent's arguments, the one who saved me. Without her, I would probably be dead. Sometimes, now that I'm almost 19, I think that maybe it would have been a good thing if I died back then.

I stared at the picture throughout the car ride as my hand bent taking the small image with it. I rethought my decision and relaxed. In that second it would have felt so good to crush it and throw it away, yet, I couldn't bring myself to do so. It was all I had left of her. Then again, I never knew whether I would see her again or not. As we passed her house, I put my hand against the car window, like I was reaching out to her, like I was saying goodbye. She was probably asleep in her room without a care in the world. Not knowing what was happening with me, not knowing I was leaving the town.

Saying goodbye was something that I couldn't handle. I didn't want to leave her. I wanted to stay with her. I never wanted to abandon her. But at that time, I was too young.

The two kids in the picture smiled at me. My smile was mocking me. Her smile was full of pity. But I know that wasn't the truth of those smiles. My mind was just messing with me. And slowly, this darkness that was living in my head had finally begun to spread uncontrollably, making me think things that I never thought I would think, making me act out of control. I guess you could say that's how the relationship between my mom and I had shattered. What could a ten-year-old do anyway, right?

It was a long car ride, that's for sure. I needed to take a piss. That is how long it took. My mom never stopped driving, not even at a gas station so that I could piss. It felt like I was going to piss my pants that night, I swear.

"Mom, come on, please?" Still, she wouldn't listen to me. That's when her phone rang. The caller ID popped up on the screen that the car had. I always thought that little screen was cool. I saw my dad's name. My dad was calling. "That's dad. Are you going to pick up?" She wasn't talking to me. "At least say something!"

It was when she turned around that I raised my voice at her. Her eyes looked scary, worried, scared. "Shut up, kid! This is all because of you that things ended up like this!"

Me?

I never knew what my mom meant back then since she never gave me a clear answer to everything. I'd like to think now that she just said that because she was scared and needed something to blame everything on. I was there so that something was me. She let out all her anger on me. The one I called my mom. The one who gave birth to me. I never saw her as my mom again after that night. Things kept on getting worse. Our relationship got worse. Now I was just a kid who was following around the one person I knew would keep me alive. That did not last long.

"Why can't she just understand. It's simple." Muttering incoherently to no one but myself, yet someone was listening, I could feel it.

We were in a different state, I think. I didn't know exactly where we were, but I knew it was far away. From how long the car ride was, from how many stops we made to get gas. We went a long way.

The indecisive silence shadowed my small, yet not skinny figure as I sat alone for the millionth time deciding what I should do next. Sitting in an alley, I didn't want to be in that strange town I didn't know, with all of these people I didn't recognize. It was scary.

"Why did she do this to me? She ruined it. She ruined everything. Why did she take me away?" That was when it all started. The hatred kept on growing towards my mother until one night.

I did something that started my career as a murderer. That attribute I probably got from both of my parents.

I was only a young boy, so when they found her body, her death was ruled an accident. Not like I was in sight when they found her body anyway. Her son—Jameson Smith— was declared missing. That's why everyone eventually forgot about me. Everyone probably thought I was dead. Everyone forgot about me. Even Serina.

I hid in the shadows, watching through the small hole in the wall. I hid, not making myself known. Not wanting to make myself known. I was scared. Of course I was. The first kill I made was my mother.

I wanted to be alone, and being alone felt right. The darkness was the only way, right?

Since I didn't know where I was, I didn't know the way back home. I didn't even know where the one person I could talk to was. I didn't know where my only friend was.

Now I was alone, with the darkness, with my thoughts. Everything was bottled in. I couldn't yell. I didn't want to get caught. I couldn't run for help because then I would be put into an orphanage or something. So what I did was I lived on the streets. I made a living by stealing food.

After a year, I kind of got used to doing what I needed to live. I killed a cat once for money. I regret that decision. It was tough, let me tell you that. But the thing that hurt me the most was not being able to see Serina. To make the hurt go away, I became fixated on finding my way back home without getting caught.

At age eleven, I used a nickname. I went by the name Jimmy Coral. Of course, my stupid young mind thought that using Jimmy was a good idea. Now that I think about it, it's way too close to my real name. At the time, that didn't matter to me. I didn't talk to people anyway.

Find my way home, find Serina. That was my plan.

My teenage years were something, that's for sure. I remember my crazy teen years more than my happy childhood memories. I mean, a lot did happen. I don't blame myself. I imagined a whole plan. Once I would get home, I would finish off high school, reunite with Serina, and live a happy life. Many of my nights were filled with dreams— some were nightmares—of getting back to my hometown.

For example, I arrived and everyone seemed to welcome me with tears in their eyes. The only person I looked out for was Serina though. She did end up showing up. Her eyes were teary, and as much as I hate to say this, I loved seeing the water as it came. Knowing that she missed me, it was heart warming. Knowing that she was thinking of me and possibly dreaming of me too, knowing that she had waited. I would love that.

Another one, however, was the complete opposite. I arrived, and I was shunned. Somehow everyone knew that I was a murderer. Everyone knew I killed my mother. They all avoided me. Of course, as always the one who most affected me was her. Seeing her face like that in my dream, I don't ever want to see that expression. I just want to see her smile just like how things used to be in the tree house.

Another one was where I arrived back there, and she wasn't there anymore. She either died, disappeared, or moved. It was confusing. I do not remember much of this dream. Or would it be better if I called it a nightmare?

That's one of the many things I wouldn't want to happen to Serina. I don't want her to die or be hurt, physically or mentally. Soulmates, am I right? If only. If Serina were my soulmate things would have gone so much better. Why is it so hard to get someone to love you just as much as you love them? Love is a crazy word, but in this situation, I would use that word over and over again because it's true. I love her.

My journey was something. I met a girl. I am pretty sure she was in love with me, but I couldn't give up on Serina, never. But in the end, Maya got a lovely boyfriend. So I guess it worked out. Until I killed them both, of course.

Let us start from the beginning, shall I? Buckle up your seat belts because you are in for a jarring ride.

SIGMA'S BOOKSHELF

Sigma's Bookshelf (www.SigmasBookshelf.com) is an independent book publishing company that exclusively publishes the work of teenage authors, who are between the ages of 13 and 19. The company was founded in 2016 by Minnesota teenager Justin M. Anderson, whose first book, *Saving Stripes: A Kitty's Story*, was published when he was 14, and has since sold hundreds of copies.

"I know there are a lot of other teenagers out there who are good writers and deserve to have their work published, but don't have access to the kinds of resources I do. I wanted to help them," he said.

Sigma's Bookshelf is a sponsored project of Springboard for the Arts, a nonprofit arts service organization. Contributions on behalf of Sigma's Bookshelf may be made payable to Springboard for the Arts and are tax deductible to the extent permitted by law. Donations can be made online at www.SigmasBookshelf.com/donate.

CPSIA information can be obtained
at www.ICGtesting.com
Printed in the USA
BVHW071519290322
632749BV00002B/157